The Meyersons of Meryton

Mirta Ines Trupp

Cover illustration:

The Dubufe Family by Claude-Marie Dubufe

This is a work of historical fiction. All characters and events in this publication are fictitious or are used fictitiously. Although the author writes from a Jewish perspective, not every belief and doctrine expressed in this book may agree with the beliefs and doctrines of any of the three major Jewish branches.

CONTENTS

To my children: you are my greatest inspiration.

If you are not a better person tomorrow than you are today, what need have you for a tomorrow?

~ Rebbe Nachman of Breslov

CHAPTER ONE

13th of October, 1812

Elizabeth gently placed her ungloved fingertips upon Mr. Darcy's forearm, now that Society would sanction the gesture, and attempted to absorb the gentleman's forbearance as they listened to her mother rail, yet again, against the injustice and extent of Lady Catherine de Bourgh's reach. Elizabeth grimaced in recalling the lady's virulent diatribe when she condescended to pay an unexpected visit to Longbourn, a se'nnight Sunday.

"I shall know how to act!" she had avowed. "I will carry my point!"

And by that very same affirmation, Elizabeth and Mr. Darcy had suffered their first cut direct. How was it possible that so many things transpired in such short amount of time—Lady Catherine's unforeseen attack, Mr. Darcy's renewed declaration...*her acceptance*? To be sure, her father was all astonishment when he realized she was not indifferent to the great man, that she liked him—that she loved him, but her mother's rejoinder was the true surprise. When the first blush of incredulity rescinded, Mrs. Bennet was as a soldier called to arms. Calling out for Hill to supply fresh ink and a sharpened quill, she readily began spewing instructions to her bemused audience as she formulated her list of tasks.

"You must and shall be married by special license, my dearest love. And we shall send an express to your uncle Gardiner post haste; he, of course, knows the best warehouses for your wedding clothes!"

But the special license was not to be had. The Right Honorable Lady Catherine de Bourgh was intimately connected with the Archbishop of Canterbury and, more importantly, she was Fitzwilliam Darcy's almost nearest relation. She declared, in the name of honor and prudence, the match should not be granted any distinct privilege. With the shame of the bride's familial connections, not to mention the alarming behavior of the girl's youngest sister, the Mistress of Rosings implored the archbishop to refrain from indulging her nephew's request. Indeed, the lady made her feelings quite clear, nearly overstepping the boundaries of proper conduct in addressing His Grace with such fervor.

Lady Catherine had been rendered so exceedingly angry upon being crossed by her own flesh and blood that the sudden removal of Mr. Collins and his wife came about in a most propitious manner. Charlotte, of course, rejoiced in the match of her dear friend and Mr. Darcy—she had long guessed Eliza had become an object of some interest in that gentleman's eyes. Wishing to remove herself from Hunsford and the ravings of the great lady, Charlotte convinced her husband that writing a congratulatory note to Mr. Bennet was all well and good, but what felicity it would bring to the party if they should away to Meryton and bestow their good wishes in person. If the occasion coincided with her upcoming confinement, it was all the sweeter. Mr. Collins would not consider such a course of action without first applying to his noble patroness, for their untimely departure would smack of disloyalty. The lady, in her outrage, was only too happy to see them gone—she did not care to be reminded of their Hertfordshire connections. Seen in this light, Mr. Collins allowed his good wife to scribble a note, alerting their cousin of their imminent arrival.

"I still cannot credit how a man of ten thousand a year, would fail to find favor with the Archbishop of Canterbury!" Mrs. Bennet cried, startling Elizabeth back to the present conversation.

"Mama, we have discussed the matter at length. Given Lady Catherine's passionate disapprobation of the match, Mr. Darcy and I would be required to request a personal interview or, at the very least, present a letter of introduction to His Grace enumerating the reasons for soliciting such a courtesy..."

"But Lizzy, everyone who is *anyone* is able to obtain a special license to wed expeditiously and wherever they please! I do not see how you, a gentleman's daughter, and Mr. Darcy, a man of wealth and property, should be denied."

"Not everyone, Mama," Mary interrupted, peering up from her book. "Methodists are exempt from the Archbishop's rules. For that matter, so are Quakers and Jews..."

"Pray, what does that signify? *Jews?* To be sure, I have not met one in my life!"

Mr. Bennet guffawed at his wife's remark, as Elizabeth sighed and once more attempted to bring closure to the heated debate.

"It is all for the best," said Elizabeth, as gently as she could manage. "Do you not see the impropriety of requesting special dispensation? Lydia was wed under questionable circumstances. I would not wish to cast aspersions upon Miss Darcy's impeccable reputation, or that of my sisters, by giving rise to gossips at the sight of a hurried wedding."

"That will do, Lizzy!" Mrs. Bennett exclaimed. "I will not hear another word against our dear girl. Had I been able to carry my point in going to Brighton, nothing would have happened, but poor Lydia had nobody to take care of her. Who was there to watch over my child—the Forsters? La! I had always thought they were unfit to have the charge of her, but I was overruled, as I always am and my poor dear child suffered for it."

"Pray, heed me, Mama—Jane and I are of one accord. We will wait the required three weeks, during which time the banns will be read both in Hertfordshire and Derbyshire, and we shall be wed in our parish church thereafter. That will allow you plenty of time to prepare," said Elizabeth with not a little concern. Heaven only knew what plans her mother could have in store.

"The banns!" Mrs. Bennet cried. "The banns, you say? That *my* daughter and Mr. Darcy of Pemberley should be made to post marriage banns as if they were common villagers—like those radical Quakers or those foreign Jews!"

"If you do not include Quakers or Jews in your society," asked Mr. Bennet, "how would you know them to be common, or radical?

"Or foreign for that matter?" Elizabeth rejoined, unable to check herself.

"Jews are no longer to be considered foreigners, Lizzy. While they had been banned from the country for centuries, you should recall Cromwell allowed for their return."

"Mary, do please quit the room if you cannot refrain from interjecting such fiddle-faddle. And Mr. Bennet! How can you jest at a time like this? Nobody feels for my poor nerves. Why must you dwell on this subject? I say, I do not know anyone of the Jewish faith and I stand by my word!"

"Then you would be mistaken, my dear. Consider Hellerman, the apothecary, who replaced Mr. Jones upon his retirement to

Ramsgate. And what of the book vendor? You oft times patronize Jacobi and Sons whenever you wish to purchase a Radcliffe novel—or some such."

"My aunt Phillips told us all about the new linen draper and his wife," added Kitty, wanting her share of the conversation. "Mr. and Mrs. Schreiber are recently arrived from London having purchased the warehouse and the living from Sir William."

"I am all astonishment!" Mrs. Bennet gasped.

"Are you truly? You know very well Sir William had long been in trade and made a tolerable fortune. Since he quitted his residence and his business—with great fanfare, I might add—and relocated his family to Lucas Lodge, it behooved him to sell the property and be done with it. After all, what would *a knight* need with place of business in a small market town such as Meryton, I ask you?" Mr. Bennet quipped, his eyes all a-twinkle.

"Mr. and Mrs. Schreiber? I do not believe I have had the pleasure..."

"Perhaps, my dear, it is time you put forth some effort in getting to know our neighbors. After all, those on the other side of the counter are also flesh and blood."

Mr. Darcy lightly squeezed Elizabeth's hand. Sheepishly she turned to gaze into his eyes and could only imagine what clandestine message he wished to impart. How she longed to shield the gentleman from the indecorous outbursts and silliness of her relations, for they had had so little time together as a betrothed couple. She was yet uneasy in his company and unsure of his reactions as a whole. Elizabeth looked forward to the time when they should be removed from her family's society and be safely ensconced at Pemberley. There, shielded and secluded, they would learn from one another and garner little confidences that surely would bring them pleasure.

"If we may come to a right understanding, Mama," Elizabeth persisted, "the date has been set. We four are in agreement. We shall be wed on the eighth of November. This will allow for our dear family and friends to join in our felicity. Colonel Fitzwilliam and Miss Darcy will, of course, be in attendance and will need to make their arrangements."

Jane, who had sat in silence, her sweet disposition unable to reconcile the animosity between a most beloved sister and her own mama, sought Mr. Bingley's unspoken encouragement. She was obliged to take part in the conversation, to be sure, for her nuptials were involved in the matter, yet how could she choose sides and be satisfied?

"Miss Bingley and Mr. and Mrs. Hurst shall be joining us," Jane ventured to say, as Mr. Bingley's eyes shone with great admiration. "My aunt and uncle Gardiner will wish to be present, Mama, and they too will need sufficient time to prepare."

Mrs. Bennet, stunned by the shocking statements uttered in her parlor that afternoon, was only capable of nodding, causing her cap, copiously trimmed with ribbons and lace, to flounce comically upon her head.

Mr. Bennet stood and bowed to his family as he made to quit the room. Having had the opportunity to taunt his wife sufficiently, the solitude and silence of his library now beckoned as no other temptation could. Mr. Darcy, seeing at last the matter had been resolved and desiring a few quiet moments alone with his beloved, came to his feet as well.

"Miss Elizabeth, might I ask you to see me to the door?"

"It would be my pleasure, Mr. Darcy," she replied, as the handsome pair made their escape. "Will you return to dine with us tomorrow evening? I must advise you—I have had a note from

Charlotte. She and Mr. Collins will be joining the party, and the Lucases as well, I'm afraid."

"No doubt you will find it exceedingly diverting to observe my weak attempts at making conversation."

"Never say so!" replied she, feigning dismay. "Do you suppose I would reference such a shocking lack of talent?"

"Do not distress yourself, dearest. Your quick wit is a quality I much admire."

"And what of my beauty?" she had the temerity to ask. "May I presume you now find me at the very least *tolerable*?"

"Ah—of that, there can be no question. I have never ceased to meditate on the very great pleasure which a pair of fine eyes in the face of a pretty woman can bestow."

"You flatter me, Mr. Darcy. I was of a mind that you were not so easily tempted."

"My comments that night at the assembly, I suppose, will haunt me to no end in the years to come." Mr. Darcy smiled as he tilted his head and gazed upon those fine eyes. "In matters such as these, I would beg you to recall your *own* philosophy."

"Pray, enlighten me, sir," she said with a giggle.

"Think only of the past as its remembrance gives you pleasure," Mr. Darcy said as he gently took hold of her hands. "I would entreat you to recall my finer moments, dearest, for I have long considered you the handsomest woman of my acquaintance."

Delighting in the easy banter they now were able to share, their silly conversation was easily discharged as Mr. Darcy bent to deliver a tender kiss on lips which were still smiling.

It was many hours later, in the darkest part of night,

when a series of harried knocks were heard upon the door that caused the Bennet family to stir in alarm.

"What is it, Mr. Bennet? Who is at the door?" cried Mrs. Bennet pulling the bedclothes under her chin.

"I have not a clue, but I doubt we will learn the meaning of this rude interruption by hiding under the linens!" Mr. Bennet declared in a huff as he pulled on his dressing gown and stuffed his feet into his slippers. Carefully managing the staircase as he held a flickering chamberstick in one hand and wiped the sleep out of his eyes with the other, the master found himself at his front door just as Hill came from behind with a few coins from the household funds at the ready.

"For the runner, sir," she said with a shaky curtsey.

"Thank you, Hill," he replied gratefully, for he had not thought of compensating the errant messenger.

Mrs. Hill bobbed once more and stumbled back to her quarters as the master made quick work of opening the door. The messenger grinned an apology at the lateness of his arrival. Handing over the missive, he touched his cap and bounded off into the night. Mr. Bennet, now fully awake and justifiably curious, held his hand high and allowed the candle to illuminate a path to his library. Once there, he quietly shut the door, sat down in his familiar welcoming chair and was adjusting his spectacles when Mrs. Bennet came rushing in, followed by his two eldest daughters.

"How cozy you are, Mr. Bennet!" cried she. "With no consideration to my poor nerves, you have sequestered yourself without further thought of your wife or children who lay trembling in their beds. What has happened?" she beseeched. "Is it from Lydia?"

As he unfolded the object in question, Mr. Bennet peered over his spectacles and looked at his girls. "Jane? Lizzy? Were you all a tremble?"

"No indeed, sir, but we are anxious to know what news comes at this hour," Elizabeth replied, taking hold of her sister's hand.

The women gathered in front of Mr. Bennet as he silently read through the brief message. Satisfied that he was at liberty to share the contents, he cleared his throat and turned to his fretful wife.

"I trust you have ordered a good dinner for tomorrow evening, my dear, for I have just been informed we may expect an addition to our family party."

"Pray, who would be so indelicate as to awaken us in the middle of the night for such a matter? Who, may I ask, wishes to trespass on our hospitality without so much as a by your leave?"

"'Tis your brother who has written..."

"Edward? Whatever is he about?"

"If you would but calm yourself and allow me to read the letter, all will be explained."

Jane gently guided her mother to a seat, as Elizabeth lit the candles on the mantelpiece to better illuminate their surroundings. Mr. Bennet hemmed and hawed before commencing:

Gracechurch Street, London

Dear brother, I know you will understand when I say things are well in hand here in town. I have met with Mr. Moses Montefiore and found him to be the best of men, brilliant as he is honorable! Upon his expert understanding of the current situation, Mr. Montefiore conveys the Meyersons to your good care. This letter is to be accepted as means of an introduction for the rabbi and his family into Meryton society. You can expect a party of three—husband, wife and child—to arrive by four o'clock on Wednesday. I have assured them of my sister's fine hospitality, but tell Fanny not to fuss for their accommodations; they will only be staying the night. Montefiore has made arrangements for a living to be had in town.

Fanny, I have no doubt, will be happy to know the Meyersons have need to be settled in that establishment by Friday afternoon! Now, with regards to...

Mr. Bennet stopped at this juncture, folding and placing the letter most purposefully in his pocket.

"I believe therein lies the crux of the matter. The rest involves business that I will need to attend in the coming weeks."

"How extraordinary!" exclaimed Jane. "Whatever does my uncle mean by 'things are well in hand in town'?"

"Are you at liberty to divulge anything further on these people and their business in Meryton?" Elizabeth asked, covering a yawn with the back of her hand. "Who is this Montefiore? Can he be a sensible man, ushering these people to us in this manner?"

Mrs. Bennet had more pressing matters to discuss and would not be silenced. "We are in the midst of planning our daughters' weddings! My poor nerves cannot take much more agitation, Mr. Bennet. What does my brother mean by sending strangers to our home? And what, pray tell, is a *rabbi*?"

The hour being late and with no desire to entertain any further debate, Mr. Bennet stood and waved his hand, signaling towards the door. "Off with the lot of you. Tomorrow is another day and it will come soon enough. I am to bed and will brook no argument, Mrs. Bennet. Good night, Jane. Good night, Lizzy," he said, with a kiss to each daughter's brow.

Elizabeth blew out the candles and followed her father and sister as they wearily climbed towards their warm and welcoming beds. Mrs. Bennet, alone in the darkened room, sat down on Mr. Bennet's favorite chair and indulged in a good cry, presumably relieving her poor nerves.

CHAPTER TWO

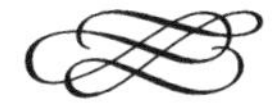

14th of October

With the household in turmoil in preparation for the unexpected guests, Jane and Elizabeth escaped towards the cherished wilderness on the side of the lawn, hoping to find some much needed privacy. Proceeding along the gravel path that led the sisters beyond the copse, they walked in silence, not wishing to be overheard by their frenzied mother or eavesdropping siblings.

A roughhewn door groaned as the sisters entered a confined and unassuming space. The humble hermitage, framed with trailing ivy and pink wood sorrel, had long been a place of respite for the Misses Bennet. Lavender and larkspur and Queen Anne's lace were suspended prettily from the rafters, filling the air with a fragrant and welcoming aroma. Borage and bugloss—and foxglove too—were potted and placed about, each according to their natural requisitions. Elizabeth, ever the naturalist, tended them all.

She shut the door and joined Jane on the cushioned bench they had placed underneath a back window many years ago. Picking up a forgotten piece of ribbon, Elizabeth twirled it about her fingers and gazed at her sister from underneath her dark lashes.

"I am not in the least prepared to ask Mr. Darcy for assistance in purchasing my wedding clothes and Jane, knowing you and I are of the same mind, I can only assume you will not humble yourself in such a manner before Mr. Bingley."

"I would never dream of doing such a thing. Whatever brought the notion to mind?"

"Our mama—naturally! She would have us wed in such finery the papers in Town would speak of our nuptials for weeks on end. We *must* be adamant on this point: Papa should not put out money on fine clothes when we can make do with a new bonnet and perhaps a few yards of trimming lace."

Jane nodded silently, knowing full well their dear papa struggled to live within their modest means.

"Dear Lizzy, your words shame me, for I had already begun to imagine what fine materials our draper might have in store. I was going to suggest a walk into Meryton tomorrow morning to visit the shops but, of course, you are right. We will make do. I may be able to complement the gown I wore to the Netherfield ball with some beading. Your own cream silk would only want for a bit of color..."

"I knew it!" Mrs. Bennet cried as she threw open the fragile door. "I knew the two of you would be scheming against me and my good intentions."

"Mama..."

"This is your work, Miss Elizabeth Bennet," she said with dismay. "My sweet Jane would never have the heart to disappoint me so..."

"You misunderstand, ma'am—we only wish to spare Papa the extra expense..."

"Extra expense? Are we discussing the purchase of a new milk cow or the necessity of refurbishing the roof? No, I think not!" Mrs. Bennet stomped her foot to strengthen the point. "We are speaking of my daughters and their wedding day. Extra expense indeed. If ever there was a time to spend his precious coin on a worthy cause, it is here and now. It is his duty...*it is your right*!"

"I do not see the point, Mama," Elizabeth replied.

"I would have you recall, not so long ago, you and your sisters were all agog at the illustrations of some noble lady's wedding clothes and that of her party. We, all of us, examined the types of lace, the usage of flowers, the patterns and various shades of materials."

"Forgive me ma'am, but I beg to differ. I was not all agog. If you recall, I found it rather humorous—such nonsense!"

"Do not dare to feign superiority over me, miss, for I know you too well, You *do* appreciate the finer things in life—I have been clothing you for nearly one and twenty years and know your likes and dislikes. There is no shame in wishing to be dressed elegantly on such a day...a day that can only be considered the pinnacle of your life!"

"I dare say I may have one *or two* such days before I give up the ghost."

"Obstinate, headstrong girl! You speak out of ignorance. Heed me Lizzy. This may be one of the last decisions you make without your husband's interference. Can you say for certain that your Mr. Darcy will allow you free reign in matters of your household, your apparel, or of your person? Mr. Bennet does not wish to appear the tyrant in front of his girls, and I perhaps should not depict your dear papa as such, but in these matters, allow me to say; I have had little liberty myself."

"Perhaps Papa has only meant to offer a hand of guidance," Jane submitted.

"My sweet girl, guidance may be what you would call it at the beginning of your marriage, but after twenty-five years, you may find a stronger word would suit! I would have you understand. Your wedding clothes will serve as a social marker to proclaim your new status."

"Weddings, even *fashionable* weddings, are sparsely attended," Elizabeth rejoined. "Pray, whom do you wish to impress? There will none there but our closest relations and possibly a handful of curious villagers. It shall not be a lavish affair. We will be married before noon as the Church dictates and return home for the wedding breakfast soon after."

"It is not a matter of impressing the villagers. You have earned such accolades by marrying *such men*." Mrs. Bennet closed her eyes and sniffed at her handkerchief, scented with lavender and lemon verbena.

"Mama, pray do not distress yourself so," Jane murmured.

"I was the daughter of a poor attorney when your father made an offer of marriage. My heart had been won, you should not doubt me on that score; nonetheless, I was not insensible to the fact that my elevated status would play a crucial role in the lives of my future children. *Your* lives have been much improved because I married out of my social sphere. I have spent my life attempting to live up to that challenge. Do not believe for one moment that I am not aware of what is said behind my back."

"Mama, I do not see how this concerns..."

"Lizzy, your father has the honor of giving his beloved girls in marriage. Allow me the honor of seeing you dressed in a manner befitting the daughters of Longbourn."

Torn, once again, Jane found herself in the middle of a debate between her dear sister and her trying parent. "I beg you, Mama, do not ask my father to overspend—"

"And for my part, ma'am," Elizabeth added, "I pray you do not mention this subject to either of the gentlemen."

"I will think upon it, but I cannot tell you how deeply aggrieved I find myself. Unfortunately, I have no more time to discuss the matter for I must design the courses of our meal. I would not shame my brother, now that he has spoken so highly of my housekeeping, nor would I wish to disappoint Mr. Bennet."

"What have you planned?" Jane asked sweetly, attempting to have her mother think on something more pleasant.

"Tonight's dinner will be as well dressed as any the Meyersons' *or* the Lucases' have ever seen! I would not have any flibbertigibbet spreading the word that my table was not fit for London folk. Already my sister Phillips has been to call, sharing what she has heard on the streets this day."

"What news could my aunt possibly have learned so soon?"

"Jane, dear, you know very well, nothing happens in Meryton without your aunt's knowledge. The town apparently is in an uproar, for these Meyersons are associated with people of prestige. I dare say, our guests might very well be quality, even though the circumstances of their arrival are questionable at best!"

WHEN THE CLOCK IN THE BENNET DRAWING ROOM WANTED ONLY a quarter of an hour, the family gathered in anticipation. Elizabeth tried to keep her eyes upon her needlework but could not help herself from repeatedly gazing out the window and, as for Mr. Bennet, while he seemed quite content reading his afternoon periodical, a discerning eye would have noted that not once did the gentleman turn the page. Mary sat at the piano forte attempting to learn a new passage in a particularly difficult piece. As her technique was rather wanting, a black key was struck when, more often than not, it should have been the white. Instead of soothing her mother's nerves, the results, to the party's chagrin, were ineffectual. Without Lydia's liveliness, therefore, it was left to Kitty to break the tension with her youthful mix of naiveté and candor.

"Do you suppose the Meyersons are much like the Romani gypsies in the woods?"

Mr. Bennet chuckled as he smoothed out his paper. "I dare say you will find them to be much like others of our acquaintance."

As the grand clock struck four, a carriage was heard making its way along the gravel drive. Kitty jumped from her seat and was for the window, only to be stayed by a stern reprimand from her mother. Mary turned from the pianoforte, indignant at her younger sibling's lack of propriety.

"Continue to act in such a manner, Kitty, and you will forever be treated as a frivolous and irksome child. It would behoove you to look to your elders and attempt to emulate the proper etiquette so becoming in a young lady of quality."

"Mary, dear, do *try* to be sociable," Mrs. Bennet petitioned. "One does not know what sort of people these Meyersons are. Jews or not, I would not have anyone say that they were ill received at Longbourn."

Kitty, hiding behind an embroidered silk pillow, proceeded to stick her tongue out toward her sister as Hill opened the door and announced the awaited visitors.

"Mr. and Mrs. Meyerson, madam."

A family of three entered the room. The gentleman bowed and the lady curtsied. A child clung closely to her mama, so much so that she nearly was concealed by the lady's skirt. The little miss peeked from behind, her large hazel eyes taking in a room full of strangers, and she proceeded to place her thumb into the safe confines of her cherubic mouth.

"You are most welcome," Mr. Bennet said as he eagerly extended his hand. "Allow me to introduce Mrs. Bennet and my daughters, Jane, the eldest, followed by Elizabeth, Mary and Catherine, or Kitty, as we call her—she is rather too silly yet to be called her proper name."

Mrs. Bennet, ashamed for her daughter and how the girl's silliness could reflect on her own maternal talents, silently performed a welcoming curtsey.

"We are grateful for your hospitality, Mrs. Bennet," said the gentleman as he bowed over her hand. "It is a blessing to be received with such amiability and on such short notice, too! I do hope you will accept our apologies for any inconvenience..."

"Ahem..." the elegant lady murmured.

"Ah, but I am forgetting my manners—Jacob Meyerson, your servant, ma'am." He extended his hand to his side, before continuing, "My wife, Mrs. Meyerson, and our daughter, Rachel."

"We are delighted you have arrived safely," said Mrs. Bennet, and she was surprisingly sincere. Her guests, although quite unknown to her in every conceivable manner, were fashionable and appeared to be exemplary specimens of London society.

"Are you the *rabbi*? You do not look at all as I expected," Kitty exclaimed.

"You were expecting a rather exotic fellow with a flowing kaftan and an impressive growth of a beard," Mr. Meyerson responded amicably with a great bellow of a laugh. "The great Maimonides once said there is no commandment requiring Jews to seek out clothing which would make them stand out as different from what is worn by Gentiles. Therefore, Miss Catherine, as you find my appearance in keeping with Hertfordshire society, it would seem I am in good standing with the great philosopher."

Mortified, Kitty blushed and retreated to the corner. Mrs. Bennet rolled her eyes at her daughter's unrefined comportment, although, if she were to be truthful, at least with herself, she would have admitted to sharing the very same thoughts. However, not wanting to appear ignorant or worse yet, unsociable, Mrs. Bennet quickly attempted to make amends.

May I offer you some refreshment? You must be tired after so long a journey. Ring the bell for tea, Kitty."

"Tea would be most welcome," Mrs. Meyerson said with a gentle smile as she took the proffered seat. "Your kind housekeeper showed my maid and the child's nurse to their rooms, but I would have Rachel stay by my side, at least until she is a bit more acclimated to her surroundings. May I beg your indulgence madam?"

The child had already made herself quite at home, having found a comfortable spot at her father's feet. Elizabeth stole a glance and observed her mother's reaction. La! The child had a bit of Lydia's tenacity. Certainly her mama would recognize the similarities and not request the child be removed. Having spared any discipline towards her youngest daughter, Elizabeth could not think that the mistress of the house would do any less for her guest.

But then her thoughts turned to Mr. Darcy. Had he been in attendance, what would he have decreed? Would he be of the opinion that children were to be seen and not heard?

Her own upbringing differed greatly from what Mr. Darcy had experienced at Pemberley House. Five daughters brought up at home without a governess—Lady Catherine had been scandalized at the notion and, indeed, compared to other families, she and her sisters had been quite at liberty to run amok. It seemed that today would be no different.

Mrs. Bennet gazed uncomfortably at her good rug before smiling at her guest. "But of course little Rachel should stay, Mrs. Meyerson."

The lady nodded her gratitude to her hostess and then, turning to her husband, she chastised, "Mr. Meyerson! You, sir, have caused Miss Catherine to feel uncomfortable in her own home. How is the young miss expected to know of rabbis and medieval philosophers? If you are going to preach, at least let there be a lesson so that others may benefit from the experience."

Mr. Meyerson laughed once more and joined his wife on the settee. "I do beg your pardon, Miss Catherine. My wife is quite right."

"Please do not worry on my account," Kitty stated. Thinking better of her comments, she added, "It was idle curiosity, nothing more."

Mrs. Bennet, unaccustomed to such easy behavior between man and wife, had become quite undone. Within moments of making their acquaintance, Mrs. Meyerson chastised and teased her husband and he accepted her admonishments with good humor and grace. Her mouth suddenly dry, Mrs. Bennet found she lacked sufficient conversation and began waving her delicate handkerchief towards her daughter. "The *bell*, Kitty," was her fervent plea.

Mrs. Meyerson brought her daughter onto her lap and with a delicate yet swift motion, removed the child's thumb from her mouth. Reaching into her reticule, she produced a length of linen and proceeded to unravel a packet of sweetmeats, which she promptly handed to the child before turning her attention to the Misses Bennet.

"I had the privilege of meeting your aunt and uncle Gardiner before leaving London," she said. "Miss Bennet, Miss Elizabeth, you may be interested to know there is a package in the foyer addressed to your attention. Naturally, after the Gardiners came to our aide in procuring our lodging for this evening, we were more than pleased to act as their courier."

"How very kind you are, Mrs. Meyerson," said Elizabeth.

"It is just like my brother and his wife to send presents for my girls. Kitty dear, make yourself useful and bring the gift to your sisters."

"Perhaps Lizzy and I can retrieve the package when we go up to dress for dinner, Mama," Jane suggested, not wanting the embarrassment of opening the gift in front of company.

"Nonsense. If my brother sent a gift, I am sure we may all take pleasure in sharing your good fortune." She nodded her head in the direction of the door and watched her youngest do as she was bid.

"I believe Mrs. Gardiner included a note. It is just there, tucked under that length of ribbon," said Mrs. Meyerson as Kitty came rushing back into the room.

Jane espied the message but, being in harmony with her sister's wishes, swiftly removed the missive and placed it in between the pages of a book readily at hand. Just at this pivotal moment, Hill arrived with the tea tray. Elizabeth, determined to allay the party's curiosity, eagerly went to her aid. By all accounts, it was her mother's place to pour and offer the small plates of seedcake and lemon biscuits but, Elizabeth appropriated the task with the hope of coaxing a new and infinitely more interesting topic of conversation. In this manner, Elizabeth secured her goal. She and Jane would open their aunt's letter, along with the package, in the privacy of their own bedchamber.

"We would enjoy learning more of your people," she said, handing the gentleman his tea. "We are rather ignorant of your customs and history."

Mr. Meyerson graciously accepted the cup and saucer and smiled at his hostess. "Where does one begin?"

"Ah, I see I have posed a rather insuperable question," Elizabeth laughed. "Allow me to ask something decidedly more to point. Do I detect an accent, Mr. Meyerson?"

"Quite so, Miss Elizabeth! I am of German ancestry. I am an *Ashkenazi* Jew."

"I am not familiar with the term, sir."

"I do not doubt it, but it is fairly simple to explain. When the Israelites were taken from their land thousands of years ago, my people eventually made their way to the eastern part of the Continent, some settling in Germany, others in Poland, others in Prussian territories. These Jews are known as *Ashkenazim*. My grandfather came to England in his youth. I was raised speaking the language of his birthplace along with the language of my new homeland. As much as I have worked on perfecting my speech," he said with a chuckle, "the accent still lingers."

"As a student of our family's ancestry, I find your history to be intriguing, Mr. Meyerson," Mary acknowledged. "Imagine tracing your lineage to the ancient Israelites!"

"Ah—we have a genealogist in our midst. Miss Mary, as the topic finds your favor, you may be interested to know Mrs. Meyerson has a different story altogether. She is a *Sephardic* Jew. Her ancestors and others from the Iberian Peninsula have been in England since fleeing the Spanish Inquisition."

"But that is extraordinary!" Mary exclaimed. "It must have been Divine intervention that brought your families to our country."

"Yes, quite." Mr. Meyerson grinned knowingly at his wife. "And a good thing too. However, *that* is a story for another day."

Mrs. Meyerson nodded her approval, knowing her husband ever to have a sermon at the ready but not always at the most appropriate time.

"What brings you to Hertfordshire, sir?" Mrs. Bennet asked. "I dare say that you will find life in Meryton to be quite unsophisticated and rather dull—especially if you are accustomed to socializing with The Upper Ten."

Oh Mama! Elizabeth thought, as she bit her lip in exasperation. It seemed such a personal question. They had not been made privy to the particulars of their guests' status in London. But Mr. Meyerson's response put her at ease, and so Elizabeth held her tongue.

"I would not have you believe we dined every night at St. James or attended the assemblies at Almack's. Vouchers are not easily obtained, as you very well may know. Nonetheless, Mrs. Meyerson and I enjoyed our social set, which indubitably is due to my good wife's familial connections. As to life in Hertfordshire, we are come to enjoy the simple life and to improve and perfect a friendship and intimacy with the growing Jewish community in Meryton...a community which has been increasing in numbers, and constraints, with each passing day."

"Constraints?" Mary asked. "How so?"

"Judaism, Miss Mary, is a religion that cannot be practiced in isolation. There are rituals and commemorations that are meant to be experienced as a community. While we can pray individually, the presence of a *minyan*—a quorum of ten or more men—is required for certain portions of our services."

Aghast, Mary insisted on further elucidation. "Do you mean to imply, sir, there is some sort of impediment whereby your people may not gather together in their house of worship?"

"By no means! It is my understanding that obtaining the required amount of congregants in Meryton has proven to be difficult. While I can certainly appreciate why that is so, as the rabbi I hope to rectify the situation and, in doing so, bring a sense of fulfillment to my brethren."

Mr. Bennet nodded and shared a knowing look with his guest. The two men had not been afforded any privacy since the family arrived. Only that which was previously shared in Mr. Gardiner's letter was immediately open for discussion. He would have to be patient for the rest of it. The particulars would be shared over a brandy once he and Mr. Meyerson were safely secluded in his library.

"The situation in its entirety was my cousin Montefiore's doing," said Mrs. Meyerson. "My cousin, you will understand, serves on a committee which administers the development of Jewish communities throughout England. Although we are a small minority, our people are spread throughout the land and are in need of schools, clergy, and houses of worship. Rabbi Ash of Dover, for example, has been performing services there as well as in Canterbury and Chatham under the auspices of the Chief Rabbi in London. My husband was leading a community in Town and had been there for quite some time when the offer of the living in Meryton was made. It was all quite sudden!"

"Yes, we were scarcely given any notice," added Mr. Meyerson. "Montefiore had made the arrangements and informed us the house was ours for the taking. We were made to understand it would not be ready for occupation until Thursday. With our Sabbath observance starting on Friday evening, the directors of the committee wished us to depart post haste!"

"What exactly *is* a rabbi? I have an image of Levitical priests." Mr. Bennet quipped."

Papa! Not you as well? Elizabeth groaned internally.

"Nothing as splendid as that. I am simply a teacher," said Mr. Meyerson with a shrug of his shoulders. "I have studied our laws, our language and the practices of our faith. As a rabbi, I simply lead a congregation."

"But you do not presume to be addressed as such?" asked Mary.

"No, Miss Mary, I tend not to impose my title on those not of my flock. Even then, I have had some congregants choose to call me some other, rather unfortunate names—"

Mrs. Meyerson coughed into her handkerchief and raised a delicate brow. Mrs. Bennet observed the exchange with not a little incredulity, but then the grandfather clock struck startling the party who had been mesmerized by Mr. Meyerson's speech. Mrs. Bennet came to her senses and resumed her duties as mistress of the house.

"Oh dear! Look at the time," she said. "We will retire to dress for dinner and gather in the drawing room at half past six. Pray, Mr. and Mrs. Meyerson, allow me to show you the way."

The party quit the room with the two eldest daughters trailing behind. When well ensconced in their bedchamber, Jane and Elizabeth took the opportunity to open their package and read their favorite aunt's letter.

My dear girls,

I trust you will not think me presumptuous. I have acted with only the best of intentions. Enclosed you will find sufficient materials for your wedding clothes—I suspect your announcements are on their way to Gracechurch Street, as you read this note. With the understanding that your local shops, charming as they may be, might not stock the quality or selection that your dear mama would desire, and you would not have sufficient time to come to Town, your Uncle Gardiner and I decided to forward our wedding gift without delay! I have no fear your local dressmaker and milliner will see to an impeccable design. Before you dare to think it, Lizzy, 'tis not too much, 'tis not by far too much, for who better deserves this felicity?

I dare say Mr. Bingley and Mr. Darcy will be overcome when first they lay eyes upon their beloved brides. To be sure, your uncle and I will be hard pressed to contain our emotions. May God be with you, my dear girls, and continue to bless your days with good tidings and immeasurable joy! Most affectionately~

"How kind of our aunt and uncle!" Elizabeth cried.

"There, you see?" Jane murmured, as she gingerly caressed a length of silk with her fingertips. "Mama will be pleased, and we will be spared. There will be no need to shame ourselves in front of our soon-to-be husbands."

Elizabeth nodded silently and sent up a prayer of gratitude for her thoughtful relations. She was certain the generous gift had not been sent merely to circumvent a costly trip to town or to avoid quibbling with local shopkeepers with empty shelves and who, themselves, were at the mercy of smugglers or worse. With a keen understanding of the machinations of her dear sister-in-law, their aunt had surmised the situation to be dire and, by providing the necessary and appropriate goods, she saved the girls hours of vexation and irritabilities.

Seeing that Jane had all but completed her *toilette*, Elizabeth disallowed any further woolgathering and made haste to prepare for their dinner engagement. It would not do to keep Mr. Darcy waiting in the drawing room. Just the thought of the gentleman stranded and surrounded by Kitty, her mother *and* Mr. Collins had Elizabeth dressed, coiffed and skirting down the stairs speedily and without delay.

The family and guests had just gathered when Hill announced that Mr. Darcy and Mr. Bingley had arrived. The gentlemen were shown into the now confined and intimate space, and they were quickly followed by Mr. and Mrs. Collins as well as Sir William and Lady Lucas. Introductions were made and all the customary sorts of pleasantries were exchanged as the ladies took to their plush and cushioned seats, while the gentlemen made do with an assortment of chairs brought in for the occasion.

The Bennet household boasted two sitting rooms and, while the one being utilized for the evening's affair was the superior option, accommodations for such a large party were exceedingly lacking. Mrs. Bennet's poor nerves were all aflutter, for she knew that Lady Lucas would have the gossip all about town by tomorrow noon. Her only saving grace would be that soon her daughters would be mistresses of Netherfield and Pemberley. Lady Lucas could not equal that proclamation, for her daughter's humble home was merely a parsonage bestowed on her son-in-law with great condescension.

With nothing for it, Mrs. Bennet held her head high and turned her mind to other thoughts. Charlotte Collins née Lucas was not fit for company, thought she. Indeed, in her day, a woman so close to her confinement would have thought better of the situation and would have chosen to remain at home. However, *her girls*—how well they looked tonight! Dressed in an elegant gown of cream silk, Jane looked every bit the angel, smiling sweetly as Mr. Bingley made his way to stand alongside his betrothed. And even Lizzy, not half so handsome as Jane, nor half so good-humored as Lydia, looked quite acceptable this evening in her rose net gown with chenille embroidery. Mrs. Bennet had witnessed the look of sheer admiration upon Mr. Darcy's countenance as he gazed at her Lizzy. *Darling girl.* She had done well in securing his affections.

Sir William made his way across the confined space and bowed low before Mr. Darcy. "Good evening, sir. Allow me to reiterate my felicitations to you and Miss Elizabeth. You are carrying away the brightest jewel of the county. We wish you happy, to be sure!"

Mr. Darcy bowed in return and smiled, knowing full well Elizabeth would be attempting not to roll her eyes. "Thank you for your good wishes. I believe I *and* Mr. Bingley are, indeed, the luckiest of men."

Sir William, realizing his error in singling out one of the Bennet daughters over the other, was awash in shame and mortification. With a bit of hemming and hawing, however, the gentleman quickly rallied and was soon speaking with the other guests newly arrived from London. Having learned of Mr. and Mrs. Meyerson's connections to the House of Rothschild, Sir William was convinced that improving his acquaintance with his new neighbors would certainly bode well.

"Are you much at St. James, Mr. Meyerson? Mayhap our families will meet the next time we are all in Town..."

Mr. Meyerson smiled cordially. "I am afraid we do not have any immediate plans for visiting the palace, sir. Indeed, there is little call for a humble clergyman to be presented at court."

While the gentlemen spoke of possible mutual acquaintances, Elizabeth turned to her dear friend and, speaking *sotto voce*, enquired about her health.

"I am so very glad to see you Charlotte, but was it wise to come all this way in your condition?"

The lady placed a gentle hand upon her great belly and smirked. "Dearest Lizzy, can you truly ask me that question, having experienced our neighborly relations with Rosings? To be sure, once Lady Catherine heard of your betrothal, there was no living in Kent. The rantings and ravings...Lizzy, you must promise me that a room awaits me in Pemberley if ever I run away from home again."

The two friends shared a laugh, as the Meyerson child made herself known to the company by bursting through the door with her nurse in frenzied pursuit.

"Mama!" Papa!" she cried, her sobs echoing through the corridor.

In her brave escape from the nursery, the errant adventurer had dragged her favorite counterpane along for protection, much like a knight with his chainmail or shield. However, in the child's despair to reach her parents, she tripped on the overlong coverlet, tumbled across the floor and landed quite soundly at Mr. Darcy's feet. So startled was she at the sudden encounter, the little miss ceased sobbing immediately and scurried up a pair of extraordinarily long legs, making herself quite at home on the gentleman's lap. The party at once was all astonishment as the child reached up and ran her hand over the stranger's face.

"You are not my papa," she said quite emphatically.

Mr. Meyerson appeared at once and attempted to remove his daughter from Mr. Darcy's person. "Come now, Rachel," he said sternly. "It is back to bed for you and your good nurse."

But the child now refused to go. Burrowing her curls deep into her protector's broad chest, Rachel's hot tears flowed unrestrained, sullying the gentleman's impeccably styled cravat. Her mother, aghast at this impetuous exhibition, was quite beside herself and, although the father demanded immediate obedience, the unruly daughter would not submit. The threat of having to return with Nurse to a dark and unfamiliar bedchamber sans her dolls, books and fripperies was more than she could tolerate—especially when the adult persons were assembled for an evening of entertainment and delights.

"Rachel Naomi Meyerson! You will cease this intolerable display at once!" Mrs. Meyerson commanded. But with each call from her anxious parents, Rachel wept with that much more vigor.

"Pray, be at ease, madam," Mr. Darcy said, surprising one and all with his calm demeanor.

Elizabeth watched the proceedings as if it were all in a dream. When Mr. Darcy removed his handkerchief from his coat pocket, she felt her mouth drop open in a most unbecoming manner, as he did not wipe away the child's tears but instead fashioned a makeshift puppet together with a ribbon taken from Rachel's curly mop.

As the sobbing ceased, the room was suddenly, unnervingly silent. Mr. Darcy peered from under his furrowed brow to find the party entranced by his quick thinking and talented exhibition.

Elizabeth gazed at him with a deeper sense of admiration than she had previously thought possible.

Who was the gentleman before her? Certainly not the same proud and arrogant man she met at the Meryton assembly. Mr. Darcy caught her stare and found both affection and amazement in her eyes.

"I used to make these little dolls for Georgiana," he explained with a boyish grin. "She would wake in the middle of the night, frightened and crying for our mama."

"That is very well done, Mr. Darcy," Mr. Bennet said with a resounding slap on the gentleman's back. "I would never have believed it, had I not seen it with my own eyes. Ladies and gentlemen, I give you the Master of Pemberley!" He applauded and urged his guests to join in.

Mr. and Mrs. Meyerson had composed themselves sufficiently to cease placing the blame on each other for the child's misconduct and began begging the pardon of their most bewildered hostess.

"I have never witnessed such behavior from any of my children," Mrs. Meyerson confessed. "To say that I am ashamed is putting it rather mildly. I can only believe that the child is overly tired and utterly confused in these new surroundings."

Mrs. Bennet herself was at a loss for words. She had believed them to be such elegant company, and yet they had proven to be very much like her own family. "Rachel is not your only child then?" she enquired.

"No, we have three daughters married and a son—David," the lady said, regaining some pride.

"*Three daughters married?*" said Mrs. Bennet, her admiration growing for the lady with every syllable she uttered. "My goodness! I commend you, Mrs. Meyerson, for I know only too well how difficult a thing it is to bring about. I will be equally blessed when Jane and

Elizabeth are wed, for my youngest, Lydia, has already been married off."

Kitty, uninterested with all the talk about married daughters, turned to the child, who was now playing quietly with her rag doll.

"I am looking forward to the Christmas season," she declared with great eagerness. "Are you anticipating what pretty dolls and special presents you shall receive on Boxing Day, little Rachel? When my sisters and I were your age, we made paper flowers and strung them about the drawing room. Mary had a set of figurines representing Joseph, Mary, and baby Jesus."

Elizabeth would have kicked her sister if she had been close enough to impart the punishment without censure. She glanced at Mr. Darcy and watched in dismay as he closed his eyes and grimaced.

Rachel removed her thumb from her mouth and looked at the young lady who was kind enough to address her directly. "Mama says we do not celebrate that holy day."

"You do not celebrate Christmas?"

"No." She shook her raven curls to and fro. "We celebrate *Chanukah* with *dreidels* and *latkes* and chocolate coins!"

Mrs. Meyerson, laughing uneasily at this new outburst, quickly enlightened the party. "Pray understand that Rachel is schooled in all of our holidays as well as several of the Christian faith. She is, after all, the daughter of a rabbi and should be well versed in such matters as these."

Kitty found that although she was once again discomfited by her actions, she could not resist posing another question. "But what *is* Chanukah?"

Finally leaving the safety of Mr. Darcy's embrace, Rachel went to stand by her mother and removed her thumb from its favorite position. Her eyes wide and expressive, she responded to Kitty's question.

"Evil men came from far away with armies and elephants and poured pigs' blood all over our books and ruined everything!"

"Goodness! Perhaps if they had been faithful followers of Jesus, they would have been spared such atrocities," Kitty suggested with sincere astonishment.

"He had not been born yet," said little Rachel and promptly returned her thumb to its happy home.

"Miss Catherine," Mr. Meyerson provided hurriedly, "this event takes place nearly *two hundred years* before the birth of your savior..."

Mary chuckled and caressing the little girl's cheek, whispered, "Out of the mouths of babes..."

Hill entered the drawing room, only to find the inhabitants stunned and silent. Skirting her way to Mrs. Bennet's side, the housekeeper whispered dinner was ready to be served.

The lady of the house arose, bringing the gentlemen to their feet, and without further ado, proceeded to invite her disconcerted guests to the dining room. "Wine," she thought. "We are in need of copious amounts of Mr. Bennet's good wine."

CHAPTER THREE

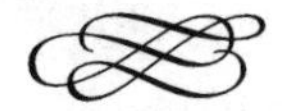

A fine table had been set, and the guests were tempted with one course after another of Cook's best work. To everyone's immeasurable satisfaction, Mrs. Meyerson had successfully sent her impish child off to bed, and the evening progressed without further interruption from that quarter. Mrs. Bennet, beaming from her end of the table, espied Jane and Mr. Bingley whispering shyly to each other, while Elizabeth teased and cajoled Mr. Darcy until finally he laughed at her witty repartee.

The evening, decidedly, would be a success in spite of its unusual beginning. If Lady Lucas spread the word about town of the shocking occurrences that took place in the Bennet parlor, Mrs. Bennet would be the first to own it—after all, she was not at fault, but rather the culpability belonged to her elegant guests.

Laughter and the clinking of glasses brought Mrs. Bennet's attention back to her fine table. While she was woolgathering, she had missed Mr. Meyerson's comment. Her husband's enquiry allowed her join in the conversation once more.

"Tell us about your son," asked Mr. Bennet. "Does he follow in his father's pious footsteps?"

"No, nothing could be further from the truth," replied Mr. Meyerson. "Our David is a pugilist and a disciple of Mendoza the Jew."

"I beg your pardon?"

"My son is a professional fighter following in the footsteps of that bare-knuckle fighter who captivated London. You may have heard of the fellow. Though he was only sixteen years of age and stood just five foot seven, he defeated far heftier opponents with his style of boxing. His secret weapon was the so-called *jab.* He became so famous, a plaque hangs outside his house on Paradise Row in the East End."

"The East end, you say?" Mr. Collins interjected with a phlegmy cough. "I dare say my noble patroness, Lady Catherine de Bourgh, would not call it the best of neighborhoods."

Elizabeth shared a quick look with Jane who also had noticed the affront.

"Very true, sir. Unfortunately many in my community have been delegated to that area. Although I do not take pleasure in seeing my son make his way in this world in this manner, I understand his angst. There are only so many avenues for our young people. Harassment and frustration tend to build up in a young man, you must own. David emulates Mendoza's mannerism and philosophies, as have many others. Samuel Elias, *Dutch Sam* as he is known, was such an adherent."

"Yes! I am familiar with this man," exclaimed Mr. Bingley enthusiastically. "I attended a fight with a few gentlemen from my club and witnessed his famous moves..."

"Never say so!" Jane cried.

Mr. Bingley grinned and looked to Mr. Darcy for assistance

before continuing, "It *is* a gentleman's sport, my dear. I will not attend again if it troubles you, but the fight was extraordinary. The man invented something called an upper-cut." Mr. Bingley, forgetting himself momentarily, jumped to his feet, putting his fists in the air to demonstrate what he had learnt.

"Mr. Bingley!" cried Mrs. Bennet.

"I do beg your pardon, madam," said Mr. Bingley, as he retook his seat next to his startled betrothed.

Mary, wishing to pursue an altered course, maneuvered the conversation in a different vein. "I wasn't aware that Jewish people intermingled with the rest of Society in that manner. I mean to say, it was my understanding that the Jews secluded themselves and kept to their ancient traditions."

"As Christianity takes on many different forms and customs, Judaism does the same. We seem to be experts at the art of contemplation and reform. Remember Miss Mary, we have had longer to do so!"

"If I may expound on the matter," Mrs. Meyerson interjected, "my husband is a follower of Moses Mendelsohn, the father of the *Haskalah* movement. This philosophy encourages our community to avail themselves of the new possibilities of social, educational and economic integration."

"Indeed?" questioned Mr. Darcy, startling the party with his interjection. "In what way are they new?"

Having not participated in the conversation thus far, Mr. Darcy's simple rejoinder appeared incompatible with the general party's friendly banter. Elizabeth understood he lacked the talent which some people possessed of conversing easily, and she grimaced at the thought that their guests would misinterpret his meaning—especially after having won them over earlier with little Rachel.

"Pray, forgive Mrs. Meyerson for being so bold, sir, no offence was meant, to be sure! Our community, *praised be He*, is living in an...enlightened era of unprecedented freedoms, thanks, in part, to the removal of legal discrimination and forced conversions. I am determined to spread this philosophy, this *Haskalah* ideology, so that my congregation and others begin to take part in the world around them, contributing to and benefiting from society, as any other citizen would be apt to do."

"Forced conversion?" Sir William asked. "How can such a thing exist?"

Noticing Mrs. Meyerson's sigh, the rabbi attempted to curtail further discussion. "The retelling of this history is not suitable for the dining room. Perhaps, sir, we may discuss it at another time?"

"I have read the works of William Wilberforce," Mary continued, "which speaks of the London Society Promoting Christianity Amongst the Jews."

"La!" Kitty exclaimed. "You mean to say you have forsaken Fordyce and read something written by another's hand?"

Not wishing to acknowledge her sister's outburst, Mary continued with her point. "It is my understanding that he and his followers believe their organization a benevolent one—one whose purpose is to rescue unhappy Jews from the state of moral degradation."

"I assure you Miss Mary, we are neither *unhappy*, nor do not desire rescuing," Mr. Meyerson said with a bitter chuckle.

"But I would agree with you, sir! While I am aware this is a charitable attempt to convert the Jew, I do not condone the action. Let the convert come to Christ on his own volition, not by reprimand or coercion. Surely the example of our Savior has shown us the way of it."

"This shows a great deal of intellect and generosity of spirit, Miss Mary. Jewish emancipation is making it possible for my people to become active and productive citizens. Where in the past my community has seen outright restrictions placed on them with regards to occupations or education, we are living in a new day and age."

Mrs. Bennet fidgeted in her chair, uncomfortable with the topic and uncertain if was proper to speak of such a delicate matter in one's dining room. Attempting to direct the conversation to something to which she could contribute, she grasped at the flittering thoughts that crossed her mind.

"Pray tell me, sir, how are you acquainted with my brother?"

"It is rather a complicated story, ma'am, and it all began thanks to the machinations of two enterprising ladies."

Mr. Bennet snorted and muttered something mercifully imperceptible. However, its meaning did not escape his wife, whose disapproving mien conveyed her thoughts. Mr. Meyerson noticed the looks exchanged by his hosts and decided it was best if he continued with his anecdote rather than attempt to modify his *faux pas*.

"Let me see if I can unravel this web of familial connections and Divine Providence," he said, rubbing his hands together as if preparing for a great feast. "As I believe we mentioned, my wife is related to Moses Montefiore, a Sephardic Jew. They are cousins through mutual relations with the Mocatta family—who, if you are interested, Miss Mary, settled in this country in the 1670s! In any event, Montefiore took to wife a lovely young lady from a prominent Ashkenazi family by the name of Judith Barent Cohen."

"Jacob, perhaps you should get to the point," Mrs. Meyerson encouraged.

"Quite right, dearest. You see, Miss Judith, nay, Mrs. Montefiore, is a patron of the Jewish Ladies' Loan and Visiting Society and an officer of the Jews' Orphan Asylum, as is my Sofia! Both ladies participate in a veritable host of philanthropic organizations. While they are from different communities, they soon became friends without knowing they were related—distant cousins, of course but, nonetheless, related."

"I believe Mr. Montefiore is connected to Nathan Mayer Rothschild, a man of some importance in London's financial world," Mr. Bingley added.

"Indeed! The men are connected by marriage. Mrs. Montefiore's sister, Hannah, is married to Mr. Rothschild, but it does not end there. Moses Montefiore's brother is married to Rothschild's sister."

"I say!" Sir William exclaimed.

"It is exceedingly diverting, striving to follow the branches of this family tree, and most particularly because marriages between Sephardim and Ashkenazim have been frowned upon...until recently, that is. My own union was much criticized," he said with a wink towards his disapproving wife. "Yes...well—I digress. Because the two ladies were much thrown together organizing charitable balls and philanthropic events, Mr. Montefiore and his wife have been frequent visitors in our rather unfashionable neighborhood of Cheapside."

"Ah," Mrs. Bennet said, waving a delicate fan about her heated face imagining the illustrious society of said 'charitable balls' and 'philanthropic events.' "And now I see. You met my brother there."

"Precisely, but not for the reason you might think. Mrs. Meyerson's brother, Aaron, owns a factory near Gracechurch Street. He was recently blessed with a generous military contract and will have need of employing many people who would otherwise be destitute."

"Unfortunately," Mr. Darcy said dryly, "war is good for business."

"The military requires a host of goods and in massive quantities, to be sure. Everything from tents, knapsacks, and uniforms, to muskets, gunpowder..."

"Jacob—" A gentle prodding was whispered.

"I believe you take my meaning," said Mr. Meyerson with a sheepish grin. "In any event, it was Montefiore and a few of his colleagues who came to Cheapside and introduced my brother-in-law and many other merchants of the East End to Mr. Gardiner and his business partners. Your brother, Mrs. Bennet, and my brother-in-law have put their heads together for a grand business venture! Aaron will produce the merchandise and Mr. Gardiner will use his warehouses to store and distribute accordingly."

"I would not have expected such maneuverings and assignations," exclaimed Mrs. Bennet, "but of course, I wish them much success—anything to bring Little Boney to his knees!"

As the meal had been completed, Mrs. Bennet asked the ladies to join her once again in the drawing room, leaving Mr. Bennet and the gentlemen to enjoy their port and cigars. Elizabeth grinned at Mr. Darcy and mischievously rolled her eyes at the obligatory exodus of females. Although she was loath to leave Mr. Bingley's side, Jane made no attempt to mimic her sister's frivolity. It was not in her nature to do so, and surely the men would prefer to enjoy her father's last bit of smuggled spirits within the confines of masculine solidarity.

As the door shut behind the last lady quitting the room, Mr. Meyerson posed a question to the secluded party. "Gentlemen, what can you tell me about the local militia?" he asked, twirling a fine goblet by its delicate stem. "I was informed they are stationed in Meryton."

"Ha!" Sir William exclaimed. "They seem to come and go as they please. I do not know that there is much need for such men. They are supposed to serve the homeland while the Regulars are off fighting on the Continent, but to what end?" He stopped only to take a long puff of Mr. Bennet's exceptional cigar. "Meryton has not seen any rioting or criminal activity. At least, *it did not* when I was mayor. Needless to say, seditious actions are kept to a minimum in Hertfordshire!"

"Then, the militia are not in town?" the rabbi insisted, disregarding the gentleman's attempt at humor.

"They removed to Brighton a se'nnight Wednesday for training or some such and, if you were to believe the ladies," Sir William quipped, "our local society has suffered for their retreat. I dare say they will return soon enough."

"I should not speak harshly against these good men," Mr. Darcy reproached. "While the Regulars, including my cousin Colonel Fitzwilliam, keep Napoleon at bay, the militia lie in wait in the event of an attack here on the home front."

Mr. Bennet nodded his agreement. "I am an ardent supporter of the militia, truth be told. As a landowner, I was asked to lead a local troop when this horrible business began years ago. The Lord Lieutenant of Hertfordshire himself offered the post when he came round to fill his quota of Protestant volunteers. Needless to say, I declined and I have deeply regretted that decision. But you see, I did not feel properly equipped for such a responsibility. I fear I took the cowardly road."

Mr. Darcy commiserated with this sentiment, for he knew only too well the heavy burden of administering justice among his tenants and villagers. "As the local magistrate at Pemberley, I confess the responsibility is great, but it does not follow that one is a coward for not wishing to accept that particular yoke. What would your position have necessitated?" he enquired.

"Oh, I would have been named colonel or some such and, while my men would have been practically guaranteed not to see any actual fighting, I could not risk their lives *or* mine. If anything were to happen to me—well, on this point, it will be as well to be silent," he said raising a sardonic brow as he glanced at Mr. Collins.

"I dare say, Mr. Meyerson, not being of our faith and a Hebrew clergyman to boot, you have found yourself exempt from duty," Mr. Collins decreed.

"Very true, but that does not change the fact that there are able-bodied men, *dissidents*, if you will, who are eager to sign on. And the Crown needs men. Parishes have been fined for not raising the required numbers. You would think that they would be happy to have anyone fill the rosters—*even* a Jew!"

"I would tend to agree; the Crown is in dire straits. Just this past April, Wellington's men saw heavy fighting with high numbers of casualties in Badajoz. The fortress was taken, but at a great loss," Mr. Darcy observed bitterly. "There were nearly five thousand British casualties in that theater alone. I gave thanks to the heavens above when my cousin was returned to us."

"Praised be He!" exclaimed the rabbi.

"Our troops rallied over the summer," continued Mr. Darcy, "when Wellington gained a complete victory at the Battle of Salamanca..."

"But now the army has retreated, disorganized and ill-prepared, to winter in Portugal," said Mr. Bennet, "and my son-in-law is somewhere in Newcastle playing card games or attending an assembly with my silly daughter."

"It is my understanding," Mr. Darcy said, "the Exchequer has been in negotiations to secure the distribution of funds for Wellington's troops."

"Indeed," agreed Mr. Meyerson. "Not only for the campaign in Portugal, but the funds are to subsidize our allies as the *Corsican Monster* blazes a trail across Europe."

"I am at a loss," Mr. Bingley conceded. "The Crown is in negotiations with *whom?*"

"With Rothschild, sir," replied Mr. Meyerson.

As the gentlemen seemed perplexed and ill-informed, Mr. Meyerson was more than happy to indulge their curiosity. Satisfied that the information he shared was not considered confidential by the War Department, he proceeded to relay the particulars of the Rothschild connection.

The long and the short of it, he explained, was that the British government had been vastly disappointed with the more traditional, more established, London firms. While they were renowned and accepted by the wealthiest of men, they did not have the means to provide the government with what they required at this crucial time in history. Rothschild had established an international network for moving funds throughout the Continent, thereby proving himself a veritable asset to king and country.

"Due to their affluence and connections across Europe, men such as Rothschild, Montefiore, the Cohen family and the Goldsmid brothers," he concluded, "have become an indispensable element in society."

"My father has been in trade for quite some time and yet, I have never heard of these families," said Mr. Bingley.

"That does not surprise me, sir, but please do not take offense—many are not aware of their existence. The perfect example is my benefactor, Mr. Montefiore. His relations are positioned to grace English life in every field of banking, industry, law, and politics for centuries to come. But, for the ignorant or small-minded, they are *simply* Jews. While their wealth has provided an indispensable entrée into the corridors of power and the drawing rooms of the *ton,* it will take some time before these families are completely accepted and acknowledged as British citizens as well."

"Are you well acquainted with these giants of your community?" Mr. Bingley enquired. As someone newly admitted into the world of the aristocrat and the landed gentry, he was fascinated to hear how these newcomers forged their path into the exclusive and incredibly rigid social hierarchy.

Mr. Meyerson chuckled, as he swirled the last bit of golden liquid still in his glass. "As a simple clergyman, I am not exactly in the same sphere as these gentlemen. But due to my wife's connections, we are indeed acquainted."

Mr. Bingley was at once eager to hear more of these enigmatic men. They were the epitome of all that he wished to be. Of course, his friendship with Darcy had been a gift from above. No one could be as generous and willing to lend a hand as Fitzwilliam Darcy had been. Nevertheless, he was the son of a merchant and knew all too well the stench of trade would bar many a door for generations to come.

"I can tell you this, Mr. Bingley," the rabbi obliged, "Nathan Rothschild is as different from Moses Montefiore as the sun and the moon! They are, of course, brothers-in-law and business partners, but Nathan is famously slapdash and a risk taker, while Moses is meticulous and instinctively cautious."

"And yet it would seem, they are the best of friends." Mr. Bingley grinned at the stern Mr. Darcy, for between the two was a very steady friendship in spite of the great opposition of character.

"Indeed! Despite, or mayhap *because* of their differences," laughed Mr. Meyerson. "Shortly after their marriage, the Montefiores moved to New Court, where they live next door to the Rothschilds on St. Swithin's Lane. Mrs. Meyerson and I have had the pleasure of visiting their home on one or two occasions for holidays and other celebrations."

Mr. Bingley began enumerating the vast similarities between the two aforementioned men and his own association with Mr. Darcy, much to Sir William's amusement and Mr. Collins' reproof. With a slight tilt of his head, Mr. Meyerson suggested meeting his host at a side table where Hill had placed a tray lavished with fruits and sweetmeats.

"I would have a word with you, sir—in private, if you please?"

Begging his guests to excuse him momentarily, Mr. Bennet escorted the rabbi to his library. Once there, he gestured for the man to have a seat as he quickly made his way around the desk to his awaiting chair.

"I have it on good authority I may be perfectly blunt with you, and so I wish to clarify the situation in which we find ourselves."

Mr. Bennet sat quietly, waiting for the man to proceed without restraint.

"While it is true that Mr. Montefiore arranged for the living and has spoken to the rabbinate in London on my behalf, I am come to Meryton for a decidedly different purpose. I have been sent on business for the War Office."

Mr. Bennet nodded his understanding, not wishing to interrupt.

"I do not need to tell you, sir, this war with France has been raging continuously for nearly twenty years. Wellington is poised to be victorious, but at great cost."

"As I am sure you are aware, Mr. Meyerson, I have had a hand in the courier network established throughout the country and have been witness to the many messages crossing to and fro. That being said, I am not privy to the current situation."

"I thought as much. I would expect that a man of integrity such as yourself would not risk the safety of these missions by attempting to gain information not meant for the general public."

Never had Mr. Bennet known such satisfaction. He had set out to be of service and it seemed that his humble offerings had been well received. Red-faced, Mr. Bennet hemmed and hawed before petitioning his guest to continue.

"As Mr. Darcy mentioned, the Chancellor of the Exchequer has been responsible for financing and equipping the armies in the field but, since he has failed to deliver, the government has sought out Rothschild. With the man's ever-increasing consociation, the funds had begun to be disbursed, much to the great relief of Wellington and his men."

"I can well imagine! But what has happened? Are you here to tell me Rothschild has failed to keep up his part of the bargain?"

"No sir, to be sure, the deliveries *are* being made. However, the last two shipments received were found to be supplemented with counterfeit coin. You can understand the merchants and tradesmen on the Continent were none too pleased to be cheated in this manner. What do they care if our men live or die? They demand to be paid for services rendered."

"I fancy an investigation is under way," Mr. Bennet whispered in astonishment.

"Indeed, the investigation has brought me to Hertfordshire," responded the man with great solemnity, "and it is due in large part to your observations. Headquarters received your communiqué regarding the unusual behavior of a certain ensign, a Bartholomew P. Wakefield, to be exact, and they have found it most enlightening."

"I am honored to have been of service, although all I did was pass on a bit of information—rather odd to see a lowly ensign spending so much blunt in our bucolic shire. But tell me, sir, what does this all mean?"

"There are traitors in the militia, Mr. Bennet...the militia which has been stationed, up until recently, in *Meryton*."

"Good heavens!"

"My instructions are to follow this ensign's trail. He is sure to lead us to the leaders of this dastardly scheme. There will be questions to be asked, notes to be taken. I do hope that I may rely on your assistance."

"You may depend upon it, sir!" he said, shaking the gentleman's hand with great enthusiasm. "For the time being, my good fellow, I fear we must rejoin the ladies. Heaven only knows what they have been about, left alone for so long with only their conversations of lace and ribbons."

Mr. Bennet need not have been concerned overmuch, for the ladies, happily situated in the drawing room, were deep in private conversations that had naught to do with fripperies.

"Tell me, dear Charlotte," asked Elizabeth, as they sat secluded in a cozy corner, "how are you, truly?"

"I am well, Lizzy," her friend replied, caressing her rounded form. "Your visit to Hunsford should have set your mind at ease. I have done well for myself and am satisfied with my lot."

"Yes, but..."

"You mean to ask me about Mr. Collins, I suppose."

Elizabeth had been determined to pose the question, however indiscreet it would seem. The tell-tale blush that colored her face gave her away, and Charlotte was too good a friend not to understand.

"The ends justify the means, Lizzy. If I desire a large family, I must see to my wifely duties and...I find I can bear it most effortlessly. Addressing the subject in a sensible manner, *it* may have to occur but once or twice a year."

"Charlotte! What are you saying?" Elizabeth was startled by such a confession and, although she knew the technicalities of what had to occur, she was quite unacquainted with the subtleties of what took place between man and wife.

"It is quite simple, really. In one form or fashion, I will either be *with* child or *caring* for one for the next several years. Mr. Collins made it clear from the beginning of our marriage that he would keep to his own chamber as soon as I revealed I was in the family way."

"My own parents do not keep separate chambers..."

"Mama says men are simple to sway. One only needs to cry or complain, and they are only too happy to leave one at peace."

"I am astonished, Charlotte!" she exclaimed, mortified at her own disappointment if she would not share Mr. Darcy's bed. "Can you be happy in this manner?"

"I find that happiness in marriage is entirely a matter of chance... and good planning."

The two friends laughed quietly, not wishing to alert their mothers and provoke their questioning. They needn't have bothered, for Mrs. Bennet was otherwise engaged wresting information from her guest with the hope of discovering her societal connections.

"Do tell us about your good works, Mrs. Meyerson. Your husband mentioned such provocative activities. I would hear it from your own lips."

"Mr. Meyerson tends to flatter when, in truth, I am the fortunate one. Charitable works are a blessing for the giver as well as the receiver."

Mary nodded her agreement and quoted a favorite verse, "One who is gracious to a poor man lends to the Lord, and He will repay him for his good works."

"Truly, the repayment, if it may be considered as such, is the great privilege to work alongside generous, intelligent women such as Judith Montefiore. Currently we are working on establishing a school for underprivileged Jewish girls. They will learn a trade and be able to find work in Jewish houses which, you must understand, are always looking for employees who are familiar with our ways."

"Pray, enlighten us," Lady Lucas said. "While it is true that good help is hard to come by, why should standards be any different in a Hebrew household?"

"The girls are taught to work in *kosher* kitchens for the elite in our society who keep our dietary regulations," Mrs. Meyerson replied. "Others are prepared to be ladies maids and are skilled in all manner of cosmetics and hair styling. Next year, we hope to begin a program for nursing."

"Nursing?" Kitty exclaimed. "Is such a menial chore acceptable for young ladies?"

"There is a great need for such skills, Miss Catherine, with so many of our men returning ill or injured from the Continent," Mrs. Meyerson answered with a gentle smile. "These girls are not of your sphere, my dear. They must earn their living."

Jane could not help but notice that Kitty had become mesmerized by such commentary and discreetly called Elizabeth's attention to their younger sister's countenance. How odd it was for Kitty to be so attentive. Perhaps it was due to Lydia's withdrawal from their society, Jane reasoned.

"If your people wish to socialize with The Upper Ten, they must needs learn to adapt to British fare and give up their dietary regulations altogether!" Lady Lucas retorted rather emphatically.

"Many families, sadly, have done just that, and others, such as in my household, attempt to find a solution that is appropriate for their circumstance. My husband and I, as well as Mr. and Mrs. Montefiore, do not concern ourselves overly much with *kashrut* when we are away from home—that is to say, observing the rules regarding mixing dairy with meat or partaking of certain foods such as shellfish, pork and the like. In truth, I tend to make do with what is put before me, but Judith is quite formidable! She is ever experimenting and creating new recipes, refusing to lower her standards, for she is adamant we need not suffer by keeping faith with our laws."

"I dare say, if these Montefiores are truly in society, they would not venture to impose their peculiar ways upon the *ton*."

"You would be mistaken, Lady Lucas, for my cousins entertain many prominent families of the highest social circles and, even more astonishing, their Christian acquaintances are demanding their own chefs learn to prepare a *kosher* cuisine. It appears The Upper Ten find it not only satisfying, but a delight to their fastidious digestion."

"It is most inspiring," Mary interposed, "that your people cling to their traditions."

"I would not have you believe the majority of the Jewish elite are stringent in their beliefs. In my experience, it is the middle class which maintains a certain level of orthodoxy. In general, my husband's philosophy, as well as those in my cousin's circle, is to attempt to find a suitable compromise, one which works with the social and financial demands of society."

Mrs. Bennet smiled at one lady and then the other. While Lady Lucas was a person of some import in Meryton, it was clear the Meyersons had notable connections in Town. Who was to say that their acquaintance would not prove to be advantageous for her girls? It was necessary to speak a little; it would be odd to be entirely silent on the subject. Therefore, Mrs. Bennet, in her effort to appease both parties, believed she had found some common ground.

"Perhaps," she suggested, "these recipes would not only benefit ladies of the Hebrew persuasion. Pray recall, Lady Lucas, we are ourselves charged to make dishes without meat or dairy many times throughout the year such as during the Lenten or fasting holy days. Perhaps it is not *so* peculiar as it appears to be at first glance."

Elizabeth overheard this exchange and was astonished. Why, her mother's words were practically revolutionary! Mrs. Meyerson herself could not help but laugh. She explained that Judith Montefiore and the ladies of her sphere were proponents for the betterment of all women, be it through their culinary skills, their domestic talents, their *toilette,* or their education.

"We believe those females who are the most solicitous about their beauty and the most eager to produce a favorable impression should cultivate their moral, religious, *and* intellectual attributes. This makes for the finest cosmetic..."

"I would endeavor to become a student in your school," Kitty quipped, "if I could become half as accomplished as all that!"

"Frivolous activities and imperfect sentimentalities spoil the finest face, Miss Catherine. Body and mind are so intimately connected that it is futile to embellish the one while neglecting the other."

"I do so heartily agree, Mrs. Meyerson, for the highest order of beauty *is* intelligence." Elizabeth looked about the room and smiled as her gaze settled upon Lady Lucas. "If I am not mistaken, someone once said it is the mark of an intelligent mind to be able to entertain a peculiar thought without necessarily accepting it."

Jane was much in accord with this dictum, though in a quieter way. Her thoughts in general were not likely to be discovered by society, since Jane united, with great strength of feeling, a certain composure of temper and an unvarying cheerfulness of manner which guarded her from accusations of impertinence. Jane merely smiled at her outspoken sister, acknowledging her sanction.

Elizabeth raised the cup to her lips and wondered what in heaven's name the gentlemen were discussing. Surely, they could not have partaken in such interesting deliberations as the ladies had had that evening. Goodness! They had discussed marital relations, assisting the underprivileged and educating the fairer sex. What would Mr. Darcy opine?

CHAPTER FOUR

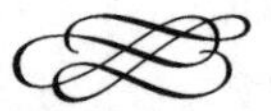

16th of October

The sunlight peeking through the draperies danced across the bedchamber, causing Elizabeth to awaken perhaps earlier than she would have liked. Stretching in a most unbecoming fashion, Elizabeth raised her hands to her head, releasing her mane from its nocturnal braid. An image came to her mind as she pondered how she would go to bed once she had become Mrs. Darcy. Would she don a wifely nightcap, or would Mr. Darcy prefer her tresses to be loose and flowing? Elizabeth felt her face burn at the thought.

She could well hear his reprimand at calling him *Mr. Darcy*. They had spoken at length about what name would suit. She had confessed that *Fitzwilliam* did not feel endearing and *Mr. Darcy* seemed too reserved. Mr. Bingley and Colonel Fitzwilliam referred to him as Darcy, but she felt that was too mannish. She had settled on *William*, knowing Miss Darcy herself had favored that name in reference to her beloved brother and, while Elizabeth's feelings toward the gentleman were anything but sisterly, she felt more at ease in pronouncing a name which he had become accustomed to associate with love and admiration.

Removing her bedclothes, Elizabeth instantly felt the morning chill. Long gone were the warm summery days, as Longbourn was covered in tawny leaves and withered hedges. Calling for one of the maids, she prepared to dress quickly, for the day would slip away soon enough and there was much to do. Choosing her favorite sprigged muslin and its matching pelisse, for when she ventured outdoors, Elizabeth completed her morning ablutions and made her way down to the breakfast room.

She bade a good morning to all as she kissed her father on his cheek before taking her seat alongside Jane. Sharing a knowing look with her beloved sister, Elizabeth knew no words were necessary. Her mama had begun the day with her list of tasks in preparation for their wedding day. Elizabeth buttered her toast and spooned a generous amount of Cook's fine preserves upon it before attempting to acknowledge her mother's requests. It wasn't until she sipped her coffee and allowed herself to feel fortified by the infusion that she deemed it necessary to speak.

"Very well, Mama. Where would you like us to begin?"

Mrs. Bennet nodded her head in acknowledgement of her daughter's acquiescence. "Your wedding clothes and trousseau must be seen to immediately.

Jane shared a smile with her sister as they replied happily, "Agreed!"

Completing their meal, the ladies gathered in their mother's favorite sitting room, lately fitted up with greater elegance and lightness than the principal drawing room, which was used to receive company and where they family gathered in the afternoons. There, on the center table covered prettily with her mother's fine embroidery, Jane placed the packages recently received from Cheapside.

"Your aunt and uncle have provided you girls with a lovely selection," said Mrs. Bennet. "How will you choose?"

Elizabeth had known immediately which material she favored but, knowing Jane would be generous and withhold her own decision until her sister had made her selection, Elizabeth pretended uncertainty and begged Jane to choose first.

"If you do not have a preference, Lizzy, then I believe I will choose the ivory silk. Perhaps this lace-trimmed tulle will do for an overlay about the bodice? What do you think, Mama?"

"I should like to see the dressmaker fashion a heart-shaped neckline, Jane dear. The detailing would complement your lovely features. What do you think about this eggshell blue for a cloak?"

Elizabeth was overcome at her sister's evident happiness. She was so deserving. "Yes, do take it, Jane. It will match the coloring of your eyes. And how do you like this lace for your bonnet?"

"Oh, Lizzy, it would be lovely!"

Elizabeth smiled. "Then you should have it. And this netting will do for the veil."

"And what do you envision for yourself?"

"The cream damask is quite extraordinary," she replied, peering up under her eyelashes with not a little doubt. "Are you certain you do not wish for yourself?"

"Be assured, Lizzy, I much prefer the simplicity of the ivory. The leaf pattern does not suit me, I think."

"Then I will be most happy to make it my own. I will pair it with the striped silk and have the *modiste* fashion a matching pelisse. The silk net will be lovely for the bonnet…"

Mrs. Bennet, delighted to see her girls enthusiastic and so amiable, could not help but add a suggestion or two. "Why not add a few decorative flowers, dear Lizzy. You have always favored being about in nature."

Elizabeth bowed her head in appreciation and kept her amusing observations to herself. How considerate her mother had suddenly become *now* that she had accepted a gentleman's offer. Had she known her estimation would rise in her mother's eyes, perhaps Elizabeth might have entered into the marriage state sooner. But she knew this to be an absurdity, for only the deepest love would have persuaded her into matrimony. Knowing that she would have that sort of union with Mr. Darcy made all of her mother's planning very much worthwhile.

"Well then," said Jane, "it seems we are ready to meet with the dressmaker. Although, seeing how knowledgeable and well-prepared we are, perhaps *we* should open up our own shop."

"Our own shop?" Elizabeth teased. "Do not think of it, Jane dear —not with *five thousand a year*!"

The walk into town was easily done, the weather being considerate and the roads dry and clear. Mrs. Bennet was happy to accompany her girls, for it was not every day that she was welcomed in their society. She realized then how deep she would feel it when at last her girls would be wed and far from home. Of course, if Jane and Mr. Bingley remained in Netherfield, she might be able to visit with some frequency, seeing that the property was only a distance of three miles. Elizabeth, however, would be another matter entirely. Pemberley was a great deal further.

Mrs. Bennet sighed as she walked the familiar path, now sprinkled with fallen leaves of russet, gold and brown. She could not complain, she *would not* complain, for her girls would be safe and happily situated. What more could a mother ask?

Walking past The Red Lion, Mrs. Bennet spotted Mrs. Brown traveling in her chaise down the hamlet's main thoroughfare and waved enthusiastically. "Oh, my dears, your father was correct! I do need to come into town more often. It has been some time since I have the pleasure of seeing Mrs. Brown. I do so miss her society, for she ever seems to have the most interesting topics to discuss."

"She does not live far, Mama. You should write a note and invite her to tea."

"You are quite right, Jane. Harpendenbury is a stone's throw away. It is just the matter of crossing the River Ver. I will feel the loss when my three girls are gone. Perhaps it would do me good to get out and about. I shall invite *myself* to tea and ask Mr. Bennet for the carriage. While our brave Lizzy was able to trek three miles to Netherfield, I cannot credit making the journey across St. Michael's Bridge afoot."

Coming upon the dressmaker's shop, Elizabeth recalled her father declaring that Meryton was now the home of Mr. and Mrs. Schreiber, the new owners of Sir William's warehouse. Her curiosity was piqued. She wondered what sort of people they might be.

"Perhaps we should stop in and introduce ourselves?" she asked but quickly reassessed her judgment. "On second thought, our visit might not sit well with the new merchants seeing that we are already laden with material."

"Still, it would be the neighborly thing to do," said Jane, "but look! Is that not Mr. Meyerson? Good heavens! Whatever are they doing?"

Mrs. Bennet and the girls turned to witness a most unusual sight for, indeed, Mr. Meyerson was dancing *and* singing and lovingly carrying an odd looking sort of scroll in his arms. Mr. Jacobi and his three sons supported a striped canopy with long wooden posts sheltering the rabbi as he made his way. To be sure, Mrs. Bennet was surprised when she witnessed Mr. Hellerman and other gentlemen dancing along their side, but when she espied Mrs. Meyerson accompanying the public processional with several ladies clapping and carrying timbrels, she gasped in astonishment.

"Whatever could be the meaning of such a display?" asked Mrs. Bennet.

Singing in a foreign tongue, the men danced along while the rabbi lifted the venerated object to and fro. The people of Meryton opened their windows and doors to witness the goings-on. Some clapped along, others scratched their heads in wonderment, and others still, including Mrs. Phillips, shook their heads in reproof.

As the women in the procession danced by, Mrs. Meyerson recognized her new friends standing with their mouths agape on the street corner, and came to a most welcomed stop. "Good morning to you!" she said breathlessly. "It is a happy day for us in Meryton."

Mrs. Bennet curtsied her greeting as propriety required, although she could not help but enquire as to what was taking place. Meryton had only once before seen such a public display, and that was when a set of players had come through the village and set up a small amphitheater in the wilderness. Her sister, Mrs. Phillips, had been none too pleased at that occurrence, she recalled. Perhaps Kitty had been right—perhaps these Meyersons were like the gypsies that lived in the woods.

Mrs. Meyerson acknowledged their celebration appeared rather astonishing but, it was the custom to accompany a *Torah* to its new home with much gaiety and even a festive meal. Knowing that her new friends would be unfamiliar with the term, the lady explained that the Five Books of Moses were most likely known to them as Genesis, Exodus, Leviticus, Numbers, and Deuteronomy.

"Understanding that the community was without the holy scroll," she stated, "my husband was given the honor of transporting one from London. This particular scroll was brought out of Yemen hundreds of years ago."

"And all this merriment and spectacle is commonplace?"

"Yes, Miss Elizabeth, indeed it is so! Our community lives by the Torah. Our lives revolve around the readings, for it is read in sequence throughout the year, commemorating our holy days and commanding us to observe certain life cycle events. Ah—," she paused as another lady approached and the men carried on. "Mrs. Bennet, Miss Bennet, Miss Elizabeth, allow me to introduce Mrs. Schreiber."

"How fortunate a meeting. We have not had the pleasure of making your acquaintance, ma'am," said Elizabeth, "but you will find the Bennett family is oft' in Meryton and will be sure to patronize your establishment."

"You will be most welcome," replied Mrs. Schreiber. "The *Rebbetzin* told me of your kind hospitality to her family. It warms my heart to know that there are such kind and generous people in Hertfordshire."

"Mrs. Bennet is in preparations for a blessed *simcha*," Mrs. Meyerson informed her neighbor. "I mean to say *celebration*, of course. The Misses Bennet are to be wed in a double ceremony."

"Oh, but I have already heard the villagers speaking of this great event," said Mrs. Schreiber. "I wish you both happy and...how fortuitous! We have recently received a lovely selection of fabrics in honor of our grand opening. It has been challenging to find anything of quality—heaven only knows how difficult it has been, what with the war and the blockade of Parisian goods."

Mrs. Bennet shook her head in sympathy, knowing how trying it was to run a household while at war with one's suppliers, but at the same time her thoughts were whirling, trying to recall the strange words she had overheard.

"My daughters have received a plethora of material from their aunt and uncle in London," explained Mrs. Bennet. "We are just now on our way to see the dressmaker, but I would be happy to inspect your goods for my own gown. It is not every day a mother sees two daughters married and I would have a new gown for the *seem-ha,*" she cautiously pronounced, not with a little pride.

"But of course. The mama should be dressed appropriately for such an occasion! I have the perfect shade of peach. It will compliment your coloring. And, if I may, I would suggest swan feathers—in *great* abundance! All of London is dressed in swan feathers this season."

The ladies nodded and exchanged promises of returning to the establishment as soon as they were able. Mrs. Meyerson begged to be excused from the impromptu meeting, for her place was with her husband and the congregation at this time. Mrs. Schreiber nodded her feathered bonnet in agreement.

"Yes, of course, I do understand," Mrs. Bennet replied, although she was not quite certain if she did, indeed, understand. "I am delighted to see you are acclimating yourself into Meryton society. Perhaps I will walk into town on the morrow. I would be happy to introduce you to my sister, Mrs. Phillips."

Mrs. Meyerson smiled, uncomfortably so. She explained she was still in the midst of unpacking and organizing their new home, and she had yet to prepare for their first *Shabbes* in Meryton.

"I do beg your pardon," said Mrs. Bennet.

Mrs. Meyerson laughed and brought her hands to her face, covering her blush. "Pray, forgive me. While English is my native language, it is difficult to separate from one's mother's tongue!

Sometimes a *Yiddish* word works best; at other times *Ladino* comes to mind—"

Mrs. Bennet simply nodded, having now to add two new words to her vocabulary. *Yiddish*? *Ladino*? Perhaps, she thought, they were similar to Welsh.

"How astonishing, Mrs. Meyerson, to have such a wealth of knowledge," said Jane. "I sometimes struggle to find the correct word in the King's English. I can only imagine having multiple languages from which to choose."

"Shabbes," Mrs. Meyerson offered, "is what we call the Sabbath, which for us begins at sunset on Friday evenings and ends when the first stars appear on Saturday night. As you can well imagine, I have much to do before then, for I would have my table set with our traditional foods and my family heirlooms about me. It will make the transition to Meryton that much easier when we can welcome the Shabbes bride according to our traditions."

"*The Shabbes bride*?" Mrs. Bennet queried.

"Mama," said Jane, rather hurriedly while glancing at her sister for assistance, "we must not detain Mrs. Meyerson any longer, and I am afraid we too must be on our way."

Elizabeth laughed at the unusual encounter, finding humor in how little she and her family knew of the world. "It was a pleasure making your acquaintance, Mrs. Schreiber, and we will be sure to frequent your shop." She could hardly keep from smiling as she assured the lady. "Indeed, now that you have enlightened us of the London fashion, I am certain Mama must not rest until she is swathed in peach plumage!"

The ladies bobbed their salutations as they departed and quickly followed the others entering Mr. Hellerman's place of business. As Mrs. Meyerson and Mrs. Schreiber rejoined the congregation, voices could be heard singing out from the apothecary's shop windows:

Baruch ata Adonai Eloheinu Melech ha'olam, shehecheyanu, v'kiyimanu, v'higiyanu la'z'man ha'zeh! [1]

"Meryton is coming up in the world!" Elizabeth laughed. "We may need to carry a primer about when we pay our calls!"

Mrs. Meyerson had, indeed, quite a list of things to do before the sun would set that evening. While the nurse played with little Rachel and Mr. Meyerson prepared the sermon for his new congregation, she, along with the cook and the housemaid, continued to unpack, prepare the meal, and set the table as befitting the new rabbi of Meryton. When at last she was able to sit at the table, surrounded by her own dear mama's candlesticks and other traditional accoutrements, Mrs. Meyerson was well pleased with what they had been able to accomplish.

A fine Shabbes dinner had been placed before her family. Her husband sang her praises as never before. Rachel, being well schooled by her elder sisters, joined her mother in blessing the candles and the two loaves of braided *challah* bread. It had been a good day, Mrs. Meyerson thought—an eventful day—for they brought the Torah to its new home and placed it in a fine cabinet lovingly made by Mr. Shaffer, an excellent craftsman when he was not out shepherding sheep. Tomorrow they would join the congregation in the little *shul* that had been created in back room of the apothecary's shop and all would be well.

Indeed, the next morning, the Meyerson family made their way to the makeshift synagogue, grateful for the space the Hellerman family had allotted the community. Eventually they would see a separate location constructed, possibly with room for a school, but

Rabbi Meyerson knew, as they walked along the way, everything would be done in God's own time. Even his long overdue conversation with Sofia could not be rushed. He would have to confess when the time was right. He would have to tell her all, tell her *all* that had occurred, and her surprise would be great. But today was not the day to think of such things. Today was Shabbes, and everything was good. Everything was as it should be.

They had met the families of the congregation. Albeit few in number, they were strong in their dedication. Mr. and Mrs. Jacobi owned the local bookshop. They had come from London when their first son was born seventeen years ago. The other two boys had reached their majority, being over the age of thirteen, which meant the rabbi could include them in the necessary quorum. And there were Mr. and Mrs. Schreiber; they had grown children spread throughout Essex and Kent but came to Meryton when the opportunity arose to purchase Sir William's business. Mr. and Mrs. Hellerman had two lovely daughters, and Rabbi Meyerson could not help but wonder if there could be a possible match made with the Jacobi boys.

Oy! Just arrived into town and already he was match making! Mrs. Meyerson would tease him if she knew what he was about, for she always said that a rabbi's imagination was very rapid. It jumped from admiration to love, from love to matrimony in a moment. But what felicity it would be for the community.

Lest he forget, there were two farmers and their families which rounded out the congregation. Rabbi Meyerson was the tenth man and he completed the *minyan.* This Sabbath, with a quorum of ten, they would read from the Torah, and what a blessing that would be.

Hellerman's back room had been prepared for the morning's service. The mismatched chairs, donated by the congregants themselves, were neatly aligned, and the room had been divided with a crocheted coverlet separating the men from the women as tradition dictated. In the center of the room, they had placed a table and the rabbi presumed one of the ladies had embroidered the white covering with the phrase *Gut Shabbes*.

The handsome cabinet constructed by Mr. Shaffer had been placed on the eastern wall such that, in facing it, those praying would face Jerusalem. A small bookcase with an assortment of prayer books completed the room. Rabbi Meyerson had noted that each family had contributed treasures from their own family library and immediately thought he would write to London and ask for additional reading material.

As the congregation gathered, the morning prayers rang out in joyous unison. At the appropriate time, the Torah was removed from the cabinet and the rabbi called up Mr. Shaffer, the sheep farmer, for the honor of chanting the Torah blessings. Mr. Shaffer, as it was made known, was a *kohan*—a descendant of the priestly tribe and was therefore deserving of such an honor. His voice sang out proud and true as he recited the words his father, and generations before him, had the honor of chanting.

Bar'chu et Adonai ham'vorach,[2] he began and the congregation responded: *Baruch Adonai ham'vorach l'olam vaed!*[3]

Rabbi Meyerson continued with the reading of the assigned portion for the week. It warmed his heart knowing that, from London to Morocco to the tip of Argentina, he and his brethren would be reading the same exact words. The Babylonian Exile had driven out Jews from the Holy Land until they were dispersed across countless foreign nations. More than lineage, more than social status, they were united by the words given them in this treasured scroll. It seemed providential that today, of all days, there in Meryton, Rabbi Meyerson was to read the Torah portion of *Lech Lecha*.

Before uttering the first few words, he breathed in deeply and allowed himself to cherish the moment that God had provided...and then, he began chanting in their ancient tongue:

"And God said to Abram, Go forth from your birthplace and from your father's house, to the land that I shall show you. I will make of you a great nation and I will bless you and make your name great."

CHAPTER FIVE

17th of October

Jacob Meyerson observed as his wife extinguished the *Havdalah* candle. Their Sabbath rest, with all the whirlwind activity preceding it, had come to an end with the recitations of the final prayers that separated the holiness of their rest from the mundane work week. How he admired his Sofia, he thought. How blessed was his portion. He knew not of another woman who would be able—who would be *willing*—to pack up their belongings, close down a London home and move to the country simply because the rabbinical council had suggested he open a house of worship in the small market town of Meryton. They had left behind their beloved children, their acquaintances and relations, and she had not questioned him. They were required to trespass upon a family of strangers and impose on their generosity whilst their new home was made ready, and still she did not complain.

With not much more than a day to prepare, his wife had him

comfortably ensconced in his study while she and the one servant that accompanied them from London set the house to straights. Just prior to sunset, he had donned his frock coat (which had been cleaned and pressed for the occasion) and made his way to the dining room, where he found his wife and daughter awaiting his arrival.

The resplendent table had been lovingly prepared for the Sabbath. A white linen cloth which his mother had embroidered so many years ago was the setting for the candles, *challah* and traditional meal. Sofia had seen to everything, and now he would have to break her heart.

"Come, my love, and sit by me," he said with an outstretched hand. "I would speak to you."

"Yaacov, there is still much to..."

He sighed and grinned. "And it will all be there, waiting for you once we have chatted."

Mrs. Meyerson harrumphed but nevertheless sat beside her husband, laying her head upon his shoulder.

"Do you know how dear you are to me? Have I praised you sufficiently so there can be no doubt?"

"Oh husband! It must be something dire if you feel the need to shower me with compliments," she said softly, as she turned to meet his gaze.

"They are not empty compliments, for I mean every word. Nonetheless, you have the right of it. I do have something of great importance to relate, and *not* disclosing it has caused me great agony."

Mrs. Meyerson crossed her arms and waited for the distressing words to come, for distressing they must be.

"I am for Brighton, dearest, and do let me explain before your outrage makes an absconder of me and I give up the scheme entirely."

With a sense of foreboding, she simply nodded her acquiescence.

"Sofia, the synagogue is only one reason we are come to Meryton," he began.

"Yes, dear, we had thought the fresh air would help Rachel with her asthma—"

"No, it is not that, well—yes, it is, but there is something more." Mr. Meyerson stood and began pacing about the room. She had never seen him so uncomfortable. "Sofia, I am working on a project with Mr. Gardiner..."

"Yes, and well I know it. Everything was to be done with no delay! I hardly had time to say farewell to my friends and neighbors. Yaacov, what is it you are trying to tell me?"

"You are speaking of the *beit tefillah* that the council secured for us, but I am speaking of something different all together. I am here on a mission—for the War Office."

"I do not understand your meaning, sir! Pray, what sort of mission with the War Office would require a rabbi?"

Seeing he would have to start from the beginning, Mr. Meyerson sat down beside his wife and, taking her hand in his, confessed it all. For over a year, he had been working with Montefiore and Rothschild in a grand scheme. A network of couriers and messengers had been set up across the country to assist the War Department in their attempt to shut down Napoleon once and for all. He and others like him had been recruited for a simple reason: they would never be suspected of being informants.

"I cannot credit you have kept this from me for over a year!" she cried. "What compels you to own it now—now that you have separated me from my home and family?"

"Forgive me, my love, but I was not at liberty to speak beforehand."

"What has changed that you are now *at liberty* to inform your wife, the mother of your five children, that you are not the person she believed you to be?"

"Try to understand...Wellington's men are starving—they are without supplies. Rothschild has supplied the Crown with the means to pay the troops their salaries, to purchase food, clothing and ammunition. The gold was delivered, *miraculously so*, but more than half of it was found to be counterfeit! They have traced the traitor to a group of men currently serving in the Hertfordshire militia. Montefiore and Mr. Gardiner believed them to be stationed here in Meryton, but they have gone to Brighton, and I must follow."

Mrs. Meyerson placed her head in her hands and wept tears of anger, tears of dread. "You knew all along! You knew, yet you did not confide in me. I should have known something was awry when we left in such a rush. It was so unlike you to leave one home when the next had yet to be prepared for our arrival."

Mr. Meyerson attempted to take hold of his wife's hand once more, but she would not allow it. He was heartbroken at this rejection, yet he continued with the hope of persuading her to understand.

"I could not risk speaking of it while we were still in London. I thought we would have time to discuss the matter once we settled here, in our new home...and this can be our new home, if we wish it. It will be much healthier for Rachel, and we are close enough to visit the children in London. They will come in the summer when the heat is unbearable. You will see, Sofia. This *will* be home."

"That is all very prettily said, sir, but I do not comprehend how this business came about! You are a man of peace, a man of faith. Why have you involved yourself in such a dangerous scheme?"

Sensing that she needed to hear from his heart rather than from his head, Mr. Meyerson sought the words which would win her to his side. He could not make a success of it without his wife's support—without her faith.

"We have had generations of ancestors leaving hearth and home seeking out a peaceful existence. Putting their lives in God's hands, our forefathers found their way to this land. It has been a difficult journey, one paved with blood and tears. Nonetheless, I am *grateful*, Sofia, grateful for what my family has been afforded in this, our adopted country. Even through the bitterness of exile, even through the pain of rejection, amid the taunts and the limitations placed upon our people, we have survived. We have flourished. *The people Israel live*! Our son fights with his fists to prove himself—to show the world our people are courageous. I have a different way. These wars must stop, the gold must be delivered, *and I* must track down the blackguards who have betrayed their countrymen."

He had done his best. There was nothing more to add to his soliloquy. His heart clenched in agony as she calmed her breath and wiped away her bitter tears.

"Rachel and I will be all alone," she whispered.

Mr. Meyerson sighed and drew her near. "I will send for David. He will be a comfort to you while I am away. Let us pray that my absence will be short-lived. If you should need anything; you are to seek Mr. Bennet's assistance."

CHAPTER SIX

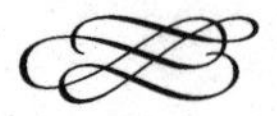

One morning, as Mr. Bennet and his daughters sat together in the dining room (Mrs. Bennet still abed) their attention was suddenly drawn to the window by the sound of steps upon the graveled path. Kitty quickly observed it was Mrs. Meyerson and her daughter approaching their front door. Although it was quite early for calls, the lady had been a guest in her master's home and therefore Hill felt quite at liberty to announce the unexpected caller to the family. Mr. Bennet, perceiving straightaway that something had gone awry, waved the housekeeper away and stood to greet his Meryton neighbor.

"Good morning, Mrs. Meyerson. Good morning Rachel. Have you broken your fast? Please join us," he said as the servant set down extra place settings.

Mrs. Meyerson bobbed up and down in a silent greeting and became quite pale. Indeed, it appeared the lady would faint and, had it not been for Jane's quick thinking, Mrs. Meyerson might well have found herself on the Bennet's hand-knotted, woolen rug. Jane, taking her gently by the hand, assisted Mrs. Meyerson to her seat while Elizabeth quickly provided the lady with a strong cup of coffee.

"Kitty, I think Rachel would very much like to see your collection of dolls," said Jane. "Ask Hill to send up a tray of hot chocolate and biscuits to your bedchamber."

For once, Kitty did not question her sister's directive but simply nodded and took the little girl by the hand. Mrs. Meyerson had, by now, regained her coloring and thanked the party for their attention.

"I fear I must once again trespass on your hospitality, Mr. Bennet, and I see that Mrs. Bennet has not yet come down. It is dreadfully early for visitors, I know, but I simply could not put this off!"

Mr. Bennet waved away any concerns and explained that Mrs. Bennet had been suffering from a nervous stomach. "I have nothing but respect for my wife's nerves. They have been my old friends for over twenty years. I assure you, there is no need to concern yourself. Now, madam, tell me what brings you to Longbourn."

Mrs. Meyerson smiled guardedly, looking hither and thither until Mr. Bennet realized the unspoken message. "Girls, pray take some tea to your mother and inform her that we have company. Perhaps that will provide sufficient incentive for the lady of the house to arise and see to the day."

Jane and Elizabeth reluctantly did as their father bade, bobbing a quick curtsey before quitting the room. Mrs. Meyerson did not tarry in informing her host about what had taken place.

"My husband, I believe you understand, has been away on an errand for the Crown. It has been a week complete," she concluded, "and I fear for the outcome of such an undertaking. He is wholly unprepared for a predicament such as this."

"Come, come Mrs. Meyerson! Your husband would not have been asked to fulfill a task of this magnitude without proper preparation." That being said, Mr. Bennet hesitated only a moment to consider the ramifications of his next statement. "I will make for Brighton and see if I cannot be of assistance."

As he completed this declaration, Mrs. Bennet walked through the doors, pretty as a picture and eager to receive her guest. She was therefore surprised to see Hill escorting Mrs. Meyerson into the drawing room as Mr. Bennet requested a private word. Glancing nervously at her host, Mrs. Meyerson expressed her gratitude for his assistance and begged pardon for interrupting their morning. The mistress of the house stood astounded waiting for an explanation of the curious proceedings.

Upon the lady quitting the room, Mr. Bennet went straightaway to his library, calling again for Hill and shuffling his wife towards the door of his sanctuary. Unaccustomed to being granted such a dispensation, Mrs. Bennet situated herself comfortably by the fire, hoping for, rather than expecting an explanation. Poor Hill, who had had quite the morning, appeared at her master's request, ever ready.

"Ah, Hill! Pray, prepare a portmanteau suitable for several days away from home. I am for London this afternoon. Oh! And have Jane and Lizzy join us at once."

The housekeeper nodded and went out the door, keeping her instructions as well as her questions at the forefront of her overtaxed mind.

"Where are you going, Mr. Bennet?" Mrs. Bennet cried. "And at such a time as this? Your daughters are to be wed in less than a fortnight! Have you lost your senses?"

"I do not wish the others to overhear what I am about to say, nor do I have time for silly questions or nervous reactions," he responded as he closed the door. "I mean to be on the coach to London this afternoon. A matter of grave importance has arisen and I must provide whatever assistance is at my disposal."

"But, what could possibly take you away from Longbourn at this time? Do you have business in London? Have you invested in some sort of speculation? Oh, Mr. Bennet! Pray, tell me at once that you have not gambled away what little we have set aside," she cried in despair.

"Calm yourself, my dear. You have no need to fear on that score," he replied. "But, I do owe a debt of gratitude to a certain fellow. My assistance was implied from the onset of our acquaintance, you must understand. He had been entrenched here in Meryton, but now that the militia has decamped, I find that I must follow."

Although she cried copious tears, Mrs. Bennet found, much to her dismay, her husband would not change course and remain at home. He instead insisted that she attend Mrs. Meyerson and see to her well-being. Taking pride in being Longbourn's mistress and the neighborhood's foremost hostess, Mrs. Bennet (to her husband's astonishment) arose from her seat and quitted the room with nary a word. Jane and Elizabeth passed their teary-eyed mother in the corridor. The sisters shared a fearful glance, uncertain what awaited them in their father's presence.

"Shut the door, Lizzy," said Mr. Bennet as they sequestered themselves in the confines of his library. "Although I have said naught to your mother, I would share the truth of the matter with you two—my sensible girls—lest things go awry."

The master of Longbourn, heretofore known to his family and friends as an odd mixture of sarcastic humor, reserve and caprice, explained in short and curt terms that for several months now he had been working for the War Office in conjunction with his brother-in-law, Mr. Gardiner. His daughters, understandably shaken and bewildered, could not countenance such a brief communication and, although he had not given them leave to question him, Elizabeth could not abide by this restriction.

"How did this come about, Papa?" she asked. "It is wholly unexpected and not in keeping with your character."

Mr. Bennet, ill at ease, began pacing the room, faced now with the truth of the matter and having to articulate his perceived failings to his beloved daughters.

"I have long been desiring to do *something*, to act upon an overwhelming sense of duty which I can no longer squelch," he proclaimed. "I have failed to produce a son," Mr. Bennet raised his hand to stay an interruption, "and I have failed to protect my family from a life of penury and homelessness in the event of my death." He paused to take a generous swallow of port before continuing. "England has suffered for years with an unending war and yet, again, *I have failed* by not serving my country. When I found that your uncle Gardiner had undertaken work for the Crown, I could not look the other way. I will readily admit, my portion has been small and by no means dangerous—I merely have been assisting messengers crisscrossing the countryside, or informing on strange behavior—but I have never before felt so useful!"

"You have never mentioned a word of this to any one of us!" Elizabeth exclaimed, not a little disappointed he had not confided in her. "What has occurred that you now make this extraordinary declaration?"

"I know what you must think of me, Lizzy, but I could not disclose my association with the matter," he replied. "I would not have your mama or the rest of the household informed of my whereabouts, but I will share this much: Mr. Meyerson was sent to Meryton to establish a front. While it is true he is meant to serve the growing Hebrew community in town, he was sent by the War Office. There has been a cessation of communication amongst the Crown's couriers and, more to the point, the Government has found traitors in our midst. Mr. Meyerson is on a mission to seek these men out."

"But, what has that to do with you, Papa?" cried Jane. "You have said that your position does not entail danger, and yet you speak of traitorous men!"

"Mr. Meyerson has followed the militia to Brighton, for there is where the traitors appear to be entrenched. He has been gone for far too long and may be in need of assistance. There's nothing for it, Jane —I must go."

While Elizabeth and Jane had attempted to stay their father's departure, Mrs. Bennet had regained control of her faculties and joined her guest in the drawing room.

"Madam, what is to become of us?" Mrs. Meyerson beseeched her hostess. "Pray, forgive my emotional state, but you see my husband has been called away. Rachel and I are far from home and are quite friendless here."

"Who can say they truly understand their husbands, Mrs. Meyerson? Surely, it is a truth universally acknowledged that a woman's place in the home is to secure her husband's comfort and her children's future *and want for nothing more*!"

Mrs. Bennet rang the bell for tea and joined her guest on an adjoining wing chair by the fire. Chilled to the bone, she knew her present condition was due to the shock she had just endured and not the chilly seasonal weather. Still, she rubbed her hands together to stimulate some warmth while frantically thinking of something comforting to say.

"There is nothing so bad as parting with one's friends but, Mrs. Meyerson, you will make new acquaintances. We are not without good neighbors—we dine with four and twenty families."

"You cannot begin to understand my distress. I was torn from my home, from my children and community to start anew in Meryton—with no real explanation, mind you; with *no* opportunity to opine!" she cried. "Never have I felt so put upon."

"Oh, but I *do* understand. You are not alone!" Mrs. Bennet proclaimed, feeling herself at once akin to the lady. "You may depend on my friendship, my dear. As it is not in our power to dictate the comings and goings of our husbands, we may at least find comfort in each other."

The two ladies condoled with one another in their collective abandonment, while Jane dutifully assisted with her father's preparations. Knowing there would be no objection to her presence, Elizabeth remained secluded in the library behind closed doors.

"You must not endanger yourself on our account—you have nothing to prove. You need not go."

But hearing his daughter's words only served as further incentive. Mr. Bennet had very often wished, before this period of his life, that he had done his duty to family and country. Never had he been at a loss for words, yet he struggled now to articulate these emotions. "I have made too many mistakes in my life, Lizzy. I have been reprehensible as a husband and a father."

"You are too severe upon yourself," she said tearfully.

"Let me, once in my life, feel how much I have been to blame!" he exclaimed. "When I made the decision to offer my services, I felt the beginnings of something quite foreign beating in my heart. Do you know what it was, Lizzy? Hmm? *It was pride!* I finally was doing something worthwhile, something that I could point to and say: 'I had a part in that.'"

"But to leave now..."

"Do not be angry with me, daughter. The wedding may have to be postponed, I fear, if I run into complications, but let us hope it does not come to that. Needless to say, there will be talk in the town when word gets out that I have quitted Longbourn."

"What care I what people say?"

"Be truthful, dearest. At least, be so with me. Gossip is the way of village life, is it not? For what do we live, but to make sport of our neighbors and laugh at them in our turn?"

"I fear, sir, I am not in mind for laughing," she said falling into her father's embrace.

"All will be well, child, fear not."

It was shortly after Mrs. Meyerson collected Rachel and headed for home that Mr. Bennet said his goodbyes to his wife and daughters. Not one for tearful departures, he barely gave them the opportunity to wave him off before he was away to catch the London transport. Although he dreaded the four-hour journey boxed up in an airless coach, submitting to other miserable passengers and obliged to listen to their drivel, Mr. Bennet accepted this great wretchedness as part and parcel of the task he had undertaken.

Arriving in London that evening, the driver brought his passengers to their final destination on Gracechurch Street. Disembarking from the conveyance, Mr. Bennet espied the coaching inn and made his way into the establishment, where he requested a room and ordered a good dinner. Once situated, Mr. Bennet penned a quick note to his brother-in-law to come meet him at the Spread Eagle, for although the family lived on that very street, Mr. Bennet did not wish to make his presence overly known.

Seated cozily by an open fire, Mr. Bennet was well into his beef stew and suet dumplings when he looked up and recognized Mr. Gardiner. The gentleman made his way past other travelers and local diners and soundly greeted his brother-in-law with a slap upon his back before joining Mr. Bennet at his table. As he was unaccompanied by his overly cautious wife, who seldom allowed him to indulge, Mr. Gardiner ordered himself a plate of the good innkeeper's stew with extra dumplings, just in case the cook tended to economize.

"Thank you for meeting me here, Edward," Mr. Bennet said, as the bar maid set down two pints of ale. "I will be gone in the morning and did not feel it necessary to incommode your household—particularly given the circumstances of my travel."

"I have to admit, I never imagined that your participation would lead you to this, Brother. I do hope you will proceed with caution. You may wish to notify the constable—"

"You know as well as I do, I cannot notify anyone until we are certain we can name the culprit. I doubt that a lowly ensign is capable of organizing such a scheme; however, Wakefield would be our best hope in finding the leader. We cannot allow the blackguard to escape, and he surely will attempt to do so if he feels he is being watched."

"Where will you go? Do you have a place to stay?"

Mr. Bennet laughed, dipping a piece of brown bread into his stew. "Well, I will not be staying at the Royal Pavilion, to be sure!"

"Probably not a good idea, especially if the prince and Mrs. Fitzherbert are in residence," Mr. Gardiner rejoined. "In all seriousness, what are your plans?"

"I must find Mr. Meyerson. That is my primary objective. He left Meryton over a week ago. His wife has had no word since."

"I wish you Godspeed, then. I will find a way to notify Mr. Montefiore's people. They should be at the ready if things get out of hand."

Nodding his agreement, Mr. Bennet finished off his plate, satisfied and quite ready for his feathered bed.

CHAPTER SEVEN

27th of October

Mr. Darcy's arrival the following day was awaited with a heavy heart, as Elizabeth was uncertain how to elucidate the series of events which had unfolded since last they met. She and Jane had spoken of it well into the night, for an explanation of some sort was equally necessary for Mr. Bingley. Ought they make their betrotheds fully aware of the dire circumstances in which the Bennet family found themselves? Their father had opined on the matter only with regard to their sisters and household. Jane, having given the matter considerable thought, had replied in her own unpretentious manner.

"Surely there can be no occasion for *not* exposing Mr. Bingley and Mr. Darcy to our dreadful news. They are to be our husbands, Lizzy. We need not withhold our confidences."

From her chamber's window, Elizabeth watched as the handsome men dismounted and walked up the gravel path to the front entrance. Jane had gone down to greet the gentlemen, accepting Mr. Bingley's arm as they took a turn about the garden. A bitter smile crossed Elizabeth lips as she peered into the looking glass to adjust an errant curl and contemplated the newest imbroglio they had yet to endure. Here they were, at the cusp of beginning their lives as man and wife, having come at last to an understanding, having reconciled and healed. Yet again; they were met with an obstacle! *This will never do,* she thought as she marched down the staircase to meet her beloved.

"Good afternoon, Miss Bennet," he said with a gallant bow.

"Good afternoon, Mr. Darcy," she answered with a proper curtsey.

Laughing, he made quick work of crossing the few steps to come to Elizabeth's side. Bringing her hand to his lips, Mr. Darcy gently brushed a tender caress there, causing her heart to skip and her breath to halt in anticipation. She closed her eyes and nearly sighed when his lips found hers. Soft and tender at first, the kiss grew in intensity, forcing Elizabeth to cling to him as her knees weakened, and she was filled with sensations previously unknown to her. She returned the kiss without compunction and then, thinking the better of it, blushed prettily, yet unaccustomed to such abandon. Nonetheless, it was not this emotion which caused Elizabeth to release herself from his embrace.

"What's this?" he declared, misunderstanding her withdrawal. "We are to be wed, dearest."

"And, I long to be your wife," Elizabeth replied breathlessly before inviting Mr. Darcy to join her on the settee, "but it seems there may be yet another deterrent to that happy day."

Knowing that Mr. Darcy would favor a clear and concise report, she provided the facts as they were related by her father. The incredulous nature of her father's involvement in such cloak and dagger proceedings should have been diverting had it not instead imposed a judicious sense of trepidation.

"I fear our plans may be postponed, for I cannot wed without my father safe and sound by my side, and he cannot know for certain when he and Mr. Meyerson are to return."

Mr. Darcy arose from his cushioned seat and began pacing about the room.

"Is there nothing to be done? To stand idly by while two men are thrown into such a dangerous situation cannot be borne."

"My father believes that they must act alone. It is a matter of great confidentiality, and they are working under orders from the War Department," she replied and then laughed nervously. "I confess, I never would have credited my father in this line of work. All this time, we believed him to be hiding away in his library, happily ensconced by the fire with his books."

Elizabeth arose and rang the bell for tea. It was evident the situation called for rational thought. Perhaps partaking in some refreshments would calm her nerves, for the thoughts racing through her head would never do.

"Do you believe in the Fae?" she asked and laughed immediately seeing the look upon his face. "Do not scowl at me, sir! We here in the country tend to be a superstitious lot. Perhaps it is *they* who wish to keep us apart."

"I do not scowl and I would have you recall that I, too, am from the country. Pemberley is not quite Grosvenor Square," he said with a grin.

"Very true. However, I would venture to say your education was rather limited with regards to local folklore." Unable to resist, Elizabeth brushed a lock of hair from his brow before continuing with her lesson. "I will happily be your instructor on this point. The fae, for your information, are horrid creatures who most enjoy creating havoc amongst poor, unsuspecting humans such as ourselves."

He bowed his head, begging her to continue for, although he was besotted with the sparkle in her fine eyes, Darcy was indeed perplexed with her meaning.

She laughed at his expression. "You need not be uneasy, sir! I do not truly believe in that sort of magic yet, it *does* appear we are meant to be star crossed lovers. You cannot discount that every step forward we have made throughout our acquaintance has been met with an impediment."

"Nonsense!" Mr. Darcy declared with more vigor than he intended, and quickly determined to temper his tone. "Do not worry overmuch with thoughts of mischievous creatures and legends of yore. In truth, our own mortal qualities have proven to be our undoing and yet, we have met our challenges. We have faced our shortcomings. If anything, my love, I believe in Fate. Nothing or no one—neither Caroline Bingley, nor my Aunt Catherine, *nor* the wee ones of the woods—will deter me. You will be Mistress of Pemberley and I will be the happiest of men."

His countenance had become hard and fierce. Elizabeth nearly laughed at his determination. Her words had been meant as a joke, a salve to calm her own state of anxiety, but she realized that, while he admired her for her liveliness, he was not yet accustomed to her particular form of humor. She would have to remember to temper her words until they had become comfortable with one another.

"The matter remains before us: my father and Mr. Meyerson are caught in the middle of a national crisis. I regret their business has interfered with our plans and I cannot begin to fathom how we are to get on with our daily lives worrying and wondering how they fare amongst those scoundrels and lowlifes in Brighton!"

Taking her hand once more, he tantalizingly brushed his lips across her fingertips. "I was planning on going to London to see my man of business. Your father and I were to review the marriage settlement, and I wished to bring you my mother's ring and a few select pieces—"

"I am heartened by your generosity but, I have no occasion to wear such finery," she said, fingering her simple necklace.

"Ah, but you will and, nonetheless, I *wish* you to have it. I wish you to have all of it."

"But I have nothing to offer you in return," she stated emphatically. "Does it follow, because I am a woman, and a poor one at that, I should not care to give my bridegroom a gift as well?"

Sighing, he kissed the tip of her nose. "I do not require a gift, my love. Your heart is all that I desire."

"I have my grandmother's locket, which I never wear. It is rather large for me, but..." He interrupted her with a kiss that left her breathless and unable to finish a coherent thought.

"I will bring back a few things and you will choose what you like," he said as he traced his thumb along her cheek, "and regarding your father and Mr. Meyerson: if we do not hear from them soon, I will go and search Brighton myself."

As the gentlemen were to return to Netherfield for the evening, the bittersweet interlude came to an end. With promises that the morrow would bring better tidings, the sisters bade farewell to Mr. Bingley and Mr. Darcy and watched their handsome men ride away. It was as they made their way indoors that Jane and Elizabeth heard an indecorous shout come from Kitty's chamber window.

"Someone is coming!"

Indeed, a hired post chaise had come to a stop at the Bennet's front door. Its arrival had been perceived from the dining room as well. While Mrs. Bennet was not expecting callers, given the lateness of the day, it did not follow that she was disinclined to receive company. As she was preparing to quit the room, Mrs. Bennet heard the piercing voice of her most favored daughter.

"Mama! Mama! I am home!"

"Lydia!" Elizabeth exclaimed.

"It is my darling girl!" Mrs. Bennet nearly ran down Hill in her need to embrace her dear child. Only Kitty remained silent as the family gathered in the foyer to greet their guests. Mr. Wickham, handsome as ever in his regimentals, stood aside and allowed the happy reunion to take place while he smirked and preened in front of the foyer's grand looking glass.

"Oh Lydia! Oh Mr. Wickham! What felicity is this?"

"Dear Mama! It is good to be home, and I have so much to share with my sisters," Lydia said, sporting a devilish grin. "Kitty, you will have many questions to pose and I will be delighted to answer. Now that I am a married woman of the world, I shall be your guide and teacher of all things."

Elizabeth stepped forward and glared at the interloper. "May I pose the first question, Sister?"

Lydia bowed her pretty little head in acquiescence, delighted to be the center of attention. "By all means."

"I will be succinct and to the point: Whatever are you doing here?"

Lydia gasped at Elizabeth's rudeness, being under the impression that as a married lady, accompanied by such a fine and handsome officer, she should be a welcome addition to any society.

"Naturally, we are come to join in the celebration of your nuptials, Miss Elizabeth," answered Mr. Wickham with a curt bow. "And yours as well, of course, Miss Bennet."

"We understand it is to be a double ceremony," giggled Lydia. "The townspeople must be beside themselves! Other than the militia's presence, your wedding will bring some excitement to this dreary little town."

Ignoring the childish snorts and snickers, Elizabeth addressed her new brother. "And how, may I ask, are you so well informed, Mr. Wickham? I would have imagined the post is rather slow in reaching Northumberland."

"Not at all. I am gratified to state being stationed in Newcastle has not caused my dear wife any undue apprehension. Indeed, Lydia has been corresponding with great success and alacrity with Kitty and all her particular friends."

"Kitty," Elizabeth grumbled, "I would have a word with you."

Jane, wishing to act as a balm over the irritation Mr. and Mrs. Wickham's abrupt appearance had brought upon the household, applied to her mother. "Let us ask Hill for some refreshments while Lydia tells us the news of her new home."

In this manner, Mrs. Bennet led the way into the drawing room, followed by Lydia, her husband, Jane, Mary, and Kitty, while Elizabeth remained behind and simmered in her frustration. She had purposely neglected to dispatch an invitation to her sister. It was her hope that, being stationed so far away from Hertfordshire, Mr. Wickham would not be granted leave on short notice. Elizabeth had contrived the scheme believing it would save her from doing battle with her mama. The added benefit, of course, would have been to spare Mr. Darcy from having to socialize with his nemesis.

With nothing for it, a moment later Elizabeth traced her family's footsteps and situated herself in a lonely chair in the far corner the room.

In her feverish attempt to draw attention to any subject rather than Lydia's unexpected arrival, Kitty began sharing the gossip of Meryton—forgetting that her last letter had already covered most of the town's news.

"Captain Carter, Denny and the others are now stationed in Brighton. We have a new shop where Sir William's warehouse used to stand. There are new families who have come to make Hertfordshire their home...oh! The vicar's son has returned from university and their household is all aflutter, for the parsonage is full to capacity—so many children in the Ainsely home, you understand."

"You forget yourself, Kitty. As if I would care a whit about the vicar and his familial arrangements!" Lydia laughed. "Speak to Mary about the vicar's son, for such dull gossip is better suited for her ears."

Mary, uncomfortable with her name being mentioned in such a conversation, quickly responded. "'Do not let any unwholesome talk come out of your mouth, but only what is helpful'...so sayeth Ephesians. I would also add that I care not about Gideon Ainsely *or* he for me."

"No one has implied anything of the sort, Mary. Nonetheless, the more you protest, the more diverting the conversation has become."

"He does not even know of my existence!" Mary's protest rang throughout the room.

"Dearest, there is no need to upset yourself," Jane murmured. "It is just Lydia's way..."

"Yes," Elizabeth interjected, "and well we were getting along without Mrs. Wickham's childish jokes. Tell me, Lydia, why are you truly here? I suspect a wedding breakfast would not be sufficient to tempt you away from a camp full of soldiers and the society you enjoyed there."

George Wickham glanced at his wife, and with a raised brow, reminded her to guard her tongue. He had given Lydia explicit instructions not to divulge his purpose in applying for leave. In truth, she did not know the full of it, for Wickham knew the foolish girl would be his ruination if he had given her a complete understanding of his business in Meryton. He had given his wife a few crumbs of information sufficient to appease her curiosity and nothing more.

Wickham had learned that one or two of his prior acquaintances had recently come into quite a bit of blunt. Returning to Hertfordshire to attend his sisters' nuptials allowed him the perfect alibi to investigate the matter and to ingratiate himself into the scheme. When he had applied to Colonel Leighton, the man had given his consent willingly. Having a soft spot for weddings and family reunions, he readily allowed the Wickhams to travel to Longbourn for the happy occasion. Now, all that was required was for Wickham to reestablish himself with his old friends.

"Really, Elizabeth, this assault is too much, even coming from you!" cried Lydia. "Mama, am I not welcome in my own home? Pray, where is my father? Will he not receive me?"

Mrs. Bennet, heretofore silent while her daughters bickered and squabbled, shifted in her seat and was barely able to transfer her cup and saucer onto the tray, such were her tremblings.

"Oh! Such a question," she cried. "Such a clever girl! Your father is away from home and we do not have the pleasure of knowing when he shall return!"

"Whatever do you mean, Mama?"

"My dear girl, there is no rhyme or reason to your father's withdrawal from Longbourn," she replied. "You know very well that Mr. Bennet takes great pleasure in wreaking havoc on my poor nerves."

Lydia's frown encouraged Mrs. Bennet to continue.

"It had something to do with the militia decamping, or some such. Your father insisted that he was duty bound to come to a friend's aid," Mrs. Bennet added. "As of this moment, I know not where he is or when he can be expected to return."

"But the banns have been posted!"

"We will have to wait until our father has seen to his obligations," Jane murmured softly.

Mr. Wickham, hearing that the regiment had quitted Meryton, became uncomfortable and complained suddenly of headache. Arising from the settee he shared with his wife, he put aside his cake and tea and begged to be excused.

"The extensive travel has brought on an unexpected discomposure; however, I am certain a little rest will set me to rights," he said bowing low. "Mrs. Wickham, will you show me to our rooms?"

Lydia, misconstruing her husband's suggestion, looked about the room and glancing devilishly at her sisters, purred her response. "Of course, my love. I am certain Mama will understand...even if my sisters cannot."

With their departure, Elizabeth jumped to her feet and quickly made for Kitty before she could be allowed to quit the room. "Who gave you leave to invite Lydia and Wickham to the wedding?"

"She is our sister! I did not think it necessary to ask permission to write to my own sister."

"While I do not have the authority to keep you from corresponding with Lydia, I feel it my right to presume your respect and consideration. It was not your place to extend an invitation," Elizabeth declared. "After everything that selfish, thoughtless girl has done—her actions nearly destroyed all our hopes."

"But, she is married now. I cannot comprehend..."

"You cannot comprehend the matter because you are too naive to grasp what her folly has cost our family. I did not wish to impose their presence on Mr. Darcy *or* on Miss Darcy."

"Dearest Lizzy," cried Jane, "do not upset yourself. Mr. Darcy will not be provoked by Mr. Wickham's attendance. He does not have room in his heart for anything but you."

"You are too good, Sister. Your kindness and forbearance are truly angelic, but I have nothing of your tolerance in matters such as these."

Jane eagerly disclaimed all extraordinary merit. "I am in love and simply wish to see all the world happy. All will be well, you shall see."

"Nay," cried Elizabeth, "I fear it is not possible, for the more I see of the world, the more I am dissatisfied with it." She did not speak further upon the matter, for doing so would reveal her father's involvement in a dangerous scheme. Knowing that there were men so evil, so devoid of good character that they would fill their own pockets by stealing from their own brothers, was contemptible. Knowing that her own brother-in-law was a blackguard and a rogue, made her ill.

"You must keep forgiveness in your heart," Mary pleaded. "Remember Lizzy, there are still decent men in the world."

"Because they have condescended to align themselves with our family, two *decent* men are to be brothers with such a man as Mr. Wickham," cried Elizabeth. "And on a day which is meant to be solemn and full of goodness, they will now have to countenance such a man. It is unaccountable. In every view, it is unaccountable!"

CHAPTER EIGHT

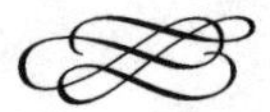

28th of October

To help pass the time and to commiserate with their new neighbor, Mrs. Bennet had sent an early note inviting Mrs. Meyerson to call. She had hoped rather than expected Lizzy might restrain herself from arguing with her sisters while they were entertaining company. But when the time came to change from her dressing gown, Mrs. Bennet begged off and returned to the comfort of her bed. Her nervous stomach would not allow her to arise, and the contemplation of partaking refreshments only made matters worse. She sent for Jane with explicit instructions that she act as hostess and to see that Lizzy kept a civil tongue.

At the appointed time, Mrs. Meyerson and her daughter were heard to arrive, and Jane happily greeted the guests as they made their way to the front door. Jane welcomed the opportunity to occupy her time with tea and chatter, as her gentle nature could not abide worrying overmuch.

Elizabeth, at her sister's behest, joined the party and petulantly took up her embroidery, although she could not keep from stabbing herself with the needle and imagined the tapestry was Kitty instead.

"I will take tea to my mother," Kitty mumbled, wishing to remove herself from Lizzy's glare.

"My mother still keeps to her room?" Elizabeth enquired.

"The possible change in our wedding plans is causing her a great deal of anxiety," Jane responded.

Elizabeth considered replying to the comment with a biting remark but had not the inclination to begin such a discourse. Her own constitution was waning after several sleepless nights.

"I must say this state of affairs is exceedingly diverting."

"I do not understand your meaning, Lydia. Pray, explain yourself. Our father has quitted Longbourn and is off on a mysterious adventure. Your sisters are suffering from anguish heretofore unknown. How is that to be construed as diverting?"

"After everything that has transpired between the lot of you, the months of misunderstandings and missed opportunities, you and dear Jane finally receive and accept your offers and yet, here you are, still unwed and, I presume—*knowing you as I do*—yet to have tasted the delights of the marriage bed."

"Lydia!" cried Jane.

"You are not going to be missish, I hope, and pretend to be affronted by my speaking of such matters. You must not be tempted to scold me Jane, for I take your place now and you must go lower. I am a married woman."

"We might be more inclined to accept your exalted position," said Elizabeth, "if you would have a care and comport yourself in an appropriate manner."

"Shall I tell you what to expect on your wedding night, Jane?

Hmm? Do you think that your wit and sarcasm will serve you, Lizzy, when Mr. Darcy takes you to his bed?"

"What has come over you?" Elizabeth demanded. "You will stop this wanton speech at once!"

"Let me tell you this, dear sisters. Once you are wedded and bedded, you will see the world with different eyes."

Mrs. Meyerson set down the book she had been perusing and cleared her throat as if to remind the others she still remained amid the party. "Mrs. Wickham," she said, "as your own dear mother is not here to offer guidance, please allow me to intervene. You are newly wed and, being quite young, still unaccustomed to your new place in society. Perhaps you do not comprehend what propriety dictates in matters such as these—it is not proper to speak to your sisters thusly."

"Why ever not? I have experienced that of which they can only dream—why should I not take care and broaden their education?"

"I thank you for my share of the favor, Lydia, but I do not particularly wish to learn from your familiarity with the subject."

"And what do you know of it, *Miss* Elizabeth? Of course, there is more to the whole business of matrimony, for Mr. Wickham has been generous of late—fine dinners, extravagant gifts, luxurious lodgings..."

"And how does Mr. Wickham pay for this lavish lifestyle? Surely he is not foolishly wasting your dowry. He will have only his military wages to support you if he continues at such a rate."

"Do you believe, because my husband did not choose *you* as his bride, he is simple or without intellect? Wickham has many schemes and is ever meeting people who know how to turn a quick profit. We are living in style, Lizzy. Do not presume to put on airs with me! What do I care about your Pemberley?" she said, with a glare. "Wickham will see me right."

"A man is not measured by his bank account, Lydia," whispered Jane.

"And yet, were we not in ecstasy over Mr. Bingley's five thousand a year?" Lydia smirked. "Naturally, as a married lady, I can speak of another sort of ecstasy...I do apologize, Mrs. Meyerson. I cannot seem to help myself, but you see, the good Lord has blessed my marriage," she said, raising her fingers and flashing her wedding band. "Consequently; I have nothing of which to be ashamed!"

"'Therefore shall a man leave his father and his mother and shall cleave unto his wife, and they shall be one flesh,'" stated Mrs. Myerson. "What you are speaking of, the marital act, is in actuality, a divine gift and a holy obligation."

Lydia snorted in her usual manner and, without compunction, replied, "Wickham is of another mind. He states the act cannot be a sin if animals do it."

"We are not animals, nor are we angels. We are flesh and blood and are made in the image of our Creator," Mrs. Meyerson replied forcefully. "I hear your words of passion and ecstasy, but I cannot discern any love or devotion. I must question how much happiness can belong to a couple who are only brought together when their passions are stronger than their virtue."

"I will say only this, and then, Mrs. Meyerson, I will beg to be excused from our little *tête-à-tête*—once you are in the arms of your husband, there is little difference between a lady of the night and a lady of the realm."

"Enough!" Elizabeth jumped from her seat and made short work of coming to Lydia's side. "You will be silent or I will have you removed from this house."

"On whose authority? *Yours*?" Lydia laughed, as she lifted her hand to fan in front of her sister.

As the gold band flashed before her eyes, Elizabeth lost what little control she had managed to preserve. With the agility of an experienced fencer, one hand flicked the offending appendage out of the way, while the other administered a resounding slap across Lydia's still-smirking face. The room was silent then. It seemed only the echo of contact lingered as the tell-tale imprint of Elizabeth's hand on her sister's cheek became evident.

The women heard Hill welcoming Mr. Darcy into the foyer and knew they had but a moment to compose themselves before the gentleman joined their party. Jane wiped her tears away and, bringing her cup to her trembling lips, attempted to sip her now-tepid tea. Elizabeth, unmoved, stood firm in her place, such was her fury, *such* was her disappointment in her sister's contemptible behavior.

"Good afternoon ladies," Mr. Darcy said as he entered the salon. Of course he had heard the raised voices, but he would not broach the subject until he and Elizabeth could discuss the matter in private. What concerned him now was that *his Elizabeth* had yet to turn to acknowledge his presence, so lost was she yet in her passion.

"Lizzy, dearest, Mr. Darcy has joined us. Perhaps he may wish for some refreshment?"

Elizabeth, unclenching her fists, turned to face the gentleman and was mortified at her hoydenish behavior. She allowed her passions to overcome her senses. Worse yet; she had struck her sister. *Had he witnessed her shameful outburst?* Had he overheard Lydia's disgraceful speech? Appalled at her own inability to control her emotions, Elizabeth burst into tears and fled the room. Jane gasped and was so taken ill, the delicate cup and saucer fell from her hands, spilling the last drops of liquid on her mother's good carpet. Mrs. Meyerson's maternal feelings stirred her to follow in Elizabeth's footsteps; however, Mr. Darcy stayed her action with a curt bow.

"Please madam, attend Miss Bennet. I will go to Miss Elizabeth."

She had run down the hall and through the kitchen, passing Cook and Hill without a word or a second glance. Overwrought, Elizabeth sought solace in the garden, where she allowed her tears to flow until she was spent. Only then, was she able to formulate her thoughts.

Lydia's reprehensible behavior had been disconcerting yet, it was not the singular source of her distress. She and Mr. Darcy had managed to overcome their initial misunderstandings, their contrived prejudices—*their false pride.* That blessed day on Oakham Mount, they had pledged their love and admiration for one another. And yet, Elizabeth's understanding of marriage had been drawn from her own family. The image that formed was not a very pleasing picture of conjugal felicity or domestic comfort.

It had been difficult to own it but, Elizabeth had confessed she had misjudged Mr. Darcy from the very start. Her cherished skills of discernment had failed her before. Was she to fail once again? *Could it be possible that she and Mr. Darcy would not suit, after all*? Could she, the daughter of Fanny Bennet née Gardiner, be the wife of the proud Master of Pemberley?

Mr. Darcy had followed Elizabeth down the now-familiar path nestled among the foxglove and larkspur but stopped and stood firm as he set eyes upon her. Guardedly, he watched as she struggled with private contemplations that seemed to pierce her with anguish. "Dearest," he said, when he could stand silently no longer. "What has happened?"

Elizabeth allowed her hands to be gently enveloped into his warm grasp, but she was unable to gaze upon his countenance. She closed her eyes and simply shook her head.

"Tell me, my love, for I am grieved, indeed, to see you so distraught."

"I fear ..." she whispered, "I fear the felicity I had envisioned for our union is fading away. Perhaps Lady Catherine was correct in her assumptions, for it is becoming exceedingly difficult to deny that I *am* of inferior birth, my family too low to be borne. I fear my blood is tainted."

"What has come over you? You are a gentleman's daughter—had we not settled all of this before?"

"While that is true, you have not been made privy to certain attributes of my family heritage. Shall I divulge some of our secrets?"

Her pale face and impetuous manner could only allow him to nod his head. Mr. Darcy waited in wretched suspense until she drew her next breath and unburdened her soul.

"You are acquainted with my father as a landed gentleman of modest income, a country esquire who prefers his library to routs or assemblies and who, unfortunately, will see his family estate entailed to a distant cousin."

"Elizabeth, my love, the facts are well known to me..."

"You know, of course, that my father's marriage did not produce a son to inherit, a fact for which he, no doubt, blames my mother. He has not been able to set aside an annual sum for the better provision of his children, a fact for which, again, he blames my mother. You see, my father was captivated by my mother's youth, her beauty and her *liveliness.* He offered for her without knowing her mind, without respect or esteem. Throughout the years, I have witnessed my mother's confidence dwindle to nothing. I am not blind to the impropriety of my father's behavior, and I fear my mother's weak understanding and small-mindedness stems from the disadvantages of so unsuitable a marriage. I have never been so fully aware of the evils arising from so ill-judged a direction of talents. They are neither one worthy of each other!" *Am I worthy of you*? she thought.

Mr. Darcy sighed. "Your parents' marriage is of no consequence. We are schooled and counseled by our elders but, in the end, what we make of our lives is in our own hands and in the hands of the Lord."

"In observing my own parents' unfortunate marriage in addition to Lydia and Mr. Wickham, I cannot help but wonder if the apple does not fall from the tree."

"Your suffering grieves me exceedingly, but I fail to understand this bewildering display of emotion. I must admit that, upon entering your home, I heard raised voices emanating from the drawing room that were disconcerting. What occurred to bring your party to this fevered pitch?"

"Lydia is a disgrace! I cannot credit we are of the same blood, for she is cold and contemptible," Elizabeth cried and wiped fresh tears away with a frustrated motion. "My sister puts me to shame, Mr. Darcy..."

"William—*you promised.* Tell me the rest of it. There is something more."

Suddenly timid, Elizabeth turned again. "It is difficult for me to speak of it."

"Surely, if we are to be man and wife," he said, turning her so she faced him once more, "you can find the words to tell me your sorrows —or is it your fears?"

"How is it to *be* with us, William?" she cried. "I yearn for your touch. I dream of your kisses! But will I be as vile as my sister?"

Mr. Darcy cupped her face and tenderly kissed away her tears. "Oh, my dearest, how could you compare our love to what they share?"

"What do I know of love or the marriage bed? My mother has spoken only of the getting of a husband, not the keeping of one," she said as a hiccup escaped her lips.

He chuckled as he caressed her silken curls. "I have professed my love for you. I am devoted to you and to your happiness. What will happen between us will be blessed and sanctioned by the Church."

"I see little affection and less respect in my parents' sanctioned union and Lydia speaks of the act in such carnal terms..." she said, stepping away from his reach, needing to create some distance.

"It is written that Adam knew his wife...."

Elizabeth raised her eyes to his at last, uncertain of what she would see reflected back—mockery or reverence.

"*I am my beloved's and my beloved is mine.* The psalmist's words express it best, I think. We will know one another as Adam and Eve and it will be transcendent, for it is not solely the physical intimacy that will unite us, but rather the linking of our souls. I swear to you on my honor Elizabeth, I will treasure you, body, mind and spirit. Fear not, for I am neither your father nor Wickham, and you, my dearest, do not—*could not*—resemble your mother or your sister."

With nothing further to add, Mr. Darcy held out his hand and waited for Elizabeth to come to him. She allowed herself to walk into his sheltering embrace. Nonetheless, the seed of doubt had taken root. Just as the creeping wood sorrel grew with abandon alongside the hermitage, her uncertainty would prove difficult to restrain.

CHAPTER NINE

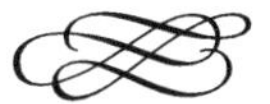

29th of October

The morning meal was quite a dreary affair, with Mrs. Bennet upstairs, unable to look at her breakfast tray, and Elizabeth and Jane concerned for their father and their wedding plans. The sisters were each so deep in their own thoughts, neither realized Lydia was missing from the room. Therefore, the screeching coming from above was both unsettling and disturbing.

"Lizzy! Jane!"

The sisters, followed by Kitty, who did not wish to miss any of the diversion, ran upstairs only to meet Lydia on the landing.

"Whatever is the matter?" asked a breathless Jane.

"It is Wickham," Lydia cried. "He has left me!"

"Whatever do you mean?"

"He is gone! Wickham is gone! He left me a note," she said frantically waving the missive about, "but I am not certain what to make of it. He is to meet a business partner, but he does not say where he has gone or when he will return."

"Do not make yourself ill, Lydia," Elizabeth sighed as she descended the stairs. "Your husband will return for you." *If he knows what is good for him,* she thought to herself.

"I am not concerned on that score. Of course he will, for we cannot be without one another."

"Then what is it?" Elizabeth asked in exasperation.

"I cannot credit that he left me behind!"

"If he went to meet a business partner, perhaps he thought you would find it dull," Kitty suggested.

"I have accompanied him before when he attended business meetings. He calls *everything* a business meeting, whether he is playing cards or betting on the ponies."

"I do not follow," Jane questioned. "How is this possible when he is serving in the militia?"

"He is not a prisoner," Lydia replied with a snort. "There is society in Newcastle. However, it *is* rather a miracle that Wickham has not been sent up the River Tick! When Kitty told me of your nuptials, Lizzy, I was tempted to ask for a loan but thought the better of it. He always manages to turn things around."

"Have you no idea of where he went?" Kitty asked.

"None whatever. He only states his business partner was not in Meryton as expected, and so he has followed him to his next destination."

Lydia was ever given to theatrics—selfish, irresponsible girl! Elizabeth could not be bothered with such distractions, for her heart and mind were wholly occupied elsewhere. Everything was dependent upon their father's safe returned and the reconciling of her own misgivings towards an ill-matched marriage with Mr. Darcy. Her restlessness increased with each passing moment. Elizabeth's last concern was Wickham and her infuriating sister. "The first wish of my heart," she whispered to herself as she walked down the stairs and out the door, "is nevermore to be in company with either of them. Their society can afford no pleasure that will atone for such wretchedness."

Elizabeth made her way to Oakham Mount, hoping that a good long walk would help clear her thoughts. As the weather was fine, she enjoyed her freedom, running when she wished or stopping to forage through the dog-violets and honeysuckle. Even as winter had announced its arrival, nature's bounty was still ever present. Elizabeth, satisfying her natural instincts, gathered samplings for her herbalist's potted garden as her grandmother had instructed her many years ago. Her grandmother had been a healer of sorts, as many of the Bennet women had been. The legend of their Norman ancestry, their skills and bravery, had long been the stuff of Elizabeth's imagination and inspiration.

How she longed to speak to her *Grandmère* and share the burdens she carried deep in her heart. What advice would she have given? Elizabeth shook her head in disgust, imagining her rebuke. *Where is your fire, girl?* She had inherited the garnet locket from her grandmother with a note that stated: *To Elizabeth, the one who shares my Norman blood.* "But look at me now," she thought, as she marched through the woods. Confused, concerned and cantankerous!

Elizabeth slowed her pace and allowed herself to take in the crisp, cool air, to breathe deeply, and to be at peace. The leaves rustled ever so slightly and a flock of birds squawked as they flew overhead. She sighed at this. It seemed an alarm to awaken and get on with the act of living! As it was her practice to be satisfied—and certainly her temper to be happy—Elizabeth determined she would find a way to resolve this unprecedented trepidation.

Returning home, feeling somewhat refreshed by the exercise,

Elizabeth reasoned her best course of action would be to speak with her sister. After all, Jane *was* her dearest and closest friend. They had shared every manner of confidences since the two had been out of leading strings. Surely, if she had been able to confess her hopeless love for Charles Thornton (the son of the apple farmer when she was nine years of age), she ought to be able to disclose the misgivings that plagued her heart this day.

Entering the drawing room, Elizabeth quickly noted that, although Kitty and Mary were suitably entrenched with their books and embroidery, Jane was nowhere to be found. The silence was foreboding and, as Lydia's presence was also wanting from the cozy scene, Elizabeth surmised there had been an exchange of words while she had been frolicking in the woods.

Retracing her steps back into the foyer, she ascended the staircase and quietly made her way to their chamber. She found her sister—or rather, she found the lower portion of her sister's person—poking out from under the bedframe.

"Jane! Whatever are you about?" Elizabeth laughed. "Are we playing hide and go seek—at our age?" She watched with continued amusement as her normally docile and dignified sister wormed and waggled her way up to a standing position. Affecting a stern mien, Elizabeth stood at the foot of the bed, arms crossed, awaiting a reply. "Well?"

Jane, who was not in the habit of such strenuous activity, rose to her full height wheezing and short of breath. "I am ashamed to admit it, Lizzy, but *your* sister has driven me to act the hoyden!"

The significance of the wording was not lost on Elizabeth, who immediately understood they were speaking of Lydia. "What has she done now?"

Adjusting her gown and pinning a loose curl, Jane regained control of her emotions and took a seat by their dressing table. Sliding her foot into the kid slipper she had retrieved from under the bed, Jane colored slightly. "Oh Lizzy. I lost my temper! I ran up to our room and was so exceedingly angry that I...I had to...*I felt the need to—*"

Exasperated, Elizabeth exclaimed, "What? What did you do?"

"I removed my shoe and threw it against the wall," Jane murmured. "I did not take into consideration the weight of the heel would cause it to rebound and fall under the bed. Lizzy, I am mortified at my behavior. Up until this moment, I did not know my own strength! I nearly toppled over our favorite water pitcher."

Recognizing her sister was clearly distraught and commiserating with the cause, Elizabeth was able to curtail her own cheeky remarks, offering empathy instead. "I am only too familiar with the emotion you encountered this day, for I struggle constantly in seeking release. Unfortunately, Jane dear, we have very little remedy for discharging our frustrations, do we not?"

The two shared a bitter laugh as Jane provided a brief summation of Lydia's latest transgression. Their youngest sister found fault with everyone and everything. Society in Newcastle, one must be made to understand, was exceedingly more diverting, more fashionable, and more enlightened than the dreary lot found at home. The gallant young men, handsome in their regimentals, paid court to all the ladies. It mattered not if the ladies in question were married or unattached. When Jane asked her sister if she engaged in such disgraceful behavior, Lydia doubled over in laughter, nearly bringing up her breakfast of poached eggs and toast.

"To say I was disheartened," Jane declared, "would be putting it lightly. I cannot imagine the sort of love Lydia and Mr. Wickham share. To tell the truth, I *would not* wish to imagine it! Mr. Bingley and I have such a tender attachment that I find myself blissfully happy in its warmth and enveloping security."

Elizabeth, delighted that her sister brought up the subject she desperately wished to discuss, continued along in the same vein. "Jane, dearest, do you not find that Lydia's comportment brings up some disturbing questions?"

"Whatever do you mean?"

"Having experienced that which we have not, could it be possible our youngest sister might have an understanding of emotions we can only feign to comprehend? Might we be judging her too harshly, condemning her as hoyden and a wanton when she is merely experiencing that which all married women are intended to enjoy?"

Gasping at such a thought, Jane shook her head in vehement opposition. "Nay, I cannot agree with such an assessment, Lizzy. My feelings towards Mr. Bingley are quite the opposite," said she, the sweet animation of her face making her look handsomer than ever. "Our love is quiet and enduring..."

"But do you not ever feel overcome with emotion, something quite prodigious—something *all consuming*?"

Jane smiled and gently took her sister's hand. "I am not like you, Lizzy. My heart does not yearn for the passionate, liberating sensations that you have always sought. Do you recall that young farmer, Charles Thornton? You imagined yourself wildly in love with him, did you not?"

Laughing, Elizabeth nodded her head in amazement. How like her sister to know her own thoughts before she had the chance to voice them.

"You had asked Grandmère if she could concoct a potion to make him return your love..."

"Yes!" Elizabeth exclaimed with amusement. "And I asked for another to make Mama approve the match."

"Grandmère was fierce with her reprimand. Do you not recall? She said in matters such as these, it was best to let the soul decide on its own," Jane whispered. "We, each of us, must be true to our own hearts, Lizzy. Remember Mrs. Meyerson's own words on the matter. How little happiness can belong to a couple when their passions are stronger than their virtue? Lydia and Mr. Wickham will have to make their own way. I flatter myself hoping their mutual affection will eventually steady their passionate nature and they will finally settle and live quietly. And now Lizzy, if you do not mind, would you make my excuses to Mama? I fear it is my turn to beg a lie-down. The morning's theatrics have gotten the best of me."

Elizabeth kissed her sister's brow and pulled the coverlet over her shoulders before quitting the room. She had much to think upon but believed herself ready to write the letter she owed her aunt and uncle. They had been so kind in sending such a generous gift for the upcoming wedding. Elizabeth had not the heart to dispel their wishes for her future happiness, although she was not yet convinced her happiness was assured.

SEATED IN THE DRAWING ROOM MUCH LATER IN THE afternoon, Elizabeth held a quill in hand and stared at a blank sheet of paper daring her to begin, when the Meyersons were announced. Mrs. Bennet had extended the invitation, knowing that the family had increased by one family member and she wished to welcome the young man into Meryton society. Mrs. Meyerson entered the room, followed by her son and her daughter, who espied Kitty immediately and ran to her at once.

"Rachel, you might wait to be asked, dearest," her mother said, knowing full well that the two had become inseparable. Kitty, for once, was the center of someone's attention and Rachel delighted in receiving the sisterly devotion to which she was accustomed.

Mrs. Meyerson addressed the family with great pride, turning to present her son. "Mrs. Bennet, Miss Bennet, Miss Elizabeth, Miss Mary, Miss Catherine, allow me to introduce my son, Mr. David Meyerson."

Elizabeth, still at the desk, arose from her seat. Mary, who had been attempting to decipher the fingering of a new musical piece, discontinued momentarily in order to greet the newcomers. Performing their perfunctory curtsies, she and her sister returned to their tasks at hand—Elizabeth because she could not formulate the words to begin her letter, and Mary because her timidity was such that she sought comfort at the pianoforte. It was therefore rather startling when, less than a quarter of an hour later, a masculine voice came from behind.

"May I turn the pages for you?"

"Oh! I did not hear you approach, sir. Please, do not trouble yourself," cried Mary, without addressing the gentleman directly. "I play rather ill and your presence will make me anxious. Rather, make yourself comfortable with a book or some tea, or perhaps it would better suit if I should leave my practice for another time."

"No excellence in music is to be acquired without constant practice, Miss Mary."

"But does it follow that every apprentice is meant for such distinction?" she replied, before she realized the words left her lips. "I have worked countless hours for such accomplishment, but I fear my fingers do not move over this instrument in the masterly manner I have envisioned."

"I cannot imagine you wasting countless hours on the pianoforte when other fine young ladies find so many interesting things to enjoy."

"I thank you for the compliment, sir, but I am neither fine or like other young ladies."

"Are you not?" he said, as he began picking out the notes of the score.

"I am the plain one in a family of four other handsome, accomplished and clever daughters. I enjoy the solitude and enrichment found in reading and in the playing of music. I fear I am not good company, especially for a gentleman newly arrived from London."

"I beg to differ!" he exclaimed. "Although we have just become acquainted, I cannot accept your description of plain or boring. My idea of good company is the company of clever, well-informed people who have a great deal of conversation, and if you will not observe it for yourself, Miss Mary, allow me to point out we have been doing an admirable job!"

He laughed and slightly turned his head to see if his outburst had annoyed his mother. It was then that Mary first witnessed the gentleman's startling features. She must have gasped aloud, for the young man turned around once more with an apologetic smile. "Ah, I had forgotten—you were not warned of my disfigurement, I presume?"

"I would not call it a disfigurement, sir, and I apologize exceedingly for my ungracious and unchristian behavior."

"Come, Miss Mary, there is nothing for which to apologize! I do not fancy you have had the opportunity to meet many young men flaunting a droopy eye and broken nose," he said, winking his one good eye. "I would have you know, last year, Mama commissioned a family portrait but, she insisted the artist capture my aquiline profile!"

Mary laughed at this, causing Mrs. Bennet to question her daughter's unusual comportment. She was not accustomed to this daughter showing much joviality, particularly in the company of an unknown gentleman. As the two young people composed themselves and returned to matter of making music, Mrs. Bennet allowed herself to continue her conversation with her new acquaintance.

"And how are you faring, Mrs. Meyerson, with your husband gone from home? What a comfort to have your son join you during this trying time."

"I am pleased that David was able to come to us, of course I am. However, nothing can replace the camaraderie and friendship I share with my husband." She placed her cup and saucer upon the embroidered tablecloth admiring the handiwork, before continuing *sotto voce.* "I am worried for his safety while, at the same time, I am angry that he got himself into this imbroglio in the first place."

"I envy you, Mrs. Meyerson, and I am not ashamed to say it, seeing that we two are in a most unique crisis which no one else in my acquaintance could understand."

"Why should you envy me, dear lady?"

"The way you speak of your husband...your relationship is something to be admired."

"I do not have the pleasure of understanding your meaning, madam."

"Oh, I suppose I am being melancholy, but—you see, I married for love, as I assume you have done as well. I adored my Mr. Bennet," she said fiddling with the *serviette* with anxious fingers. "When we were wed, I believed him to be besotted, but I quickly came to a right understanding. My husband was infatuated by my comely features, *not* my heart."

"Mrs. Bennet, men can be so unfeeling. They do not understand a woman's nature..."

"I fear it is more than a difference of the sexes. You see, I became the target of his vexation when Mr. Bennet realized he had chosen poorly. He teases and torments me—in truth, he punishes me for his own folly and I have no recourse but to accept it! I love him, but there is no making him happy. If I overspend at the farmer's mart, it is only so I may set a decent meal before him. If I exceed my pin money by purchasing fripperies for the girls, it is so they may do their father proud. It is all to no avail! There are times when I purposefully act with impropriety in the attempt that he pay me mind. *All* things can be borne, Mrs. Meyerson, with the exception of neglect."

"Oh, my dear Mrs. Bennet, it pains me to hear this. Have you no close relations who might have been able to offer you respite?

"I have a sister, Mrs. Phillips. Her husband, an attorney in town, used to be my late father's law clerk. My brother Edward, as you know, lives in Cheapside with his charming wife and young children. They each of them have their own lives to lead. No one takes my part, nobody feels for my poor nerves. I should not expect them to understand, as they only witness what is exposed. I do not know why I speak thusly to you now! It is quite reprehensible of me, but I seem to have become overly sentimental of late."

"I too have found myself crying over the most insignificant things. I fear it must be due in part to the strain of our impromptu removal from our London home. I miss my daughters, as Rachel misses her sisters. She has yet to bond with her new nurse, and it is very trying at home with Mr. Meyerson gone."

"Oh my dear, if you are in want of daughters, pray, do take one of mine!" Mrs. Bennet exclaimed. "I have several from whom to choose and I would not mind separating one or two of them, for their squabbling does nothing for my poor nerves."

"Would one of girls favor spending some time in town, helping me with Rachel?"

"Certainly—you must ask Jane, she is such an angel."

Mrs. Meyerson thought for a moment and replied. "If you sanction the idea, I would have Miss Catherine. She and Rachel are already the best of friends."

"Then it's settled. I will have Kitty come to you in the afternoons. I am certain that she will be a comfort to you. Away from her sisters, the girl can be quite pleasing."

With her mama whispering in the corner and Mary and Mr. Meyerson attempting a duet, Elizabeth found it nearly impossible to concentrate on her letter. Nonetheless, she began with her salutation and the words finally started to flow.

Dear Aunt,

Jane and I are truly grateful to you and our dear uncle for your most generous gift. Such finery! How fortuitous that the Meyerson's were able to convey the package. Heaven only knows what might have transpired had you sent it by post. In any event, the dressmaker is well on her way in creating our gowns, the banns have been posted, and all is going according to plan. Alas, that is not the truth of it—dear Aunt, you will perhaps be shocked by my news. My father has left Longbourn to aid a friend in dire need. While his actions are honorable—and I, without question, continue to hold him in the greatest esteem—I am much aggrieved! The wedding may be postponed, for we cannot know when our father will be returned to us.

Pray for us, Aunt, and write as soon as you are able. Jane and I are living in quiet desperation with each day that passes. May it be God's will that all goes well.~

Elizabeth completed her letter without mentioning anything unseemly to her beloved aunt. How could she express her marital concerns without portraying herself as an unscrupulous young lady?

Laughter suddenly coming from the corner of the room enticed her to regard her sister's blushing countenance and Mr. Meyerson's amusement. Witnessing Mary, who was usually averse to socializing in this manner, was most intriguing, indeed. As her sister played one of her better known pieces, Elizabeth took the opportunity to bring the gentleman a fresh cup of tea with the hopes of improving their acquaintance.

"Are you enjoying your stay in Meryton?" Elizabeth asked. "It must be difficult to be in such a provincial setting after experiencing the delights of Town."

"I am unaccustomed to the setting, ma'am," he admitted. "Nonetheless I find the country offers many pleasant attractions."

Elizabeth was quite unsure if he turned to set his gaze on Mary. The matter was becoming disconcerting. He had been acquainted with her sister for little more than a quarter of an hour!

"I understand you have three sisters residing in London," she continued.

"Yes, Deborah and Sarah are well established in Mayfair. I doubt very much that anything could take them away from that society. Much do they enjoy the routs, evening suppers, and balls. The eldest, Esther, married into an old Sephardic family and comes but rarely to Town. She enjoys the Season, and then quickly retreats to the family's country estate."

"Are you very close to one another? I have ever longed for a brother, you see. I imagine we would be ever finding ourselves in some sort of mayhem."

"We are all on good terms," he said, a bit wary with the lady's questioning. "I would do anything for my sisters."

"I am pleased to hear you admit as much," she whispered, "for what I am to say is quite presumptuous, and I pray you will forgive me."

"Say what you will, Miss Elizabeth," the gentleman replied, his curiosity piqued.

"My sister, Mary, is quite unaccustomed to receiving attention from gentlemen, sir, in particular—"

"From Jewish gentlemen?"

"No! That is not at all my meaning. Pray, understand. We lead sheltered lives with only family dinners, card games and the occasional assembly. Mary rarely attends even these rustic affairs, for she is quite timid and withdrawn. I could not help but notice my sister was enjoying your conversation."

"And this displeases you, Miss Elizabeth?"

"By no means. I wish to call your attention to the truth of my sister's character. She is a studious, pious sort of young lady and I would ask you not to trifle with her feelings if you only mean to enliven your short stay in Hertfordshire. My desire is not to offend, sir, but I do not wish to see Mary used ill."

"Your concern is commendable, ma'am, but I assure you, my intentions this day were merely to accompany my mother and to enjoy the charming company at Longbourn."

"You have a way about you, sir, that puts me to mind of another sort of happy man with an agreeable manner. It appears you have the same ability of making a guarded young lady believe herself to be anything but common or dull. We were all quite taken in by the charm and affability of the gentleman in question."

"Truly, Miss Elizabeth, I pray you be at ease. While I have enjoyed my brief conversation with your sister, you have nothing to fear from me on that score."

"Do you mean to say you have an understanding with another young lady, Mr. Meyerson?"

"No, *no*! What I am attempting to say and finding it dreadfully uncomfortable to articulate is that, while I may find Miss Mary exceedingly charming, I could not secure a match—I could not offer for a lady not of my faith."

Elizabeth had not prepared herself for such candid testimony. "Do you have a propensity for rejecting that which is not of your own belief?"

"Nothing could be further from the truth, Miss Elizabeth, and I would not believe you capable of willfully misunderstanding my meaning," he said setting aside his tea. "We are a relatively small community, striving to survive and carry on our ancient traditions. If we continually marry outside of our faith, slowly but surely we will find we have accomplished that which no other adversary has been able to do—my people, *my heritage* will die out. On a more pragmatic note, it seems that marriage is a difficult undertaking, even under the best of circumstances, and I would submit to you, it behooves husband and wife to have more in common than not."

"It would appear, Mr. Meyerson, you have given the matter quite a bit of thought."

"I assure you, ma'am, my mother has been broaching the subject since I was of age. While Miss Mary and I seem to complement one another; I am not of a mind to marry. You have my word, Miss Elizabeth, my intentions are for friendship—nothing more."

"Very well. I must thank you, sir, for your enlightening declaration," she said bringing the teacup to her lips. The irony of the situation, however, did not escape her discerning sensibilities.

CHAPTER TEN

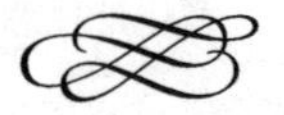

4th of November

Elizabeth had the satisfaction of receiving a prompt reply from her much-loved aunt Gardiner. She was no sooner in possession of her letter than she hurried off into the little copse where she was least likely to be interrupted. Sitting down on her favorite bench, she prepared to be happy.

My dearest Lizzy,

Where to begin? I am gladdened to know the Meyersons have arrived safely to Meryton and that they were able to convey our good wishes, along with our wedding gifts. Mr. and Mrs. Meyerson are well known and much admired here in Cheapside. They will be missed! I wonder what Caroline Bingley would think if she knew we not only conducted business but also socialized with the Jewish families that live with us here in the East End? I fear the Bingley sisters think poorly of us and our connections with trade, but we live in so different a part of town, all our connections are so different from theirs and, you well know, we go out but a little.

Now Lizzy, do not fear. Although your news is rather startling, I pray all will be well! Your dear papa must have had good reason to abandon hearth and home at such a time. You must have faith, dearest, and if the wedding is postponed, we shall have the added pleasure of spending a few more days together while we wait for his safe return. Think upon it! Mr. Darcy will be that much keener when he finally beholds his bride. I will be exceedingly pleased myself to see you and Jane wed, my dear. I took no pleasure in witnessing Lydia's vows to Mr. Wickham. Pray, how are your sister and brother-in-law? Have you had any word from that quarter?

Be of good cheer, dear Lizzy. Your happy day is nigh!

Elizabeth smiled, if not with some trepidation, and reread the entire letter from top to bottom once more. When she reached the portion where her aunt enquired after Mr. Wickham, it gave her pause. She had been so preoccupied with her doubts about the marriage and her father's leave-taking, she had forgotten about George Wickham! *What was he about?* Surely, it was not a coincidence that he too had gone missing. She supposed she ought to speak of it with Mr. Darcy, for to live in ignorance on such a point was impossible, although the telling of it would deliver pain.

Elizabeth was aware that Netherfield would be receiving guests that afternoon, for Mr. Darcy had been anxiously expecting his sister's arrival. Colonel Fitzwilliam was to be her escort, and they would be joined by Miss Caroline Bingley and Mr. and Mrs. Hurst. She was uncertain therefore if the gentlemen would call in the afternoon but, she could not suspend her arrangements. At present, Elizabeth and her sisters were for Meryton.

The dressmaker was expecting both brides for a final fitting and, while Jane was the happiest creature on earth, Elizabeth was the most hesitant. She had not the courage to disengage herself from Mr. Darcy, yet she lacked the sureness that she was entering the marriage on the best of terms. Until this moment, Elizabeth had never known herself to be so irresolute. The feeling tore at her core. Previously passing judgment against Mr. Darcy in favor of Mr. Wickham had been an egregious error, to say the least. How could she be assured her heart was not misleading her now, now as she contemplated being Mistress of Pemberley?

Jane chattered along the familiar road in to town, her delight imparting a glow of sweet animation to her face. Elizabeth believed she had never seen her sister look as handsome. Her felicity at Jane's circumstance was sincere and, although it pained her not to share a confidence with her sister, Elizabeth could not allow herself to express the anguish of her own heart. She allowed her sister to carry the conversation as she nodded when it was appropriate or supplied the obligatory *yes, Jane* or *no, Jane* as required, but her mind was elsewhere.

Elizabeth's thoughts hounded her. Words were twisted into different meanings, and gestures were seen in a different light. She recalled Mr. Darcy's fateful letter when he attempted to explain himself to the woman he had offered for and insulted in the same breath. He had related his feelings about Jane... *her look and manners were open, cheerful and engaging, but without any symptom of peculiar regard. She did not invite his attentions by any participation of sentiment.* What if he meant to imply something altogether different? Was it his intention to expose the dissimilarities between the sisters? Did he favor Jane's shy and reserved demeanor over Elizabeth's outspoken and high-spirited nature? Jane, of course, did not favor their mother; Jane did not resemble Lydia in the slightest!

Jane would make him the perfect wife, thought Elizabeth in quiet despair.

"What say you, Lizzy? *Lizzy*?"

"Yes." Elizabeth replied. "What? I am sorry..."

"I wager she was thinking of Mr. Darcy," Kitty teased. "While you were woolgathering, I spotted Mrs. Meyerson and her son. Look, they are crossing the road to greet us."

"Good morning Miss Bennet, Miss Elizabeth, Miss Mary, Miss Catherine," the lady called as she approached.

The party exchanged greetings and salutations and asked after their families' well-being, when Mrs. Meyerson at last, spoke the words all were loath to utter.

"Have you had any word?"

"No, indeed, ma'am," said Elizabeth.

"How are you managing," Mary enquired. "And what of the congregation?"

"My mother is doing extraordinarily well in my father's absence," replied Mr. Meyerson, "for she has the wisdom of Miriam and the courage of Queen Esther. She can manage quite nicely. In fact, she will be meeting with the ladies of our community this evening to celebrate *Rosh Chodesh*."

Mrs. Meyerson blushed upon hearing her son's praise. However, she was quick to explain to her friends the meaning behind his words. "We are ushering in a new month, you must understand. It is our custom to celebrate the new moon, as our calendar follows the lunar cycles rather than the Gregorian calendar, which is based on the sun."

"How delightful!" Elizabeth laughed, forgetting her misery for a moment. "Here we are, standing inches apart, but my sisters and I are in the month of November and you are in the month of..."

"*Kislev*!" Mr. Meyerson supplied, as they all enjoyed a moment of levity.

"How do you celebrate this extraordinary occasion?"

Mrs. Meyerson explained that it had become tradition for the women of the community to gather and study on this holiday.

"Every new moon brings a unique, transcendent light, one that has never shone before. We study and debate—as is our tradition—each one of us sharing our own unique wisdom which, in turn, helps us to illuminate one another's path."

"And what will your lesson be this day?" asked Kitty.

"Yes!" Elizabeth interjected. "Do share some of your wisdom with us, for we are in need of enlightenment."

Mrs. Meyerson shared a smile with her son, who simply raised a quizzical brow. "Why ever not, Mama?" he asked.

The lady was unsure how to proceed. As the rabbi's wife, or the *rebbetzin,* as she was respectfully called, Mrs. Meyerson was accustomed to speaking to the women of her husband's congregation. However, speaking to the daughters of Anglican gentry was another matter entirely. At what point would her words cease to be entertaining and instead become impertinent? Nevertheless, Mrs. Meyerson thought, the Misses Bennet were everything charming; certainly they would understand she did not mean to preach—indeed, they had insisted!

"I have chosen to speak of our inherent power of renewal," she began hesitantly. "As an example, you will notice that while the moon is the smaller of the two luminaries, it has a powerful lesson to impart. Just like the moon is compared to the sun, our lives can appear to be small and insignificant when likened to others. Indeed it may seem that one could fade into nothingness and the world would not notice our demise..."

"Truer words have never been uttered! Many have tried to destroy us and the world has said naught..."

"Whatever do you mean, Mr. Meyerson?" Kitty exclaimed. "Who has tried to destroy you?"

The young man let out a most indelicate grunt as he began counting on his fingers, expounding on his knowledge. "The Egyptians, the Greeks, the Romans, the Spaniards..."

"David!" Mrs. Meyerson chastised. "Pray discontinue this ungentlemanly behavior. Your impudent discourse is unnecessary to our present topic of conversation."

"Do go on, ma'am," Mary declared. "We are not offended by Mr. Meyerson's passionate nature. Indeed, it behooves us to acknowledge such history."

"That is well said, my dear," replied the lady. "Now if my excitable son would allow it, I would conclude with this: it is my wish to point out when things are at their darkest, *there* is where we need to have faith for restoration and renewal. I suppose the real lesson is to recognize our purpose in this life."

"Can there be an answer for such a query?" Elizabeth asked.

"In our faith, *every* question is answered with *another* question," Mr. Meyerson quipped, as he stepped away from his increasingly frustrated mama.

With marked exasperation, Mrs. Meyerson continued. "For the purposes of my lesson, Miss Elizabeth," she said, shooting a warning look to her son, "I am choosing to focus on the theme of improving oneself. Just as the moon waxes and wanes, our purpose is to grow, to learn, and to transform ourselves."

Mr. Meyerson could not help but have his share of the conversation and, with his last interjection, the son appeased the mother. "We do not suffer by accident. We must look at every unfortunate occurrence as an opportunity which may lead to a new understanding of one's strength and resiliency."

Mary nodded her understanding, accepting these words as if the Meyersons had come down the mountain with the tablets themselves, while Jane and Kitty smiled politely. Elizabeth alone wished the lesson of the moon's rebirth could illumine the dark, doubting recesses of her soul.

"To that end," Mrs. Meyerson continued, "our congregation has decided to act on the *unfortunate occurrence* of the continuing war on the Continent. We have been recently discussing the shocking state of affairs in which our military troops find themselves and have decided to take up a collection. We shall send it to the War Office along with our prayers for peace."

"But you are not acquainted with the people of this village! I cannot imagine my aunt Phillips would participate in such collaboration," Kitty grumbled. "Surely such a trivial amount would be seen as a drop in the bucket."

"As David indicated, every hardship is an opportunity for growth. We will use this occasion to meet our Gentile neighbors and to form alliances within our communities. Our contribution will be small, to be sure; however, the Ethics of our Fathers state we are not obligated to complete the work, but neither are we free to desist from it. This will be our *tzedakah,* our donation made from the good and generous people of Meryton."

The Misses Bennet shared a knowing look amongst themselves and allowed Elizabeth to speak on their behalf. "We would be delighted to assist in the first alliance betwixt the Anglican and Hebrew congregations, Mrs. Meyerson, although I cannot speak for *all* the people of Meryton, some of whom are neither generous nor good."

CHAPTER ELEVEN

Some four miles away from town, Colonel Fitzwilliam and Miss Georgiana Darcy arrived at Netherfield in preparation for the wedding, which was just days away. They joined Miss Caroline Bingley and Mr. and Mrs. Hurst who, although they had not their same enthusiasm, had also come for the blessed event. It was therefore a bit of surprise for all when the gentlemen explained there might be a slight delay.

"It seems Mr. Bennet was called away on an urgent matter," Mr. Bingley began.

"Naturally, we must await his safe return," added Mr. Darcy. "We cannot know when that might be."

"And here I thought Meryton would be a quiet, carefree sort of place," Colonel Fitzwilliam interposed. "I begin to believe, I may have been misled."

"Whatever do you mean?" asked Mr. Darcy.

"Today, when we arrived in the village, I overheard the townsfolk gossiping about the rather odd disappearance of a clergyman. The

Jewish families of Meryton recently welcomed a parson for their emergent church," the colonel explained, "but the man mysteriously quitted his post—just days after his arrival. Apparently, the Bennets had received the parson and his family when they first arrived. Quite intriguing, would you not say?"

"Jewish families...*of Meryton*? To be sure, I find it would be insupportable to pass much time in such society. The insipidity, the self-importance of *those* people! Why would anyone involve themselves with that lot?" Miss Bingley asked, accustomed as she was to think well of herself and meanly of others. "They are mostly money lenders and rag merchants. Can this village sink any lower in our estimation?"

"How fortuitous it is, Miss Bingley, that your stay at Netherfield will not be of a long duration," Mr. Darcy replied. "As to your comment about the Jews, your conjecture is completely erroneous, I assure you. My excellent father stored great faith in his personal physician, a Mr. Levine. A more intelligent, well-rounded gentleman could not have been found in all of England. I was present when Mr. Levine lectured my father on his own misconceptions. That was a sight to behold, for my father was a proud man, indeed! Mr. Levine explained many Jews had become moneylenders due to the simple fact that, during the medieval period, Christians were banned from the occupation. Jews were not allowed to own land. Their numbers were restricted in nearly every gentlemanly sort of occupation. Pray, what were they to do?"

"Try to recall, Caroline, our own good fortunate emanates from the so-called rag business," Mr. Bingley reproached. "Those wretched fellows in Whitechapel are just trying to keep a roof over their heads!"

"My observation was only meant to distinguish in between these foreigners and our old English families. Naturally, the Bennets would keep company with these newcomers; their pedigree could not be of great import," she responded.

"I was informed by Miss Mary Bennet, the family historian, that their ancestors came over with William the Conqueror," said Mr. Darcy. "I do not believe you could find fault with their lineage."

"The only *fault*, as you say, sir, is that the Bennets can trace their heritage back to France. How impolitic, considering we have been at war with that country these many years. Now, an eminent family such as the proud Darcys..."

"The correct pronunciation, Miss Bingley, is *D'Arcy*," he replied with not too little disdain. "Like Miss Elizabeth Bennet, my eminent ancestors were Norman."

Georgiana Darcy, uncomfortable with the dispute, approached her brother, hoping for a private word while Charles Bingley attempted to reason with his dumbstruck sibling who had gone off to lick her wounds. Georgiana spoke hesitantly, for she did not wish to further trouble her beloved brother. Her inherent goodness won over her timidity, as Georgiana expressed her desire to be of service.

"Mightn't I call upon the Bennets?" she asked. "I do so long to renew my acquaintance with Miss Elizabeth and, as she is to be my sister, perhaps it would not be improper to arrive unannounced? If...if *you* do not think it best, William, please let Miss Elizabeth know my prayers are with her and her family."

"That is very kind of you, sweetling. Perhaps in a day or two you may tell her yourself. I do not wish you to concern yourself overmuch, Georgiana—you feel things too deeply and it unduly affects your health."

Colonel Fitzwilliam had joined brother and sister and, in his familial manner, interlocked arms with his ward. "I will not have you ill, Georgie!" he decreed. "With whom am I to dance, if you will not stand up with me?"

Miss Darcy blushed, curtseyed and scurried away, allowing the men to converse in private.

"It is good of you to come, Richard, but it may all be for naught. There is more to this development. However, I did not feel the need to disclose the full of it to the entire party."

"What have you done?" the colonel said, with a playful punch to his cousin's arm. "Tell me you have not frightened the charming lady away with one of your scowls or bitter remarks."

"I do not scowl," Mr. Darcy growled as he rubbed his sore arm.

The colonel laughed and began walking about the room. "A looking glass! My kingdom for a looking glass!"

The others in the party laughed at the colonel's comments, accustomed to his levity when amongst family and friends. Mr. Darcy jutted his head in the direction of a quiet corner, alluding to his desire to speak in seclusion. "When you are quite finished with your theatrics," he murmured, "I would continue, for this is not a laughing matter."

"What has happened? Do not say that our Aunt Catherine has meddled in your affairs. Tell me at once! It is not dear Anne demanding you satisfy the terms of that archaic agreement..."

"No, no! I would ask you to stop inventing possible scenarios of doom. Do sit down and hear me out."

The colonel, knowing his cousin better than most, discontinued his torment upon distinguishing between the man's usual reserved demeanor and his current state of unease. Setting himself down in an opposite chair, Colonel Fitzwilliam leaned forward, his countenance grave, his attention focused as only a trained military man could be.

"Very well, I am listening," he replied.

Darcy's explanation was terse and to the point. Having heard the account from Elizabeth and not from Mr. Bennet or Mr. Meyerson, he was not quite certain that he was in possession of all the particulars.

"You practically discovered the issue at hand when you spoke of the parson's disappearance," Mr. Darcy admitted. "Mr. Meyerson followed the militia to Brighton. After a week with no word, Mr. Bennet, fearing for his colleague, followed in his path. It is evident that these two gentlemen are working as adjunct emissaries of the War Department, but how the country has come to *this* is beyond my comprehension. These wars on the Continent along with the campaign against the Americans have pushed the country to its limits. I am in earnest—I do not know how it will all end."

"I can only tell you that what I have witnessed will never fade away, neither by the passing of time, nor by grace of God. These battles have been gruesome and hard fought. Wellington himself reported he never again would wish to be the instrument of putting his troops to such a test! I, for one, would be grateful never again to shoulder such responsibility."

"Thank Providence for your safe return, Richard. But now that you are home, what have you heard? What are you at liberty to share?"

"The current Chancellor keeps such a tight rein on campaign finances that the general's soldiers and suppliers have gone largely unpaid. If not for Wellington's continual demand for more men and money, nothing would be accomplished. I have seen it with my own eyes—I have *lived* it!" the colonel exclaimed, pounding his fist onto the arm of the chair. "Shortly after returning home, I naturally reported to headquarters in London. It was there I found negotiations were taking place in order to secure more funding, thanks in part to the missing gold. There was some speculation regarding a scheme to find the culprits so that they may be brought to justice."

Darcy's countenance was grim, but resolute. "And what can be done for Mr. Meyerson and Mr. Bennet?"

"I am afraid the gentlemen may be in over their heads. Coining and counterfeiting are classified as High Treason, not to mention that altering the king's image is seen as an attack on His Majesty. Whomever they are tracking, you can be assured they will be hell-bent to remain uncaught."

"If they are not back by Sunday, which was to be our wedding day, I fear I must go in search of Elizabeth's father and Mr. Meyerson."

"Then I will accompany you to Brighton."

Darcy nodded, gratefully accepting his cousin's assistance. "I am for Longbourn. Come and let us speak with Elizabeth. She may have received word overnight and all our planning would be for naught."

ELIZABETH, HAVING LONG RETURNED FROM TOWN, WAS PERCHED in the cozy alcove by the window when she observed two horses approaching in an ambling gait. The men dismounted. Colonel Fitzwilliam looking distinguished in his military garb and Mr. Darcy, she noted, disturbingly handsome in his great wool coat. Gladdened by their arrival before the threatening storm broke, Elizabeth was yet uneasy on the infinitely more delicate matter of her own tempestuous comportment. The guests, however, were well received, perhaps not as warmly as Mr. Darcy would have desired. Elizabeth welcomed the colonel with sincere pleasure and her intended with an uncomfortable peek from under her dark lashes.

Before their arrival, she had been deep in thought, recalling her conversation with Charlotte. Unwilling to break her engagement, knowing her heart would not heal from such a drastic step, Elizabeth contemplated the sort of marriage her friend had recommended with such assurance and equanimity. Perhaps by focusing on running the household and by keeping separate rooms she would become the disciplined, serene sort of lady Pemberley deserved. Could she curtail her passionate nature? Observing the handsome gentleman before her, Elizabeth was uncertain if she could meet such a challenge.

Alone in the drawing room, which was an uncommon event, Elizabeth had not required the usual embellishments other than asking for the fire to be tended. Now in the company of the gentlemen, she made ready to call for her sister and for tea. Mr. Darcy asked she stay the request, as he wished her to relate the delicate matter of her father's absence without interruption. She acquiesced and, beginning the narrative from when her father first received the missive, Elizabeth retraced the events the family had experienced. When she felt she had divulged a full accounting, she paused and considered mentioning her dealings with her sister. As difficult as it was to relive, the words flooded back and she knew she must relate Lydia's comments and boasts.

"It pains me to address another topic, which may or may not be related to the subject at hand. I fear it bears discussing, as both of you gentlemen have experience regarding the matter," she stated, unable to meet Mr. Darcy's questioning gaze. "It pertains to my new brother...Mr. Wickham."

The men shared a knowing glance, and Colonel Fitzwilliam begged Elizabeth to continue. Mr. Darcy, hearing the wretched name, began pacing the room. She turned to face the colonel and agonizingly imparted what Lydia had shared so easily.

'My sister stated that Mr. Wickham had accrued great debt, although he had received a generous settlement when they were wed and, seeing that I was to be Mistress of Pemberley," she paused feeling her face burn with shame, "Lydia was preparing to ask for a loan. Their fortune miraculously changes from one moment to the next, although my sister does not know from whence the money comes; she alludes to Wickham's many associates and their various schemes."

"Wickham is here? At Longbourn?"

"Nay, he departed shortly after they arrived. Kitty invited them to…to our wedding," Elizabeth said, stealing a glance at Mr. Darcy, who stood apart, stoically staring out the window. "Lydia awoke one morning to find her husband missing. He left a quick note stating he had gone to meet a business partner. Is it possible that Mr. Wickham is connected with these traitors? Could he have a part in this counterfeiting scheme?"

Colonel Fitzwilliam rubbed his forehead, contemplating having to deal once again with George Wickham. One look at the stern man glaring out the window revealed exactly how his cousin was faring with the news. "Indeed, Miss Elizabeth, it *is* possible. I would pose another question: Is Wickham smart enough to think of such a scheme?"

"He is too lazy to sow the seeds of such a ruse," Mr. Darcy muttered with disgust, "but he is more than capable of attempting to reap the rewards."

Elizabeth shut her eyes, as if shutting her eyes would remove the image of Mr. Darcy's countenance. The antipathy—the revulsion was so severe she could not help but think a portion of his ire was directed towards himself for being aligned with such a family. She knew he would move heaven and earth to keep George Wickham away from his beloved sister, and here she was, his betrothed, practically delivering the blackguard to his front door.

"I am afraid you long to be away…" Elizabeth began to utter as she arose, already imagining Mr. Darcy taking his leave.

"Yes, Colonel Fitzwilliam and I are for Brighton," Mr. Darcy responded absentmindedly, his thoughts already planning for what lay ahead. "Had I known of Wickham's involvement, we would have left straight away. As it is, we will leave Monday, after the Sabbath. I will order a carriage for first light."

"The roads to Netherfield were muddy, Darcy," the colonel interjected. "I suggest we go on horseback. We will cover the twenty-four miles to London with much ease. After refreshing ourselves at Grosvenor Court, we shall take your carriage to Brighton," he continued, dictating orders in experienced military fashion. "It will be another four hours, but we will have the conveyance to accommodate Mr. Bennet and Mr. Meyerson if we find they are not fit for riding."

Not fit for riding? Naturally, if they had come to any harm, her father and Mr. Meyerson would not be fit for riding. Elizabeth felt her knees tremble and fell back onto the settee. Her resolve was sinking; everything must sink under such an assurance of the deepest misfortune. Although it pained her to own it, Elizabeth feared she was not strong enough to shoulder these burdens. On one hand, she was sick with worry for her father, and on the other, she ached for the life she might have had with *her* William. Surely he would recall his mortifying yet merited reproach when first he had offered for her hand. The inferior situation of her mother's family was objectionable, but nothing in comparison to the total want of propriety, so decidedly beneath his own. Her sense of shame was severe, and Elizabeth felt depressed beyond anything she had ever known before.

"Be so kind as to apologize to Miss Darcy and the others," she whispered. "Although it behooves us to welcome the party to Hertfordshire, it may be several days before we are fit for company. Say that family matters necessitate that Jane and I remain at home."

Colonel Fitzwilliam, being an astute gentleman, made his excuses and quitted the room, allowing Elizabeth and his cousin to say their goodbyes. Mr. Darcy, believing Elizabeth to be overwrought, wished only to allay her fears and began explaining how he would bring closure to the entire affair. She was sensible of his speaking, but his meaning was lost in her silent reverie. When he brought her hand to his lips, a terse farewell, while not intended, was what her soul perceived.

Although she felt dispirited, Elizabeth's cool mien did not betray her feelings. Mr. Darcy departed without further ado, believing she wished him on his way. His only thought was to find Mr. Bennet and restore the gentleman to his devoted family. Surely once her father was home, hale and hearty, Elizabeth would be herself again and all would be well with the world.

CHAPTER TWELVE

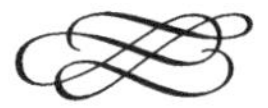

6th of November

"Where would I go if I was a Jew in Sussex?" Mr. Bennet questioned aloud. He had arrived to town on a cold and blistery afternoon ten days prior and had seen his share of the rocky coast. Long gone were the bathing machines with their dippers for Brighton's holidaymakers. These, he presumed, would see the light of day many months from now when the resort would once again welcome sea bathers to coastline. Pulling his great coat tightly about him, he determined that today would be the day he finally found his friend. Enough time had been wasted trying to locate one man in a sea of London tourists. He walked past the tall houses on the ocean's front and, when he saw a middle-aged couple out for their afternoon constitutional, he begged a moment of their time.

"Is there a Hebrew church in this locality?" Mr. Bennet enquired.

The man glanced at his wife and, when she nodded her sanction, he felt at ease to speak to the stranger. "Ay, there is, and we would know rather bettermost than other folk, seeing as we have lived here since 'eighty-nine. There is such a place on Jew Street."

Mr. Bennet was about to respond when he noticed the man's wife rolling her eyes with apparent vexation. She pulled on his coat sleeve and whispered in her husband's ear. Mr. Bennet observed the display with much diversion but said naught. He did not wish to offend the couple, especially if they were to assist him. Mr. Bennet waited as the man cleared his throat and adjusted his coat before speaking once again.

"It seems I have made a boffle of it—the wife says they outgrew the old place! The Hebrews have moved to Poune's Court," he said, pointing in the opposite direction. "You will find it midway down West Street. It is a tall structure, it is, with bungaroosh walls."

Mr. Bennet thanked the couple for their kindness, removing his hat and bowing low. The wife giggled and blushed at such a display. She tugged at her husband's coat sleeve once again, reminding him to doff his cap before they took their leave. Mr. Bennet heard her rebuke as he walked in the direction of West Street and was soon rewarded for his troubles when he came upon a signpost with a six-pointed star.

There were people wandering in and out of the building. The façade, indeed, was made in the telltale fashion of lime and pebbles and broken bricks. As he was not questioned, Mr. Bennet removed his hat and ventured indoors, where he was received in a small foyer by a craggy character handing out prayer books with a petulant air. Although the language was foreign, Mr. Bennet took the book in hand and was about to enter the main room where he saw nearly forty men standing about, when the keeper of the books pointed to his head and shouted, "*yarmulke*!" When it became obvious that he did not comprehend, the man reached into a bin, pulled out a black skull cap, and pointed to his head once again. Mr. Bennet, exceedingly diverted, comprehended the demand and, with great alacrity, did as he had been instructed.

Mr. Bennet now felt at liberty to enter the sanctuary and began to seek out his friend. He noted a second story loomed from above and heard women speaking in various levels of timbres and enthusiasm. At the center of the room stood the dais with a desk covered in white cloth. The surrounding men began to take their seats. Some chatted with their neighbors, others began their prayers, and yet others shouted at their wives who were gesticulating instructions from above. Mr. Bennet laughed at this familiar occurrence, as it seemed, no matter Anglican or Jew, the husband was always at his wife's mercy. He was still shaking his head in merriment when he espied Mr. Meyerson sitting quite on his own.

"Well, well, well! Who do we have here?" Mr. Bennet chuckled. "Half of Meryton is sick with worry on your behalf, and I find you comfortably situated away from your wife—*away from all women*—," he said, pointing to the floor above, "and with your nose quite happily stuck in a book!"

"Bennet! What on earth are you doing here?"

"*Here*? Do you mean here in Brighton, or do you mean in your church?"

"In actuality, sir, it is a *shul*—not a church—but that does not signify! I am most happy to see you."

"And I you, Meyerson!" he said, slapping the man on the back. "I do hope all is well. We have had no word since you left. Have you had any luck?"

"I have, indeed, but this is not the place to discuss the matter. The Sabbath service will be starting shortly. I will not be offended if you wish to leave. We could meet afterwards...?"

"No, no! I would stay, if it is permitted," Mr. Bennet declared. "It is not every day I am allowed to experience something so completely foreign. I am exceedingly keen on seeing the goings on!"

A robed gentleman approached the dais, his deep, rich voice reaching the rafters and beyond. The congregation joined in the song, the women from above and the men below, and so began the Sabbath service that Friday eve in Brighton.

The men returned to Mr. Meyerson's lodging later that evening and, although it was not exactly the sort of conversation one would expect upon leaving a house of prayer, it was the conversation that needed to be had.

"It has taken me all this time, but I believe I have pinpointed the lead man in this vile organization," Mr. Meyerson revealed. "Luckily for us, Ensign Wakefield has not the brains for trickery. I have seen him about town throwing his blunt around and chasing after skirts. It is a wonder Colonel Forster has not been made privy to his behavior, but I cannot approach the colonel until I have proof of the crime."

"So if Wakefield is not your man, who is?"

"I have seen our ensign following his superior like a little pup. I believe Lieutenant Thompson is the man we are after and have formulated a scheme to entrap him. Being a selfish rat and a turncoat to boot, I am certain he would be gladdened to make a few coins on the side."

"Tell me your plan, sir, so I may better assist you."

"Brighton, as you know, is Prinny's favorite retreat. He and his court have made this locality their home away from home..."

"With only fifty miles of good road, the distance is easily made in little more than a half day's journey," Mr. Bennet interjected.

"Precisely, thus making it easy for the corrupt, debauched element to follow in the Prince's wake," Mr. Meyerson completed the thought.

"What do you propose?"

"I will become what is expected. I will become a greedy Jewish merchant on holiday. The adjunct to a London official practically spoon-fed a back story to me, complete with names and all sorts of interesting tidbits to help with my ruse. I shan't want for a good tale."

Mr. Meyerson spent the majority of Saturday in the little sanctuary he discovered at the sea resort. While it was true that he was working for the War Office, he was first and foremost a Jew, and he reported to a higher authority. Mr. Bennet used the time to familiarize himself with the seedier part of town while the rabbi was at prayer.

Sunday, after the church bells rang to signal the end of services, Mr. Bennet reflected on their poignant significance. On this day, he would have had the honor of giving his daughters away in holy matrimony. He ought to have been in Meryton but instead, he and Mr. Meyerson found themselves walking down North Street and avoiding Castle Square in their bid to serve the Crown. That prime thoroughfare was known to be a fashionable location for the city's wealthiest visitors and not at all where they would be likely to find their prey. Lieutenant Thompson and his ilk were more than likely to be ensconced in a corner pub.

They found their way down another lane and, after peering in several locations, found a cobble-fronted pub teeming with red coats. Entering the establishment, they shouted out *two pints* as Mr. Meyerson masked his pleasure of espying Ensign Wakefield sitting quite alone at his meal. He motioned to Mr. Bennet to follow his lead, settling in a booth adjacent to his mark and waving away a buxom serving woman offering food and, evidently, much more. Mr. Bennet fairly blushed as she walked away, but his companion remained focused on the business at hand.

"I have come all this way, Mr. Smith," Mr. Meyerson declared in a voice loud enough to be heard at the neighboring table. "I have the coin to spend! I was sure that I could meet with the proper party in this locality."

"Patience, Mr. Cohen, you have only just arrived. With many merchants in town, you are certain to find what you require." Mr. Bennet followed along and could not help but find the play amusing.

Wakefield, taking a final swig of his ale, made his way to the bar, stopping at the neighboring booth to interrupt the two gentlemen. The ensign lowered his voice and came so close they could smell the ale on his breath. "I could not help but overhear your conversation, sir. Are you in the market for something particular?"

Mr. Cohen nodded. "Indeed, but it is something quite delicate in nature. I am willing to pay..."

"Nay, we should not speak of it here," Ensign Wakefield mumbled. "But would you care to meet at The Red Shield Thursday next? We will find ourselves better situated to discuss the matter in private."

As he turned to depart, the ensign saluted a few of his compatriots and quitted the rowdy establishment. Mr. Meyerson let loose with a resounding laugh, slapping his hand on the table with such force, that his cup tipped over, spilling his drink and earning a disgruntled curse from the bartender.

"What is it?" Mr. Bennet asked, bemused. "What do you find so diverting?"

"The Red...*Shiiiiiield*," he managed to gasp in between his cackling.

"Yes, yes, man! What of it?"

It took another glare from the bartender and a sip or two of Mr. Bennet's ale, but Mr. Meyerson soon enough had his faculties about him and was able to reply.

"*Zum rothen schild*—it means 'with the red sign'."

As poor Mr. Bennet did not seem to comprehend, the rabbi continued in a more composed manner.

"With whom is the Crown collaborating to deliver their gold?" he asked.

"Why, you have said it is Rothschild of London," Mr. Bennet dutifully replied.

"Precisely! *Rothen schild,*" he chortled. "I find it most providential!"

CHAPTER THIRTEEN

9th of November

Monday the sun shone brightly and the air was crisp and still. The trees lay barren of their leaves, and the shrill alarm of a lone raven echoed across Longbourn's park. Horses stood patiently at the Bennet door, neighing and nibbling on the surrounding strips of winter grass as Mr. Darcy, Mr. Bingley and Colonel Fitzwilliam came to address a household that was still abed.

Hill wearily climbed the stairs to announce the gentlemen's arrival, scratching softly on the girls' door, but Elizabeth had heard their voices in the courtyard and was already seeing to her morning ablutions. She thought it ironic—they would have been wed by now, but instead of traveling home to Pemberley on their bridal trip; Mr. Darcy had come to say his goodbyes. *Foolish girl*! Had her own lack of confidence tempted fate? Elizabeth felt torn by the ruthless uncertainty that taunted her throughout the day and robbed her of her sleep at night.

Jane, too, had been disquieted and distraught. Her sisters had heard her crying well into the wee hours. Nonetheless, she arose when beckoned and was now fixing her hair, as Mrs. Bennet declared she was not quite up to receiving company. Her nervous stomach continued to be a cause of relentless affliction, and she asked the girls to express her regrets. So weak was she that Mrs. Bennet's maternal concern for propriety was no longer a consideration. The girls were well chaperoned by Colonel Fitzwilliam she reasoned, and, after all, the deed was nearly done—the betrothed were only wanting the parson's final blessings.

Elizabeth met the gentlemen at the door and quickly ushered them in from the morning's chill. Mr. Darcy instead requested a private audience and, dutifully, she consented. They walked up the path until coming upon hermitage. Bitterly cold, Elizabeth hugged her woolen shawl about her, refusing Mr. Darcy's offer of his great coat with a shake of her head.

"I was certainly very far from expecting this situation to arise *days* before our nuptials," Elizabeth declared. "I am sensible to the unpardonable circumstance and fear you cannot think of it without abhorrence."

"It is not your doing. I certainly do not hold you accountable," Mr. Darcy said, holding his hand out to her and then letting it drop to his side when she declined.

"Lady Catherine was quite clear regarding her opinion of me. Do you recall her words? *An upstart pretentious young woman without family, connections or fortune*, she had said. How do you imagine she would endure this predicament? In addition to an impoverished county esquire and various relatives in trade, she may now hold the titles of spy and courier against me!"

"If you would call him a spy, at the very least, include the minor detail that your father is working for the Crown and not against," he added drily. "Do you recall what *I* said to *you* just a few short weeks ago? Hmm? I have been a selfish being all my life, and although I was given good principals, I was taught to care for none beyond my own. At the very least, your father is doing *something*! Throughout the many years our country has been at war, I have done naught save for providing financial assistance, which is an effortless endeavor. If I find Wickham is involved in this contemptible, traitorous scheme, I will know how to act."

Mr. Darcy leaned down and gazed longingly at Elizabeth. Softening his tone, he whispered in her ear. "I will return with your father, and you and I will begin our lives as planned. Pemberley will be a far happier place when her new mistress is at home." He pressed his lips onto a cold, unwelcoming kiss. Surprised at such a response, he managed to hide his disappointment but tersely enquired as to the cause.

"What is the matter, Elizabeth?"

"I am uncertain—"

"You have not been yourself. Pray, tell me, what have I done?"

Shocked by his words, she only felt more unworthy, but Elizabeth knew he expected a reply. "I feel I am not prepared, Mr. Darcy."

"Are we back to *mister*, again?" he whispered.

His sweet murmuring sent shivers down her spine, but she hardened herself and would not succumb to his charm. "A woman has so few opportunities to decide for herself, Mr. Darcy. When she is at home, she must obey her father, and when she weds, she must submit to her husband...pray allow me to reconcile my doubts. A woman ought not to enter the matrimonial state half-heartedly."

"I was not expecting such a practiced homily, certainly not of that nature—not at a time such as this."

"I am my mother's daughter," she said, lifting her chin with a decisive flair. "I am outspoken and given to fits of impertinence, and well you know it. You witnessed my unpardonable display with Lydia, did you not? Lady Catherine accused me of *being lost to every feeling of propriety and delicacy*. Perhaps she was right."

"Good God, Elizabeth! What does my aunt have to do with any of this?"

"Under the circumstances, one cannot help but be sensible to the lady's objections. Already you have had to intercede on my family's behalf, thanks to Lydia's passionate and foolish nature. Now our wedding must be postponed due to my father's involvement in espionage and heaven knows what. In reviewing my own behavior, I cannot help but find myself wanting of those talents which, surely, Mrs. Darcy of Pemberley should possess. Seen in this prodigious light, can you not acknowledge that Lady Catherine might have good reason to object to your connection to Longbourn?"

"What are you saying? Do you wish to be released from your commitment?"

She could not meet his gaze; her shame would not allow it. Elizabeth merely shook her head and whispered. "I wish...I wish us to have separate rooms, if we are to be wed. I fear that I will be overwhelmed in undertaking the duties as mistress of such an estate. I will, of course, be considerate of my wifely obligations. I am mindful of Pemberley's need for an heir."

Mr. Darcy straightened to his full height. His dark eyes focusing on anything but *her*, and declared, "I can only imagine your good sense has been affected by the strain of these last few days." Jutting his chin with an aristocratic air, he continued. "I would ask you to reflect on the matter. We will speak of it when I return."

"I will pray for your safe return, Mr. Darcy," she whispered. "More than that, I cannot ensure."

"I will have you as my wife in any way you choose. I only hope that you choose the path that would see us both happy."

The pair made a hasty return to the house, only to find an impatient Colonel Fitzwilliam mounted and prepared to take his leave.

"Come along. We must be on our way," the colonel said, his breath rising up in a cloud of mist. "Bingley has gone inside with your sister, Miss Elizabeth."

"Mr. Bingley is not accompanying you to Brighton?"

"No, we thought it best he remain in case you received word from your father." Mr. Darcy bowed and placed his hat upon his head before mounting his black steed. "In the event you should need or want for anything, you are to seek his assistance."

Elizabeth nodded quietly and smiled at the colonel, who assumed her restrained demeanor was due to the anxious circumstances. "Safe travels. May God be with you," she whispered before entering the house and seeking her sister's company.

"I suppose we should go into Meryton and condole with the Meyersons," murmured Jane as Elizabeth entered the drawing room. "We might stop and greet my aunt Phillips..."

"I dread walking into town under these circumstances. One cannot see too little of one's neighbors. Any assistance is impossible," Elizabeth cried. "Their condolence is insufferable."

"Lizzy, dearest, you do not mean that!"

"What do they know of our apprehension? I would not lay eyes on those who might triumph at our tribulations."

"You need not go," Mary advised. "I have several books to return to the vicar. I could call on the Meyerson's home, as well."

"That is generous of you," said Jane. "Perhaps you may accompany Kitty, seeing how she will be attending little Rachel again this afternoon. I dare say our sister has been fairly adopted in that household."

Mary acquiesced and made no further response to Jane's

observation. However, she felt obligated to address her sister's previous remark. "Although your sentiment towards our inquisitive neighbors seems rather ungracious, Lizzy," she owned, "I can sympathize. It *is* a demanding task, is it not, to feign composure and civility when one is feeling the complete opposite? I, for one, can bear witness to that very sensation."

Elizabeth, feeling all the more anxious for being censured so fittingly, forced herself to speak again, this time in a more penitent manner. "Thank you, Mary. I believe you have made an accurate observation. My conduct has been reprehensible. I have always felt my courage rise with every attempt of intimidation. I shall walk with you into town and face my demons...I mean, our neighbors."

Mr. Bingley had settled quite comfortably by the fire with a pot of hot chocolate and a plate of Cook's buttered scones. One look at *his angel* and poor Jane knew she could not abandon him in order to accompany her sisters, although it was she who had suggested the exercise! Elizabeth, who was not made for ill-humor and could not dwell long on her low spirits, had to laugh at the sight of the cozy pair, one who begged for forgiveness, and the other to be reprieved.

"Jane, do stay," she said, her eyes twinkling with amusement. "Mama may yet require your assistance. I shall accompany Mary to the parsonage so that she may return her books, and we shall stop and greet the Meyersons."

Jane nodded gratefully as her sister prepared to quit the room but just before she reached the door, Elizabeth leaned down with a mischievous smile and whispered. "Do not make yourself too cozy, Jane dear, for I believe I have the winning hand! You forget. Kitty and Lydia will be down shortly. Their infantile behavior will require your direction, if not Mr. Bingley's reproof."

Having seen to their grooming and their morning meal, Elizabeth and Mary made quick work of the mile walk into Meryton. As the

Meyerson household was the first to appear, they decided to stop and see if the mistress was in. To their delight, little Rachel impishly opened the door and bade them enter as her beleaguered nurse came running from behind. Dropping a curtsey, the flustered maid invited the ladies to the morning room, where Mrs. Meyerson and Mr. David had just broken their fast.

The mistress of the house greeted the Misses Bennet as family, kissing each girl on the check and offering them hot chocolate and cake. Elizabeth took a seat alongside the lady while Mary joined Mr. Meyerson, who was attempting to bring some order to a much disorganized bookcase. She observed a few selections and was puzzled at the subject matter, for several titles were on the process of professional boxing—not at all in keeping with what she had expected to find.

"Why do you pursue this occupation?" Mary asked with sincere concern. "Do you not think it an abomination before the Lord?"

"I find I am not suited for much else at this juncture in my life. I'm neither a gambler nor a rake. I am rather a serious sort of fellow and I usually have my nose in a book—when it's not getting pummeled," he added with a dashing if somewhat lopsided grin.

"But you are an educated gentleman. You must have other options."

"Not as many as you would think. It was not so very long ago, I would have had to pledge an oath on the *true faith* of a Christian had I wished for a career in politics or any manner of public office. While that is not a reprehensible ideology, it is not in keeping with my heritage and, while many in my community believe the ends justify the means, I could not comply."

Elizabeth had become curious again, sensing the seriousness of the conversation between the two young people, and found her way to her sister's side. She observed Mary to be calm and composed, not at all a blushing young maiden in peril of losing her heart. Still, Elizabeth remained attached to the pair as Mrs. Meyerson excused herself to tend to Rachel's demands.

"How I pray is my business," Mr. Meyerson continued. "I should be judged on the basis of my character and my intelligence, not by which prayer book I choose to read. My current employment is not meant to be a lifetime occupation, Miss Mary, have no fear, and when I take my final bow out of the ring, society will see past the labels they have placed on my back and remember me for my merits as a pugilist!"

Mary nodded quietly and made ready to turn, when Mr. Meyerson placed his hand on her arm, suspending her departure. Elizabeth nearly gasped, thinking her sister would be alarmed at such familiarity but, although her countenance mirrored her surprise, Mary did not seem overly distressed.

"You question me," he continued, "but what *you* are doing is also an abomination in the eyes of the Lord. Remember, I am one son in a household of daughters, I see what those closest to you *do not*."

"Pray, sir, speak clearly, for I am not accustomed to such riddles," said Mary.

With her tranquil expression, it seemed obvious to Elizabeth that her sister felt quite akin to Mr. Meyerson and openly welcomed his counsel. Curious to hear how the gentleman would rejoin, Elizabeth waited with bated breath before unleashing her own observations.

"Very well, I shall," he replied, confident now that he was given leave. "Your hair is rich and lustrous, but you arrange it in such a severe style as to not call attention to its beauty. You dress in the manner fitting a spinster, but you are not yet twenty. Indeed; you are not on the shelf by any means!"

"Sir!" exclaimed Elizabeth. "Your comments are decidedly too intimate."

"But what have I said that is not true?"

"I am convinced that pride is a very common failing," Mary interjected. "I would not relish being accused of such complacency."

"It is not prideful to wish to excel, Miss Mary," he exclaimed. "There is no sin in attempting to improve oneself."

Elizabeth was speechless; such was her shock at the discourse being exchanged. Mr. Meyerson, realizing his impropriety, attempted to explain his choice of words. "Society is not comfortable with things which are not neatly categorized and catalogued. That is why people come to see a Jew in the boxing ring—it does not fit in their characterization of what I am *meant* to be. Forgive me, Miss Elizabeth, but your sister need not be in competition with Miss Jane's beauty or your estimable wit."

"You go too far!" cried Mary. "My sisters do not impose upon me...it is my own lack of confidence which dictates my personality. I could never be as clever as Elizabeth or as elegant as Jane—"

It was precisely at this juncture that Mrs. Meyerson returned to the room accompanied by the vicar and his son. The pair had been out and about that morning, having been working on Mrs. Meyerson's collection project, and decided to pay the lady a call. While the elders settled comfortably for another round of tea, Gideon Ainsely joined David Meyerson and his charming guests. If anyone noticed Miss Mary's sudden blush, it could certainly have been attributed to their comfortable seating arrangements by the fire.

"Ah, Mr. Ainsely! I was just about to share a tale with the Misses Bennet. I wonder if you have come across the parable in your studies?"

"My studies, sir, included a vast variety of parables and proverbs, both Hebraic and Anglican in nature," replied the gentleman. "Perhaps you could be more precise?

"Yes, of course. I refer to the parable of a man named Zusha. You see, Zusha was afraid that when he arrived in heaven, the angels would ask why he had not been like Moses our Teacher. When his Day of Judgment arrived—well, do you know how the story concludes, Ainsely?"

"Yes, I believe I do," said the young man with great enthusiasm. "When his Day of Judgment arrived, the angels did not ask him why he was not more like the great leader; rather, they asked, 'Zusha, why were you not more like *Zusha*?'"

"Precisely!" David exclaimed. "Do you see, Miss Mary, we are not measured against others—"

"We are measured against ourselves," Elizabeth mumbled, recognizing at once the parallels to her own fears.

"Quite right! I only wish to champion your cause, Miss Mary. Allow the world to see *you* without prejudice, without false judgments."

Gideon Ainsely found himself at the center of what seemed to be a rather controversial debate. He was not altogether convinced he ought to participate, not knowing the essentials, but of one thing he was certain. Mr. Ainsely decided, then and there, he would give voice to his thoughts.

"I am not privy to the origins of this most interesting conversation," he began, as his face began to burn, "but having known the Bennet family for much of my life, I would tend to agree with Mr. Meyerson. Miss Mary is a paragon..."

The gentleman proceeded with his soliloquy for the better part of a quarter of an hour, recounting her sister's virtuous qualities and many talents. While Mary smiled demurely and refused to meet her questioning gaze, Elizabeth could only ponder Mr. Ainsely's comments and chastise herself once more. Her discernment on the matter of Mr. Meyerson's attentions was not all that it ought to have been, but rather a supposition based on her own preconceptions.

Elizabeth grew absolutely ashamed of herself. Time and time again she had been blind, biased, prejudiced… absurd!

Mary and the vicar's son! How natural a thing, how providential! Their union would prove to be sanctioned by all, approved by anyone who would wish to opine, for who could object? What would be the cause? They were equally matched, one with the other, not at all like she and Mr. Darcy. *Oh dear*! Where was Grandmère's fortitude and foresight, when it was quite apparent that Elizabeth was in dire need of both?

CHAPTER FOURTEEN

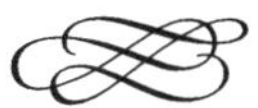

12th of November

"I have had enough of this locality to last a lifetime," Mr. Meyerson declared as they walked to The Red Shield. "I pray we may quit the place soon, for it is a den of dissipation and vice. I begin already to find my morals corrupted!"

"Hold on, now. You have made the initial contact, and once we catch Thompson with the proof, we will have done with it and we shall go home."

The men walked in silence for a moment, passing various and sundry stalls with vendors hawking their wares until finally, the rabbi found his voice.

"Tomorrow will be Shabbes. I cannot travel again until Sunday, which means I will once again forego celebrating the holy time with my family. I *miss* them, Bennet. I miss sitting at the table, watching my wife light the candles. I miss reciting the family blessings..." He paused, his countenance overshadowed by his sorrow.

"My friend, you will have to explain. To which blessing do you refer?"

"We husbands recite the *Eshet Chayil* in praise of our wives every Sabbath eve," Mr. Meyerson sighed. "You might know it—Proverbs 31, the Song of Songs? Who can find a woman of valor? Her value is far beyond that of rubies. The heart of her husband trusts in her and he lacks nothing good."

"You *are* a blessed man," Mr. Bennet said, slapping the man on his shoulder. "I envy your good fortune."

"You are equally blessed."

"Yes, I have a home and family, but my marriage is a disappointment," he murmured in shame. "We are not well matched; we do not suit! I was besotted by her beauty and her youthful vivacity, but when I realized that she did not, *could not,* share in my interests—it was far too late."

Mr. Meyerson stopped and faced his solemn friend. "You admit you did not marry Mrs. Bennet for her wit or conversation?"

"I do."

"Then how can you blame her? You secured what you desired, at least initially. Did she?"

"I do not have the pleasure of understanding your meaning," Mr. Bennet replied, not caring that passersby were beginning to stare at the two men conversing on the street corner.

"Did you cultivate an opportunity for Mrs. Bennet to share your interests or did you shut yourself away and sulk? Good God, man, she wasn't groomed to be a blue stocking! She was groomed to marry, bear children, and see them marry well. *She did her part.* The question then remains: *did you*?"

"You cannot understand—she is like a misbehaving child, ever making a spectacle of herself and the girls."

"It is my experience that an unruly child craves attention. Be attentive, Bennet. Share something of yourself with her, *admire her* for something that she has accomplished, and tell me later that you are not rewarded tenfold!"

"I readily admit, I usually try to escape her presence. It is easier than accepting my regret."

"You do not credit her for what she has brought to your life. If you do not honor her for who she is and what she is capable of, she will not feel the desire to grow into anything else. Why should she, if what she has offered thus far has been met with ingratitude and contempt?"

The church bells in the plaza began striking the hour, urgently summoning Mr. Bennet's attention to the matter at hand.

"Those bells nearly gave me an apoplexy, and your lecture, Rabbi, has me at sixes and sevens! Let us make haste, for we cannot be late and waste the opportunity..."

Mr. Meyerson pulled on his friend's coat sleeve, attempting to hold him back. "You called me *rabbi*?"

Mr. Bennet smiled and bowed low. "Why should I not? You have been my teacher this day, and I vow that my life will change for the better. Now, make haste, man! There is a blackguard out there, and I mean to stop him so we can get back to our wives."

Mr. Meyerson returned the amiable slap on the back as gentlemen often do, and they continued quickly onto their appointed meeting space.

"What will happen to these men once they are brought to justice?" asked Mr. Bennett.

"A hundred years ago, men convicted of coining were sentenced to be hanged, drawn and quartered," Mr. Meyerson grimaced. "Of late, there has been a show of leniency and most felons, including coiners, are transported, rather than executed."

"What will you say to the ensign to convince him?"

"I suspect it will not take too much effort, for he is willing and I have the blunt. I will pass myself off as a merchant in the market for tools and metals. Most of these counterfeiters are craftsmen of some sort. I would not be surprised if Lieutenant Thompson's men were not blacksmiths or some such before joining the militia."

They entered the aforementioned establishment, which indeed displayed an impressive red shield on its entry door. Mr. Bennet turned to see if his companion would again be stricken with a fit of laughter, but Mr. Meyerson's countenance was hard and determined. Spotting Ensign Wakefield seated in the corner, the two men made their way to his table and stopped short, waiting for the man's acknowledgment.

Ensign Wakefield, a short, stout man with yellowing teeth and thinning hair, stood to greet the gentlemen. "Ah, you have come!" he said, nervously looking about. "Forgive me, I do not recall your names."

"I am Mr. Edward Cohen of London," Mr. Meyerson said, "and this is my business associate, Mr. Smith."

The men bowed their greeting and took their seats.

"Gentlemen, tell me, how can I be of service?" Wakefield said, modulating his tone so as not to be overheard. "I have connections with many vendors in this town."

"I am in the market for weights, scales, and molds...cauldrons too," Mr. Meyerson said, matching his tenor with the ensign's. "And, if you know someone with a keen understanding of the metal trade say copper, silver or gold—I would be most obliged."

"Those items are particular to a limited trade. Are you a jeweler, perhaps?"

Mr. Meyerson brought a glass of ale to his lips and tersely replied. "Yes, you could say that."

"Are you certain you wish to purchase the raw materials? Would you not rather obtain the final product?"

Mr. Meyerson rubbed his hands together and considered for a moment. "I suppose, if it is cost effective—one must always keep profit above all else. I would be most appreciative if I could examine the quality and construction of this product. My clientele will only accept topnotch fabrication, you understand," he said, as he removed a velvet pouch full of coins. "Perhaps you could escort us to your warehouses? We would be glad to compensate you for your time."

Mr. Bennet left some coins on the table and the men withdrew. In awkward silence, they walked down narrow streets, crossing and turning and with each step, leaving behind the busy thoroughfares of town. Wakefield reached Old Steine Road and signaled for the men to watch their footing. The streets, such as they were, were riddled with nets the fishermen had laid out to dry.

"It would not do for you gentlemen to trip, but it cannot be helped in this here part of town."

The bitter wind seemed to push them along their way, and Mr. Bennet was relieved when Wakefield at last came to a stop in front of a ramshackle building that had seen better days. Tall and narrow, the structure appeared to have two stories and was in close proximity with the neighboring houses.

"Come in, gentlemen. The place is probably not what you are used to, coming from Town and all, but we got it on the cheap and it is rather spacious—three stories for us to spread out and work."

Perplexed, Mr. Bennet asked the ensign to repeat himself. "You say there are three stories here? I believe I only counted two."

"The landlord explained it best when he let the place. The lower story is actually set slightly below ground level. That, and the proximity of the other houses, offers some protection against the storms. We use the underground space to manufacture and store the product—"

"Wakefield?"

The men turned to see a tall military man coming up the stairs. Wiping his hands on a length of cloth, he tossed it aside and approached, his countenance revealing his ire.

"Lieutenant, I have brought Mr. Edward Cohen and Mr. Smith to conduct business. They were interested in procuring the raw materials, but I suggested they may prefer to save themselves the work and secure the finished product."

"I see," the lieutenant replied. "And what exactly did you gentlemen wish to purchase?"

Mr. Meyerson noted the lieutenant's standoffish, or rather, his reluctant mien, but he did not hesitate in providing his list of essentials. The War Office had practically given him a script to follow and he meant to stick to it.

"Mr. Cohen is from London, Lieutenant. He is a jeweler of sorts," the ensign indicated with some enthusiasm. "He is willing to pay..."

"Wakefield, be quiet, will you?" Lieutenant Thompson looked over the unwanted guests yet standing at the door, noting their age and attire. The situation necessitated caution. If there was money to be made, however, he would not allow the opportunity to pass by unexploited. "Please gentlemen, follow me."

The lieutenant led them to a room that had been set up as a makeshift office. A few simple chairs were scattered about and a plain wooden desk was set up by a darkened window. He waited until Mr. Cohen and Mr. Smith were accommodated before taking his seat behind the desk and poured out three glasses of port. Wakefield was not invited to partake in the refreshment, but instead was asked to stand guard by the door.

"Tell me, Mr. Cohen, what sort of business do you run?"

"Well sir, I am a clockmaker by trade, but we have fallen on difficult times, you understand. My wife and I and our three sons have a side business which requires the items I mentioned. In addition to those, I would add, we require a great quantity of *aqua fortis*, sand-paper, cork, and other finishing implements."

"You will forgive my impertinence, Mr. Cohen, but that rather sounds as if you are in the business of coining. Wakefield believes you would rather just purchase the coins rather than get your hands dirty with the actual manufacturing process. Is that correct, sir?"

Mr. Meyerson nodded excitedly, seeing that the script was apparently working. "Yes, if the price is right, it would save my family a tremendous amount of time and effort. I am certain we could come to an agreement. I would make it worth your while. My wife Deborah and her friend Joanna toil day and night—the children, as well."

"Mr. Cohen—"

"Lieutenant, let us come to a right understanding. I came to Brighton to purchase materials, but if you and I can come to terms, this could be a lucrative and time-saving venture. I *am* curious to see your production line."

Having heard enough, the lieutenant appeared reconciled to the situation before him. "Very well," Thompson said, as he arose. "Perhaps we can come to a satisfactory arrangement. *Wakefield*!"

The ensign appeared and was at the ready. The men were escorted to a door that concealed a separate stairwell. Wakefield led the way down, holding a thick rushlight that held an acrid candle made of tallow. When they reached thc lower level, he lit two more holders before making way for the lieutenant and their visitors. He was certain that there would be an extra bonus in his pay this month. Lieutenant Thompson was a harsh and driven man, but he was fair.

Wakefield stood aside and allowed his superior officer room to impress Mr. Cohen and his associate.

Mr. Bennet and Mr. Meyerson were speechless as they espied a most remarkable sight. The warehouse was complete with an iron press, dies, cutting tools, edging tools for milling—everything required for a lucrative business in counterfeiting coins. Mr. Meyerson approached a barrel, stamped with the insignia of the Exchequer's office and filled to the rim with the aforementioned final product. Mr. Bennet came to his side and nearly gasped aloud. Turning slightly, he beckoned the lieutenant.

"May I?" he asked, signaling he wished to reach into the barrel.

"Of course, be my guest," replied Lieutenant Thompson.

In a moment of complete abandon, both men thrust their hands into the cask filled with coins, causing the golden discs to overflow and their nervous laughter to let loose.

Suddenly, quite without notice, their felicity came to a blinding, painful conclusion as Thompson approached the men from behind, knocking them senseless with the base of the brass rushlight. Ensign Wakefield was all astonishment. Such was his frenzied reaction, the lieutenant had to slap him soundly about the face.

"Calm yourself and bring me a length of rope," Thompson ordered.

"*What have you done*? Was that necessary?"

"Are you questioning me, ensign?" he barked as he dragged Mr. Meyerson across the room. "It would serve you well to remember whom you are addressing!"

Ensign Wakefield recoiled and, almost in a trance state, walked to a cupboard to find the requested rope.

"Imbecile!" the lieutenant hissed as he made quick work of securing his captives. "Do you not realize we are involved in a *criminal* activity? What were you thinking, bringing these men here?"

"I thought we could make some money on the side," Wakefield blurted out. "Him being a Jew and all, I thought it would be safe, seeing how he was willing to pay, and I saw his blunt! He had a purse full of coins, *real* coins, and I thought..."

"Blithering idiot! These men are not who they say they are. They may be investigators or Bow Street Runners—I do not know, but they are not *Mr. Cohen* and *Mr. Smith*!"

"How do you know that...sir," he quickly added.

The lieutenant glared at the man, useless and trembling. "This one, *Cohen,* he gave himself away with all that talk about his wife and children. He even told me their names—Edward and Deborah. Edward and Deborah Lloyd, for your information, were a husband and wife team who worked with their sons and neighbor, Joanna Wood, putting off bad money for over twenty-five years. Some solicitor for the Mint had them *hanged*!" Lieutenant Thompson pulled the rope tautly against Mr. Bennet's wrists. "If you had any brains at all, you would know what you are about. No one comes here... *no one*! Is that clear? Unless I tell you explicitly, you are not to bring anyone to this place."

The men made ready to quit the room. They dragged both Mr. Meyerson and Mr. Bennet to a darkened corner and left them there, bound, gagged and unconscious. It was several hours later before they awoke and, in their terror, Mr. Meyerson and Mr. Bennet could only gesture and moan as they saw a light appearing from the top of the stairs.

"I do not know that you deserve this, but Lieutenant Thompson is gone for the night," said Wakefield. "I cannot sleep thinking of the two of you down here. It would serve you right if I let you starve after the trouble you have caused but, I do not want that on my conscious.

I will remove the rags from your mouth. You will you eat and be quiet about it."

Their throats were dry and parched. The men nodded in desperation. Wakefield was good on his word. He removed the rags and loosened the ropes about their wrists so that they could eat. He left them with one candle and the threat of returning if he heard any disturbance but, before closing the door at the top of the stairs, he turned and sneered. "No one can hear you down here anyway. That there is the beauty of this old place." He laughed and secured the door for the night.

Wakefield had thrown a plate of ham and day-old bread between them, along with a flask filled with tepid water. Mr. Bennet was able to move his fingers in such a way that he could tear the meat into smaller pieces. He offered his companion the first portion and then remembered Mr. Meyerson could not partake.

"I am sorry, Rabbi, I forgot your restrictions..."

"No need to apologize. I cannot reprimand you for not remembering something that is foreign to your ways. *Baruch atah Adonai Eloheinu melech ha'olam, shehakol nihyeh bidvaro,*"[1] the rabbi recited as he took the morsel into his mouth, blessing God for the forbidden food. "I am commanded, when faced with choosing between Life or Death, to choose *Life*. This food has not been thrown at me to question my commitment to my faith. It has been thrown at me as if I were a dog. Because I wish to live, I will eat it and be thankful for the sustenance. I will not martyr myself for the benefit of the likes of Thompson."

Mr. Bennet bowed his head and said his grace. Passing the flask of water awkwardly to his friend, he murmured, "We must find a way out of here."

With his head pounding and with growing trepidation, Mr. Meyerson agreed. "Mr. Gardiner knows of my presence here in

Brighton. Montefiore and his men must have been alerted. I am certain they are on our trail. If the Rothschild campaign is going to work, we need to get out of this alive and bring our proof to the Crown."

"Be it God's will," said Mr. Bennet.

"Amen," replied the rabbi.

CHAPTER FIFTEEN

16th of November

"If you do not unclench your teeth, cousin, I do believe your face will remain frozen in that position—at least, that is what my dear mother used to say."

"Leave me be, Richard."

"You have barely put two words together in over a week, Darcy, and while that is not completely out of character, I do believe a grunt or two every day or so is not too much to ask."

"I have much on my mind. You would not understand, and I do not feel the need to enlighten you—a hardened solider, an unattached, perpetual bachelor..."

"Well done!" he laughed, "You have managed to string together several words to concoct a cohesive, if not rational, thought. Now, out with it! What is this torturous philosophy that is driving you mad? With what unearthly dilemma are you grappling—which you believe I could not possibly comprehend?"

"Need I remind you *why* we are in this blasted place? Let us find Mr. Bennet and Mr. Meyerson and be gone!"

Colonel Fitzwilliam, without turning to face the man, simply flung out his fist and made contact with Mr. Darcy's shoulder.

"Who do you think you are fooling? I know you better than anyone in all of England. This is about Elizabeth. It is *always* about Elizabeth!"

"Do not speak of her."

"What has occurred? It cannot be about the postponement. I would not doubt her constancy."

Sighing, Mr. Darcy shook his head and appeared as if he would not give voice to his thoughts but, after walking several paces in silent accord, he began to unburden himself.

"Something has frightened her," muttered Darcy.

"Yes—of course, she is frightened by her father's disappearance."

"No, it is not that. She is withdrawn; she recoils when I am near. Elizabeth was always so self-assured, so lively, and yet she seems overwhelmed by the prospect of matrimony."

"Do you not think society has unfair expectations of young ladies?"

"*What?*" he growled.

"We require them each to be paragons of virtue, clean as the driven snow and yet, when they are to marry, they are expected to be passionate lovers, obedient wives, devoted mothers and accomplished housekeepers—all of this while they are ripped away from family and friends and everything they have ever known. It is a wonder they know how to act!"

"They are prepared to take on such a role," Darcy sighed at his cousin's theatrics. "They receive instruction and guidance—"

"They are taught the essentials, but no further," the colonel grimly replied. "We, on the other hand, are given free reign; we are sent to school, we are able to see something of the world. We are permitted to *sow our wild oats*."

"Do not be vulgar, Richard."

"I speak truth! Women are told to laugh; but not too loudly, to think, but not too deeply; *to be coquettish*, but not enough to compromise their virtue. Perhaps Elizabeth only needs your reassurance. Think of Georgie—a diamond of the first water—she was guided, instructed, prepared, and Wickham nearly destroyed her."

"I will not have you speak of him."

"We must acknowledge the kind of man he is."

"He is the kind of a man who would take advantage of an innocent! I would never do such a thing. I do not wish to speak of the matter. When we return, Elizabeth and I will set things to right. There is no question—"

"Calm yourself, Cousin, I vow to cease my tormenting if you can think of way to solve this predicament and get us back to Hertfordshire. It should not be so difficult to find two gentlemen in a town this size."

"We have circumnavigated these streets for days. I would not be surprised to find that we had crossed paths without realizing what was in plain sight," Darcy muttered. "*You* are the stratagem expert. What do you suggest?"

"We cannot apply to Colonel Forster, for we cannot risk alerting the scoundrel. We will have to continue our search without calling too much attention to ourselves."

Walking along the edge of town, the bow-fronted houses of the posh residential areas gave way to the simpler shacks and shops alongside the oceanfront. Turning onto Old Steine Road, Mr. Darcy gestured towards a promising tavern with its wooden slate swaying to and fro, inviting them to enter The Whitley Whaler by the Sea. The men entered the weather-beaten established with every intention of procuring a table, but the dining parlor reeked of frying fish so they chose instead to sit at the bar. Colonel Fitzwilliam ordered two pints as the publican came to greet them but, when the colonel tendered the payment, the landlord threw the coins upon the counter and listened to it ring.

One look at Mr. Darcy's indignant brow prompted the man to speak. "You gents are not the laborin' sort so you would not be knowin', but we who work for our daily bread are 'specially aggrieved by coiners." Satisfied with the authenticity of his compensation, the man looked up from beneath his bushy eyebrows and bestowed upon them a toothless grin. "A man works hard all day for one shillin', and if he comes to find out that it's a bad one not even worth a farthin', it'll be his wife and children who be payin' the price."

Mr. Darcy exchanged a knowing look with the Colonel, who immediately understood and nodded his agreement. Reaching into his coat pocket, Mr. Darcy removed another coin and dropped it on the counter.

"Thunder an' turf!" the publican exclaimed. "That be a *guinea*? My ale is good, sir, but it ain't worth all that much."

"It is yours—for a bit of information."

To Mr. Darcy's repulsion, the landlord tentatively picked up the coin and bit into it. "It is a real one, it is. What sort of information be you wantin'?"

"We are looking for two gentlemen," Mr. Darcy replied. "They are middle aged—one is a Hebrew clergyman."

"La! The whole tribe of Benjamin is always about this town!" the man decreed. "It is gettin' so that the streets are full of dissenters! Haberdashers, merchants and money lenders—Brigh'on has become a sort of Cheapside by the sea!"

Mr. Darcy's previous disgust substantially increased with the man's vulgar speech and he was quite ready to quit the place when

Colonel Fitzwilliam signaled with a discreet nod to the back of the room. Sitting by the bay window that faced the rocky beach was an old soldier waving them over with his one good arm. The veteran and his regimentals had apparently seen better days. Stirred by the sight, the colonel ordered another drink and made his way to greet the man.

"Looks like you have seen some action," Colonel Fitzwilliam said, taking a seat and handing the man his ale.

"Yes, sir, indeed I have! The name's Fletcher, at your service, sir. I was with the Regulars, some years ago. I put my life on the line for lousy wages and even worse food, but here you find me, with a bum arm and no one willing to take me on. Lud! But, enough about me and my sad story. I hear you are looking for a couple of gents. I might be able to help you, if you have another one of those pretty, gold coins. That is why I was waving you over, sir. Forgive my impertinence but I could use a guinea myself."

"These are difficult times, indeed, and I am sorry to hear you are down on your luck. Perhaps you can assist us, Fletcher. See if you can scrounge up any information on the streets."

"Do the gentlemen hail from London, sir? People from Town can be spotted quite easily in these parts."

The colonel shook his head. "No, they are from Hertfordshire—Meryton to be exact. Our friends are quite unpretentious, to be sure."

"I will keep my ears and eyes open, sir. I have naught else to do but sit and watch people go about their business." The corporal shifted his gaze and nodded his head toward the gentleman at the entrance. "Your friend is waiting on you, sir."

"So he is," the colonel grinned. "We will return tomorrow, corporal.

Mr. Darcy stood impatiently by the door. The stench of the place and the foul manners of the owner dissuaded him from staying any longer. As they removed themselves to the blistery chill, the colonel told his cousin about Fletcher and what had befallen the old patriot.

"Wickham is the scum of the earth," Mr. Darcy growled. "His brothers-in-arms live a life of sacrifice while he, parasite that his is, thinks of only himself and his comforts. Perhaps this man Fletcher could be of some assistance to us. I rather have him on my payroll than that ill-mannered shop tender."

Mr. Darcy and the colonel retraced their steps back to their lodgings, watching for the fishermen's' netting drying on the sidewalk and turning up their coats against the chill in the air. So complete was their fatigue, so great was their disillusionment in their inability to locate Mr. Bennet and Mr. Meyerson that they were remiss in observing those passersby who entered The Whitley Whaler just as they themselves quitted the place.

George Wickham, who had been in town wenching and gambling all the while, came to the public house that evening with every intention of reacquainting himself with his long lost companion, Lieutenant Thompson. As he was on leave from his post and thought to be in Hertfordshire, Mr. Wickham had no desire of making his presence known to Colonel Forster and given the fact he hoped to make the trip profitable; his meeting with Thompson should rather be discreet.

The Whitley Whaler had been a favorite of the men when they had been stationed previously in Brighton. Mr. Wickham was certain he could make contact with the man in some form or fashion. When he espied a red coat sitting by the bay window, he felt a *fait accompli*.

"Pardon me...corporal," Mr. Wickham, hesitating only to note the man's rank.

"The name is Fletcher, sir," the soldier said coming to his feet.

"Are you familiar with Colonel Forster's unit?"

"No, sir, I cannot say that I am..."

Bartholomew Wakefield, who was drinking away his frustration at the neighboring table, came quickly to attention. "Pardon me for interrupting sir," he asked a little too enthusiastically, "but may I be of assistance?"

"What is your name, ensign?" Mr. Wickham asked, surprised at the disturbance. "Are you with Colonel Forster's unit?

"Yes sir, my name is Wakefield, sir."

"And do you know Lieutenant Thompson, by chance?"

"Yes, sir. We are stationed here in Brighton, sir."

Mr. Wickham smiled as he haughtily adjusted his shirt sleeves from under his coat. "Pray, relay a message. I served with Thompson and Captain Denny whilst in Meryton. I am in town on business and would very much enjoy paying him a call."

"But, he be expecting you, sir!" Ensign Wakefield said bobbing his head up and down. "I have been waiting to meet you. I have orders to take you to him."

"You have been *waiting*?" Mr. Wickham was perplexed, for he had not told the ensign his name, but if Fate had allowed for the meeting to occur, who was he to snub his good fortune?

Corporal Fletcher discreetly returned to his seat and finished his ale. Oh, but the day had been eventful, he thought to himself. Every day, he sat useless and alone as people scurried about. But, not today. He had witnessed many strangers coming and going—each carrying on with no care in the world. People acted with abandon when they believed they were free from scrutiny. Perhaps his luck was about to change, Fletcher imagined, downing his final swig as he watched the men depart together.

Wakefield chattered away as the two quickly turned down one street and walked up another. The ensign was too talkative, Wickham thought to himself. *All the better for me.*

"We recently moved, sir. Them taverns and shops only be

accepting a certain number of false coins before their suspicion be aroused. This here new lodging has secret hiding places—even the chairs have been made with false bottoms to hide our coin."

"It is a dangerous game you play," said Wickham.

"Without a doubt, sir. Many have been sentenced to death for putting out false money, but the Lieutenant has been careful. He presents the counterfeit gold to the bank in exchange for banknotes and then, exchanges the banknotes for *good* coins. Them's not so difficult to trace when the Lieutenant has to buy supplies."

"Indeed?" Wickham replied with not a little curiosity. "Do you require much material for the production?"

"Oh, yes, sir! We need charcoal, copper and brass and other metals. We have a complete working production unit, you see—ah, here we are."

Ensign Wakefield opened the door and allowed his guest to enter. They had gone four paces into the room when from the lieutenant's office came a great bellow.

"Wickham!"

"I found your friend at the pub, sir!" Ensign Wakefield exclaimed as he ran to salute his superior. "Brought him straight here, as you instructed."

"You idiot, this is not the man I was waiting for—"

"Ah, Lieutenant, but I am hurt." Wickham removed his hat and placed it over his heart, feigning his dismay. "Am I not your friend?" He took a turn about the room, poking his head this way and that. "This is quite an installation, Thompson."

"Yes indeed," the lieutenant replied. "We are making buttons—for the army, of course."

"Yes, of course, I had heard of your *button* venture." Mr. Wickham picked up a stack of coins on Thompson's desk and inspected them closely. "Nice and shiny...golden, wouldn't you say?"

Lieutenant Thompson bunched up his fists and nearly snarled, knowing the jig was up for him and his mates. His previous experience with George Wickham had been beneficial, but the profit had come with a hefty price and he knew that the man standing before him was a cutthroat and a self-interested rogue. Wickham would turn him in without a doubt. The lieutenant was left with no choice.

"It's a five-man operation," Thompson admitted through clenched teeth. "The profits are distributed according to the proportion of money each has contributed towards the expenses. What are you willing to put in?"

Wickham picked off an imaginary piece of lint from his coat before replying. "I am willing, as you say, not to go to the constable and do my duty as an Englishman of the first order. Will that suffice?"

The lieutenant nodded silently.

"I am pleased we could come to terms," Wickham laughed. "Now, tell me, how did this all come about?"

His wrath towards his incompetent assistant was set aside, for Thompson's arrogance and avarice could not be suppressed. With unveiled enthusiasm the lieutenant detailed how the extraordinary opportunity had fallen into his lap. The militia had received orders to decamp from their quarters in Meryton. While the lower level soldiers believed they were stationed in Brighton to train on maneuvers, the officers were told the truth of the matter. They had been tasked to guard the gold shipment as it made its way to the Continent.

"The packet which was meant to leave this port for Dieppe has been delayed at sea," Thompson explained. "A few of us got together and quickly put our plans into action. We figured we could skim some off the top, as it were, and none would be the wiser. It is fast money, but the opportunity will not last for much longer."

"Then let us not delay," Wickham smirked. "Where can I withdraw my first installment?"

"We store the goods underground," the lieutenant replied, his mien disgruntled once again.

"Excellent. Show me the way, if you please." Wickham said, moving his arm slightly so that his dress sword could be seen.

Glaring at Wakefield as they left the front office, Thompson walked towards the hidden stairwell. Not until they reached the final steps did he recall the two men being held prisoner. It took a moment for their eyes to adjust, for even with the candlelight Thompson held high, the room was dark and shadowed. The ensign, trembling with unease, was grateful he had had the presence of mind to see to the men earlier in the day; their mouths had been gagged and the restraints tightened. Wakefield sighed in relief knowing that at least the lieutenant could not fault him on that score. Mr. Bennet and Mr. Meyerson were awake and anxious to see what was taking place but, thrown in the shadows, they were merely two moaning forms.

"I see you have been *entertaining*," Wickham said.

Mr. Bennet, hearing the familiar voice, railed against his restraints. His kicking and jouncing, however, were to no avail.

"Never mind them," the lieutenant hissed. "They stuck their noses in where they did not belong. Once this shipment has been completed, I will think what to do, but I will not risk the operation by dealing with the pair of them now."

In truth, Mr. Wickham could not be bothered with the unknown captives, for he found himself more pleasantly occupied. Lieutenant Thompson provided him with two bags of coarse homespun and pointed to the unsealed barrel.

"You would not want much more than that on your person," he

said when Mr. Wickham seemed dissatisfied. "Be careful how you dispense with it."

"Thank you, Thompson. While I appreciate your concern, I need no further instruction. I will be returning to this Midas treasury, soon enough."

CHAPTER SIXTEEN

"Hill!" Lydia called out. "Oh, where is Hill?" With little care for disrupting the family's morning slumber, Lydia slammed doors and dropped cases onto her chamber's floor. Elizabeth walked into her sister's room, only to find it in complete disarray. Muslin dresses and woolen capes were thrown haphazardly about the place. Her sister's stays and unmentionables were cast indiscriminately upon the counterpane.

"What is all this?" Elizabeth asked, her hand masking an errant yawn. "Are you going somewhere?"

Lydia did not bother to turn from the chest of drawers, where her hand searched blindly for heaven knows what. "I am going to Brighton. If the militia is stationed there, it is very likely Wickham is visiting his old friends. My husband is enjoying a holiday by the sea. It is only fair that I partake in the pleasure as well."

"You are not thinking of traveling alone?"

"I am a married woman and have the freedom to move about as I wish, unlike you, Lizzie, who still require a chaperone or should I say nurse maid?"

"Do not be foolish, Lydia," she replied, ignoring her sister's attempts to wound her pride. "If Wickham is in Brighton, it certainly is not for sea bathing—it is the dead of winter! If he is not there for pleasure, it follows he is conducting some sort of business. Can you be certain he would wish you to join him?"

"I assure you, my husband will be more than pleased to have me by his side," she replied with another slam of the dresser drawer.

"Lydia—" Elizabeth began with some trepidation, "will you cease this pugnacious undertaking for a moment and tell me, please, how can you love such a man? Would you not rather be free of him? Perhaps there is something that can be done if you wished to be released from this marriage."

Lydia stopped her feverish movements at once and turned to face her sister. Never had Elizabeth seen such a composed look upon her countenance. Lydia sighed slowly and shook her head.

"I love him, Lizzy. I know you think me childish—thoughtless—but I *love* him."

"But do you know him, truly and completely?"

"I am sensible to your opinions, I know what the world thinks of my husband, but Lizzy I accept him, faults and all. I am not proud. I know my limitations, my weaknesses—heaven knows, my father has lectured upon the subject enough. If George Wickham married me for other reasons than love, I do not care to own it. I have enough of the emotion to see us through until he learns to love me in return."

"But you are young yet. What do you know of the world? You are throwing your life away..."

"Do not judge me, Lizzy, for what does any one of us seek but love and acceptance? George Wickham took me to wife and I will not abandon him. Now, do be a dear and find Hill. I would have the carriage made ready, for I must needs be on the twelve o'clock to Town."

Elizabeth found the housekeeper, relayed the message, and made her way back to her room. She snuck back under the warm covers and contemplated the extraordinary conversation. How was it possible that her youngest sister, the silliest of them all, could see her life's path so clearly? Lydia had decided for herself and was determined enough to match even Lady Catherine de Bourgh in her stubbornness and resolve. Her sister cared not a whit what the world thought of her husband or what anyone thought of her, for that matter! She had always been a good-humored girl, Elizabeth ruminated. And although it had ever seemed a curse and a bother, Lydia had high animal spirits and a sort of natural, self-consequence that allowed her to live her life to the fullest.

It was at this particular moment that Elizabeth began to feel her own resolve grow. She allowed her mind to give way to every variety of thought—every event was reconsidered, every determination was reviewed. When she had reconciled herself to the obvious conclusion, she arose and stirred Jane from her slumber.

"Jane, dearest, please wake! I have need of you!" she cried.

Upon hearing Elizabeth's cry, Jane did awake with such a start that it took several minutes for the poor girl to regain her sensibilities. Assuring her that all was well, Elizabeth explained that their youngest sister was off to find her husband and that she herself had need to find Mr. Darcy at once.

"What has come over you, Lizzy? You cannot go chasing after Mr. Darcy in this manner."

"You do not understand. I have been remiss, Jane. I have *hurt* him. We had overcome much, he and I. We had bared our souls and admitted our failings and then, well—as difficult as it is to own it—I simply lost my faith."

Elizabeth paused just then and tempered her excitement, if not for Jane's benefit, at least for her own. The anguish she had experienced in quiet solitude had finally been resolved. The release was exquisite.

"I must go to him," she said.

Jane sat up in her bed and rubbed the sleep from her eyes.

"But cannot you wait for his return? What urgent message must you relay that is worth risking your safety—your reputation? Traveling without a male escort? What will people think?" She began to loosen her unraveling braid and, as she brushed out her golden tresses, Jane listened to her sister's remarkable confession.

"What I have to say cannot wait, and people will think whatever they wish! I certainly have no control over the matter, and, I must own, that itself has been a difficult lesson to learn."

"Dear Lizzy, what has come over you?"

Elizabeth released a heavy sigh. She closed her eyes to gather her thoughts. It had all seem so clear to her moments ago.

"Do you recall the day we met Mrs. Meyerson in town? She spoke to us about a lesson she was preparing for the ladies of her congregation."

Jane nodded and set down her brush. "Yes, she explained that our purpose was to continually renew ourselves, much like the moon."

"Her words were precisely what I needed to hear—although I was so lost in my insecurities, I was not sensible to her meaning."

"You have never been one to repine, Lizzy. I cannot credit that you, dear sister, would suffer such anxieties. Whatever do you mean by *insecurities*? Do you doubt your affection for Mr. Darcy?"

Taking up the brush, Elizabeth motioned for Jane to turn as she began brushing her sister's hair in long, even strokes. The routine was familiar and calming, and Elizabeth found the words now flowed with ease.

"Mr. Darcy and I confessed our sins to one another on Oakham Mount. We admitted our wretched shortcomings, those human weaknesses of pride and prejudice which nearly ruined all our hopes. What I failed to take into consideration, for some time past, was the possibility—the blessing—of transformation. By my openness and exuberance, his views might soften, his comportment improve. With his experience and knowledge of the world, my own education will improve; my discernment and conduct will receive the benefit of greater importance. I doubted that Mr. Darcy and I could overcome our dissimilarities, but now I realize our union would be for the betterment of *both*. I am persuaded, if William will still have me, I am his."

"It seems, while you and I are the best of friends, you share something with Lydia which I can only observe from afar," said Jane, as she turned and took hold of her sister's hands. "I have not your passionate nature. I have not that fire that Grandmère was so clever as to recognize in you! Nonetheless, I will support your decision unreservedly, but, Lizzie, may I suggest you ask Mr. Meyerson to accompany you to Brighton? It would be more seemly."

Elizabeth hugged her sister and laughed. "Oh no, Jane! That would never do! The entire town of Meryton cannot be searching for men who are supposed to be working incognito."

"I am not suggesting the *entire* town, Lizzy. Do be reasonable. Mr. Meyerson might be of some assistance, and think how Mr. Darcy, or even Papa, will react when they find you there unescorted."

"Very well, I will send a quick note. Perhaps Kitty would be willing to go into town and deliver it herself."

Jane smiled. "Kitty has been very dear of late. Mrs. Meyerson has been a great influence on our little sister."

Elizabeth nodded as she began looking for her valise and sorting through her wardrobe. "One must be grateful for such favors."

"Although, I wonder, Lizzy—do you think there is any danger of an attachment between our sister and Mr. Meyerson?"

"Why would you even consider such a notion? Kitty is full young yet. She may have followed Lydia's example by traipsing after Carter and Denny, but in truth, Kitty does not strike me as being ready for an affair of the heart."

Jane pondered her sister's reply with all due respect and consideration nonetheless, she could not help but question Kitty's sudden change.

"It is rather unlike our sister to be solicitous and generous with her time—especially if it means caring for a small child."

"Truly, Jane, I have it on good authority that Mr. Meyerson does not mean to marry, at least not for the time being. Indeed, he has told me that much himself. We should not fear for his heart, and as for our sister, I believe these afternoons in Meryton have simply afforded her a taste of freedom."

"Then, the change in her character must stem from the liberating sensation of being away from home."

Elizabeth laughed. "Oh, Jane! Meryton's flibbertigibbets might have speculated against the Bennet sisters, but we must have faith. There *is* hope for us all!"

IT DID NOT TAKE MUCH PERSUADING TO SECURE KITTY'S cooperation, once she was stirred from her sleep and presented with a cup of hot chocolate while still abed. Delightfully accommodating, Kitty made for the Meyerson household, hours before she was expected or necessarily required. The family, in fact, were just being served their morning meal when the housekeeper announced Miss Bennet's arrival. Little Rachel shouted out with glee, however, her mama bade her to show some restraint. While the child fidgeted in her chair, Mr. Meyerson sighed, set down his linen *serviette* and came to his feet. When the gentleman bowed upon her entry into the room, Kitty's heart raced and she brought her hand to her breast, hoping he would not discern the fluttering of her heart.

"Good morning to all," she murmured. "Pray, forgive the intrusion at this early hour but, my sister has sent me on a most pressing mission."

"My dear!" cried Mrs. Meyerson. "Be at ease. Sit down, won't you? Have something to eat and tell us your news."

Kitty blushed as Mr. Meyerson held out her seat but quickly recovered her faculties as she began to relate her sister's appeal. "And so you see, sir, my sisters are for Brighton and await your reply," she concluded.

Mr. Meyerson did not need to think upon the matter overmuch. He would accompany Mrs. Wickham and Miss Bennet on their journey and be glad to be of service. He was a young man accustomed to daily exercise and, more importantly, to tests and trials. This sitting about at home and taking tea with the gentry was not to his liking. Here was something to do, at last!

"I am your servant, Miss Catherine," said he. "I will pack my things at once and be at your disposal."

Having just arrived, Kitty was none too eager to return to home with his confirmatory reply. She had hoped to spend more time in Mr. Meyerson's company, he being always at the ready with insightful anecdotes and charming repartee. Little Rachel's demands provided sufficient motive for Kitty to remain, and Mrs. Meyerson gladly called for her manservant to be discharged to Longbourn in her stead.

There had been very little commentary from Mrs. Bennet when her daughters applied for her blessing. She had neither the strength to disagree nor the compunction to accompany them on their journey. Having ordered the carriage to take them into town, Elizabeth and Lydia were sent off with wet kisses and a perfumed handkerchief fluttering in the wind. Mrs. Bennet returned to her chamber for a mid-day nap, so overcome was she with tremblings and palpitations.

Mrs. Meyerson and Kitty had accompanied Mr. Meyerson to the town square. They were a quiet party, each lost in their own thoughts. The gentleman pondered what excitement he might encounter upon reaching his destination, while his mother contemplated what dangers awaited his arrival. The young miss was anxious and fretful and desperately uncomfortable with the entire business. Kitty thought perhaps she might have a word with Lizzy, hoping to unburden herself with the elder sister as she now could not with the younger, but the Longbourn carriage arrived just as the hired conveyance was ready to depart for London. Kitty and Mrs. Meyerson saw them off with a full basket containing a cold repast and fare-thee-well wishes for the entire party.

It was upon their return to the Meyerson residence that Kitty recognized a chaise and four driving hurriedly through the narrow street. Townspeople scurrying hither and thither stopped to spy on the livered servants and the family coat of arms. Although such a conveyance was an unusual sight, Kitty recognized it at once, for the same vehicle had been to Longbourn. It belonged to Lady Catherine de Bourgh! She gasped when the horses were pulled to an abrupt stop. When the door flung upon and the great lady made to alight, Kitty trembled and grabbed a hold of Mrs. Meyerson's arm.

"Whatever is the matter, my dear? Are you acquainted with this person?"

Kitty nodded, unable to speak, so terrified was she.

"You there!" Lady Catherine declared, pointing her parasol in Kitty's direction. "You are one of those Bennet girls. Come here!"

Kitty hurried to the lady's side and curtsied low.

"I was told my nephew was married in this locality nearly a se'nnight ago and yet he and his wife have not returned to Pemberley," Lady Catherine declared. "You cannot be at a loss, Miss Bennet, to understand the reason of my journey hither. That I had not received an invitation to the nuptials was insult enough, but that the newlyweds neglected their duty to call on me at Rosings...their inattentiveness is not to be borne!'

Mrs. Meyerson perceived the lady's position and her frank manner of speaking had rendered her little friend mute. Although she had not been properly introduced, Mrs. Meyerson believed she should act on Mrs. Bennet's behalf and come to Kitty's aid.

"Madam, I wonder you took the trouble of coming so far without consulting with your nephew or his housekeeper, at the very least," Mrs. Meyerson declared. "However slighted you may feel, surely you do not expect Miss Bennet to have had any say in the matter."

Kitty paled upon hearing such a rebuke stemming from her kind and patient friend. She was uncertain how Lady Catherine would reply, but she would not allow Mrs. Meyerson to be abused on her behalf. Quite suddenly, Kitty found her voice.

"You cannot know, ma'am, but my sister and Mr. Darcy are not yet wed," Kitty said with a gleam in her eye, daring the great lady to retort. "My father was called away on an urgent matter that could not be suspended—"

Lady Catherine balked at this information but could not withhold her condescension. "Your father abandoned his duty to his daughter? For shame! But this revelation can only credit my poor opinion of the match, for what family behaves in such a low manner?"

Hearing these recriminations towards her family caused Kitty's indignation to stir. "A friend was in dire need of my father's support," she said, raising her chin in defiance, "and being a gentleman and a good Christian, he could do naught but go to his aid. Naturally, the wedding is postponed until the matter is resolved and my father and Mr. Darcy return home."

"You mean to say Fitzwilliam is not here?" Lady Catherine exclaimed.

"He is gone to assist my father. I believe that proves the depth of his affections towards Lizzy. You should be pleased for your nephew. It is my understanding that happiness in marriage is not a foregone conclusion."

"You give your opinion quite decidedly for such a young person," declared Lady Catherine. "You take after your sister, do you not? I recall the Bennet family did not benefit from a governess, yet you speak *well.* Do you attend school in this village?"

Kitty lost her voice once again, and Mrs. Meyerson had to intercede. "Miss Bennet has been educated at home by her most excellent parents and is now acting as a companion in my household."

"A *paid* companion? Relatives in trade, daughters hired out..."

"Forgive me, madam, but you do Mr. and Mrs. Bennet a disservice by assuming they do not think of these things," Mrs. Meyerson interjected. "You have misunderstood my meaning. Miss Bennet has become a particular friend to my youngest daughter and a great asset to me."

"And *you* are?" Lady Catherine asked, glowering at the woman with full force.

Mrs. Meyerson curtsied and then met the lady's fiery gaze. "I am Mrs. Meyerson of London, madam. The House of Rothschild and their associates have seen fit to send my husband to lead the Hebrew congregation in Meryton."

"The House of Rothschild? I see," was the lady's stunned reply, as she gathered her wrap about her person. "In any case, I refuse to continue this conversation in the middle of the thoroughfare. Do these people have naught to do save gawk at their betters?"

The three turned to observe that, indeed, their presence had caused quite a stir. Kitty noted that even her aunt Phillips had thrown open her parlor window and was attempting to glean whatever information possible.

"I would invite you to Longbourn, ma'am, but my mother is unwell," Kitty admitted, "and I fear she would not be prepared to receive you in a proper manner."

Lady Catherine waved away her comment. "I shall return to Rosings, but I charge you to deliver a message to my nephew. I give you leave to send word upon his return. Pray, what is your Christian name, child? There are so many Miss Bennets that I fear I may lose track!"

"My name is Catherine, ma'am." Kitty blushed and lowered her eyes, ill at ease in the knowledge they shared something in common.

"Catherine, is it? Very well, *Miss Catherine,* I would have you tell my nephew I seek an audience post haste. For better or for worse, I am his eldest living relative and I would see things right."

Mrs. Meyerson and Kitty bobbed a final curtsy as the lady ascended into her awaiting carriage. "I send compliments to your mother, Miss Bennet. While I am seriously displeased at the machinations surrounding this union," Lady Catherine professed with an approving eye towards the clergyman's wife, "it appears that your familial connections are not wholly without merit."

The scene concluded, the townspeople returned each to their own toil as the women returned to the Meyerson home. "I have much to tell my mama when I return to Longbourn," Kitty murmured, still in shock. "I must confess it was your calm and determined manner that allowed me to speak thusly."

Mrs. Meyerson smiled and patted the young woman's cheek. "We are all flesh and blood, my dear. When you are in the presence of someone as intimidating as Lady Catherine, remember we are all angelic creatures and children of the Most High."

While Kitty and her mentor made their way back to the lady's warm and inviting abode, Mr. David Meyerson suffered from unforeseen torment. Although he was rather a seasoned traveler and quite prepared for the jostling and discomfort, he had not accounted for the abuse to which they would be subjected. Traveling four hours in a public conveyance was long considered a lesson in patience and restraint, but traveling four hours alongside Mrs. Wickham was enough to try the patience of Job himself.

Lydia Wickham flattered herself on being an expert in all things Brighton and found it exceedingly diverting to accentuate her elder sister's lack of familiarity with the seaside resort. "The bathing machines, the sedan chairs, and *oh*! The pleasure boats and the splashing waves against the white cliffs! Truly, Lizzy, the advantages of sea bathing are not to be denied. I read Dr. Russell's pamphlet on the subject, and he is quite convincing. Perhaps, we will have time for some sea bathing ourselves."

"But you will catch your death, Mrs. Wickham!" cried Mr. Meyerson.

Elizabeth smile apologetically and shook her head, hoping he would understand her silent message. *Pay her no mind and she may discontinue this incessant prattling on her own.*

When at length they arrived in London, Elizabeth thought it best to send a note to her uncle but, seeing that they were to change conveyances and continue on their journey almost at once, the party did not wait for Mr. Gardiner's reply.

She praised the heavens above when Lydia had exhausted her repertoire of silly observations and they were able to sit quietly, each lost in their own thoughts. However, that silent revere did not last long. They heard the driver shouting expletives as the carriage suddenly swerved off to the side of the road. Lydia peered behind the dingy drapery and gasped at the sight.

"It is the Prince!" she cried. "It appears the royal entourage is headed for Brighton."

"They nearly ran us off the road. The poor man handling the ribbons must have had an apoplexy, and for what?" Elizabeth huffed. "I wager our reasons for traveling far outweigh Prinny's engagements."

This rousing turn of events provided Lydia with sufficient fodder for the remainder of the journey. "I was practically presented to royalty," she declared, "although it would be nearer to the truth if he had actually waved. But Lizzy! I think I saw the back of Prinny's head..."

As Lydia prattled on about the Prince Regent and his fashionable society, Mr. Darcy and Colonel Fitzwilliam paid another visit to The Whitley Whaler by the Sea. Securing his preferred location with his back towards the furthest corner, the Colonel kept an experienced eye on the door while Mr. Darcy ordered their modest dinner of stew and brown bread. The tavern was not quite full. Most of the locals stayed home for their supper, so the presence of a lone boy of nine or ten walking through the thick wooden door caused Mr. Darcy to take notice.

"Evenin' sir," the child said, with a tip of his cap as he approached the landlord.

"Good evenin' to you, lad. Yer father sent you to buy his dinner?"

"Ay, and two pints, if you please. Here be the payment." The boy dug deep into his pockets, pulling out the entrusted coinage.

The burly man leaned over the bar and accepted the halfpence. "Hey now! These coins are *warm*—"

"Yes sir," he proclaimed with the innocence due his age. "My da just made 'em."

"What's this? Why, you little thief!" The man shouted as he ran around to grab the boy.

Hearing the exchange, Mr. Darcy jumped in front of the lad while Colonel Fitzwilliam pounced upon the publican, who was ready to snatch the boy by the scuff of his neck.

"Let me cover the boy's expenses." Mr. Darcy set down an exorbitant amount of money and watched as the owner quickly snatched it away.

"It's all right now, lad," Colonel Fitzwilliam said as the man backed away and returned to his station behind the bar. "The landlord was a bit confused, you see, but look now—he is preparing your da's dinner. Will you not sit with us and share our meal while you wait? You look hungry enough to eat my portion as well as Mr. Darcy's." The colonel ruffled the boy's hair and smiled reassuringly.

"He looks angry," said the child, looking up at Mr. Darcy's determined face. "Are you for cert it be alright? Seems I already am in trouble..."

"Do not pay him any mind. He growls when he is hungry."

"I do not growl." Mr. Darcy rolled his eyes.

The boy could not help but laugh and took a seat alongside the Colonel. The men watched as he wolfed down the beef stew and, when the barmaid brought over a box with the requested food, they nodded as the boy tipped his cap in gratitude and watched as he quickly made for home. Mr. Darcy and the colonel waited only a moment before arising and following the child into the night. Such was their desire to remain out of his sight, they failed to notice someone else had quietly quitted the room.

Several streets away, George Wickham walked down the cumbersome steps of the secret passage, mentally tallying his share of the take. Lieutenant Thompson, illuminating their path, led the way, silently cursing Wakefield, Wickham and whoever else had ever caused him strife. As they crossed the threshold, they were met with three other men, all busily attending the production line. Mr. Wickham was nonplussed at seeing them in action but said not a word until, he came upon the shadowy figures of men bound and secured in the dark crevices of the warehouse. When one of Thompson's men dashed passed him on a hurried assignment, his flickering rushlight shone brightly exposing the captives—nearly causing Mr. Wickham to gasp aloud.

"What are you planning to do with them?" His tone remained nonchalant, his curiosity aloof.

The lieutenant shrugged his shoulder. "I have yet to make up my mind. If I had let them go early on, they would have caused us trouble. We need to complete this shipment and see it on its way to the Continent. Only then will I see what's to be done."

Wickham nodded silently as his eyes met with those of Mr. Bennet's. Uncertain of how to proceed, he cowardly turned his back on his father-in-law and hastily filled his allotted sacks with gold, wishing everyone to the devil. It seemed no matter how hard he tried, he thought, he was always foiled in his schemes one way or another. Not this time—this time, he would win. He would see to it and no one, not Darcy or Bennet, would get in his way.

Upstairs, the young boy arrived with his father's dinner. Innocent of the goings on below, he called out, "Da, your dinner is gettin' cold!" His father laid down his tools, gathered his things, and climbed the stairs to meet his son. They left the building as Mr. Darcy and Colonel Fitzwilliam rounded the corner.

"We should have come prepared with pistols," the colonel declared.

"At least you do not look ridiculous walking around with a weapon," replied Darcy. "Carrying around this smallsword, I appear ready for a costume ball."

The colonel scoffed. "When was the last time you trained?"

Darcy did not wish to admit it, but he had been lax with his training. His last sessions with Monsieur Pierre were several months ago when he, with no success or benefit, had attempted to overcome his frustration at losing Elizabeth's hand. Recalling his first offer of marriage still caused him shame and remorse. "Do not worry about me," Darcy muttered, attempting to focus on the present course of action. "I will manage."

The men entered the main room and were looking about as Lieutenant Thompson came up the concealed stairwell. Seeing the strangers poking around, Thompson charged—not at the officer, but towards the civilian—with his blade upheld. Mr. Darcy, ill prepared, dodged the foreswing as Colonel Fitzwilliam came to his defense. The impact of the colonel's running charge sent his opponent's blade back, but not far enough to knock the blade free of Thompson's hands. The arcing shot sliced the fabric of Darcy's shirt at the midsection, tearing into the flesh behind it.

The colonel attempted to attack again as a second man came running up from behind a door. Seeing George Wickham there, Darcy roared. "He is mine!

With only a second to decide how to react, Mr. Wickham chose to retreat and ran down the stairs once more, tripping on the final step and crying out. The other two men who had been working at their posts fled at once upon hearing Thompson's shouts. A crawl space led them out through the sewer, and they were free before Wickham hit the ground.

Catching the cur, who was scrambling to his feet, Darcy delivered the first blow. Wickham returned with a furious riposte, certain of his prowess over the master of Pemberley. Darcy concentrated on his defense, letting his muscles settle into the rhythm of swordplay. After what seemed an eternity of attempting to get past Wickham's parrying engagement, Darcy rallied and began to batter at his adversary as if to pound him into the ground. Wickham had not expected an equal opponent, and his simmering anger over all he had lost at Darcy's hands now boiled at a fevered pitch.

The hiss of the blades cut through the air. Their movements came with lighting speed. Darcy knew his cousin was battling above stairs but could not spare a thought to the colonel's safety. After an exhausting parlay, Wickham's attack began to ease in its brutality. He had expected an easy victory, foolishly expending an exorbitant amount of energy from the onset. It was evident to Darcy that his opponent was becoming careless.

Their weapons caught each other high in the air, and they stood belly to belly—face to face. Darcy's training had prepared him for this hazardous position and he expected a dagger to make an appearance or a heated fist, at the very least. With a final boost of energy, Darcy pushed away and prepared to strike a final blow. Wickham stumbled at this unexpected action, losing his weapon and falling hard against an old sideboard. Colonel Fitzwilliam had defeated his attacker and rushed to Darcy's aid, only to find his cousin holding the sword to George Wickham's chest.

"Darcy..." questioned the breathless colonel.

"He is pathetic," Darcy hissed, "a disgrace to his family and countrymen."

George Wickham, seeing the colonel and preferring the military man's sense of justice rather than Darcy's sense of retribution, held up his arms in surrender.

"Why should I spare you?" Darcy raged. "There are men out there half-starved, injured,—*dying*, while you steal their earnings and moan of life's inequity."

Immobilized, Wickham still found the audacity to reply. "And what have you done for God and country? You, who sit in your fine house and lord it over the rest of us?"

"You have the right of it. I have done naught other than attempt to deal with you with honor and integrity, but no more. I will do what I should have done, when first I found you with Georgiana."

"Think for a moment," the Colonel said in deep and controlled tone. "If you make Lydia his widow, you will lose Elizabeth."

Without removing his eyes from his nemesis, Darcy growled, "What would you have me do?"

"They will hang him," the Colonel replied, "even if you don't run him through."

"And Lydia will still be a widow—"

"But not by your hand." The colonel moved slowly to Wickham's side and faced his beleaguered cousin. "Listen to me! I can make arrangements to have him transported." Colonel Fitzwilliam produced a length of rope and began tying Wickham's hands, then peered up and saw Darcy's bloody attire. "You have been injured! Stand down, man. Let me see to your wounds."

"It is nothing," said Darcy, but slowly he lowered his weapon and nodded his acquiescence.

The colonel made quick work in securing the restraints and forcing Wickham to his feet. It was then that they heard men moaning and thrashing about.

"What the devil?"

"Mr. Bennet!" Darcy cried in disbelief. "My God, sir! What has happened?"

Throwing Wickham aside, they saw to Mr. Bennet and Mr. Meyerson, who had been maltreated but, thank the heavens above, were not seriously injured. The men demanded water, which was quickly sought and provided, at which point Colonel Fitzwilliam helped them each to take a seat. Mr. Meyerson provided a brief synopsis of what had occurred and pointed out the barrels of real gold as opposed to the counterfeit product which had been marked for urgent delivery.

"We had best get above stairs and see to your wounds Darcy, and to our friends here," declared the colonel.

"I am fine, Richard," Darcy protested. "My first concern is for Mr. Bennet and Mr. Meyerson."

"Stop your grumbling, man and, for once in your life, do as I say."

"I do not grumble," replied Darcy cautiously making his way up the stairwell.

They found Thompson lying face down by the door as they led Wickham to the street. Having walked from the tavern, it was now incumbent upon the colonel to find some sort of conveyance but, as he was looking about, he espied Corporal Fletcher leading the constable and Colonel Forster to their aid.

Reporting to the officials, Colonel Fitzwilliam gave a quick and concise description of what had occurred. The constable's men entered the building and retrieved the wounded lieutenant, throwing him and Wickham in chains. Once they were taken away, Mr. Bennet and Mr. Meyerson were gingerly handed off to Colonel Forster's care. The men were to be accompanied to their lodgings under his private escort.

Finally settling in Forster's carriage, Mr. Darcy scowled and shook his head in disgust.

"I know what you are thinking, Cousin, but you need not worry. I can have him shipped to Buenos Aires," Colonel Fitzwilliam snickered. "The red coats have been struggling to get a stronghold there. Between the *gauchos* and *criollos*, Wickham will have a hell of a time working off his sentence. Lydia can follow the drum all the way to the River Plate and you will be rid of the lot of them."

"Is it fair to Lydia?" Darcy muttered.

"You can still ask that?

"I am only thinking of Elizabeth," he winced and internalized a complaint of pain.

"You need not worry overmuch. There is a small community of second sons looking to make their fortunes in that country, not to mention a handful of businessmen and their families–Lydia will have some society there."

"So be it," Darcy declared and he said no more as the military caravan made its way through the seedier part of town.

In a far more respectable quarter, Mr. Meyerson was assisting the ladies to alight from their conveyance. They had finally arrived at their lodgings. It was not a minute too soon, for Elizabeth's nerves would not support another word coming from her sister's mouth. She was determined to begin her search for her father and Mr. Darcy. However, Mr. Meyerson decidedly rejected that plan.

"Miss Elizabeth, I cannot allow you to roam the streets at this hour. Pray, see to Mrs. Wickham and settle into your rooms. I will begin making a few discreet enquiries and report back to you immediately."

Unable to convince him to do otherwise, Elizabeth heeded his words. She and Lydia made themselves at home and while Lydia unpacked and complained of wrinkled dresses, Elizabeth could only pace about the room in silent desperation. Mr. Meyerson, good to his word, directed a few questions to the landlady, but having not received any news of consequence, took to the streets instead.

Walking briskly, without any real notion of where he was heading or what he was looking for, Mr. Meyerson felt his heart skip a beat when he observed two carriages surrounded by a military escort rounding the corner just ahead. Riveted with a peculiar mixture of fear and anticipation, he watched as his father and Mr. Bennet were assisted out of the conveyance while a military officer and Mr. Darcy descend from the other.

"Papa!" David Meyerson shouted as he ran towards the assemblage. "*Papa!*"

A soldier briefly held him at bay until his father called out in return. Colonel Forster allowed the young man to approach and averted his eyes as father and son embraced. The party entered the men's lodgings as Colonel Fitzwilliam quickly dispatched a runner to fetch the surgeon. Having seen to Darcy's needs, the colonel went off to make arrangements for Wickham's sentencing and transportation. He knew his cousin would not rest until the blackguard's punishment was secured.

All the while, David Meyerson questioned and badgered his father until he was assured of his well-being. Then, remembering his traveling companions anxiously awaiting his return, Mr. Meyerson, junior, directed his attentions to the other gentleman in the room.

"I am most pleased to see you, Mr. Bennet. Your daughters will sing praises when I share the good news. I should think they would be well and settled by now. I would be most happy to bring them to you."

"My girls are in Brighton?"

"Mrs. Wickham is here, sir, and Miss Elizabeth."

Mr. Bennet shook his head in fervent denial. "I would not have the girls see me like this, and Mr. Darcy—" he paused and looked to see the great man laid low. "Mr. Darcy has been injured. I do not consent to their calling upon us at this time."

The runner arrived, with the surgeon following closely behind. David Meyerson removed himself and followed Mr. Meyerson to his chamber, where he saw to his father's comfort, ordering him a hot bath and some nourishment. Seeing first to his needs and realizing that sleep was the most effective remedy, David quitted the room and returned to the ladies.

Upon returning to their rooms, he found Mrs Wickham at the mirror adjusting her bonnet and Miss Bennet wearing a hole into the landlady's good rug.

"They are well," he assured the sisters. "I have seen them." He continued to divulge a summary of the events as they had been related to him, and reiterated that the men were resting.

"Then take us to them, Mr. Meyerson. Let us away at once!" Elizabeth cried.

Unable to raise his eyes to hers, Mr. Meyerson could only repeat what Mr. Bennet had dictated. "I do not have your father's authorization. They need their rest, Miss Bennet. Pray, allow them this evening to set themselves to right."

Disheartened, Elizabeth nodded her understanding and watched as Mr. Meyerson retired to his own chamber, spent and grateful. As Lydia sulked and grumbled, believing her sister heeded her unending complaints, Elizabeth penned a missive. If she could not see her Mr. Darcy, at least she could send word. She could not bear that he would spend another night uncertain of her feelings. With quill in hand, the words came easily, for she used his own declarations to prove the intensity of her emotions.

My dearest William, in vain I have struggled. It will not do! My feelings will not be repressed. I have searched my soul and acknowledged my affections. My wishes are unchanged! You have my admiration, my respect, and my love.

Yours, Elizabeth~

Before sealing the letter, she included a gift she had had fashioned especially for their wedding day. Enclosed in a velvet pouch was her grandmother's locket made into a watch fob for the man who had won her heart. Sending off the missive, Elizabeth released a sigh of relief. It was done. Tomorrow they would begin again.

THE MORNING CAME AND WENT, AND THEY HAD NO WORD. MR. Meyerson escorted the ladies to the parlor for afternoon tea and cakes, and still they were kept waiting.

"Why does he not come?" cried Elizabeth. "Why is there no reply?"

Mr. Meyerson, in good conscience, could no longer withhold the full of it. He assured Elizabeth he had indeed told her the truth. Both their fathers were well and resting, however, there was more to be said.

"It appears Mr. Darcy might have been injured, ma'am. Your good father wished for the gentleman's needs to be met before you were brought to him."

Elizabeth grabbed hold of the armchair in her attempt to cool her rising temper. "Take me to him at once, Mr. Meyerson."

"A man's sick room is no place for a young lady."

"I am to be his wife! Propriety must not hold sway in matters such as these. Do you think I shall faint at the sight of his blood? Men may call us the weaker sex, but heaven only knows that inaccuracy is only used to endorse *men's* beliefs. Pray, allow me the courtesy of knowing my own strength."

"And what of my husband?" Lydia finally had the courage to ask.

With no compunction whatsoever, Mr. Meyerson's reply was terse and to the point. "He has been taken by the constable, madam. I believe you will have to ask his permission for an audience."

She nodded her understanding and quietly whispered, "I will go to him." Showing more restraint than ever before witnessed by any family member or acquaintance, Lydia Wickham quitted the room.

"And I will just fetch my pelisse and gloves, sir," said Elizabeth, brooking no argument. Mr. Meyerson stood by the door awaiting her return, and when she reentered the parlor, he silently placed her hand on his arm as they walked towards the men's lodgings.

Greeting her father with wet kisses as tears slipped down her cheeks, Elizabeth sent up a prayer of gratitude that he was, indeed, unharmed. She gazed about the room, desperate and impatient to see her William, but he was nowhere to be found.

"He is abed," Mr. Bennet murmured. "I would have spared you, daughter. Mr. Darcy is having a difficult time of it."

"What has been done?" she murmured softly.

"The surgeon has come and gone, my dear. He has plied his needle and closed the wound, which he assured us was not life threatening, but when the fever came on, the surgeon let his blood in order to release the infection."

"And yet, he is unwell?" Elizabeth exclaimed, feeling her ire rise.

"Perhaps we should have the surgeon return," the senior Mr. Meyerson suggested, waving his son off to find the man.

"Nay! I will not have him bled to death! Grandmère would have recoiled at the thought of bloodletting and leeches." She began pacing the room, holding her hand to her head, pleading to God for strength and direction. "I may not know much, but I know my way around a garden. Send the cook to me at once!" Elizabeth suddenly cried. "And I have need for paper and quill."

David Meyerson went quickly in search for the cook and the requested items, returning post haste with the harried old woman and the writing materials.

"I beg your pardon for removing you from your duties," said Elizabeth, "but I must impose on your hospitality and skills. "I am in need of several items from your garden. Are you familiar with goose grass?"

When the cook nodded, wide eyed and dumbstruck, Elizabeth continued. "Pray, prepare a poultice, and I shall apply it to Mr. Darcy's wound. Might you have a tincture of goldenrod? Have you elderberry stored? I shall require copious amounts for tea. It will reduce his fever."

The woman bobbed a curtsey and was released to the kitchen to begin her assignments.

"To whom do you wish to write?" Mr. Bennet enquired.

"On our travel, we came across the royal entourage," she recounted. "The Prince is in residency, Papa, and where Prinny goes, so goes his personal physician. Write to the good doctor and ask him to attend us."

"Do you think the doctor would come, Lizzy? Who are we for the likes of him?"

"He would come for the nephew of the Earl of Matlock. Explain that Fitzwilliam Darcy has been wounded while serving the Crown. If the Prince Regent will not send his physician, he will most certainly have to answer to the Right Honorable Lady Catherine de Bourgh!"

Having dispatched her instructions, Elizabeth asked to be shown to Mr. Darcy's room. Mr. David Meyerson led the lady himself, not wasting time on any further discussion. "That was very well done,

Miss Bennet," he said as they walked down a narrow hallway. "If ever I am laid low and in need of clear and precise thought, I will call for you."

She nodded silently. All thoughts now were for her William, and when she walked across the threshold and saw him thrashing about in his bed, Elizabeth brought her fist to her lips. She would not cry. She would not faint! Although they had not said the words yet, they belonged to one another—for better, or for worse, in sickness and in health—and God willing, she would nurse him back to his full strength and vigor.

A maid had slipped into the room carrying a tray of elderberry tea and the vial of tincture Elizabeth had requested. The poultice had been prepared, and a bowl of cool water was set aside by a stack of fresh linen. The woman bobbed and took a seat in the shadows while David Meyerson silently retreated.

Elizabeth approached her beloved's bed, still refusing herself the luxury of tears. Dropping to meet him, she kissed William's forehead and felt the heat on her own lips. Without hesitation, although never having seen a man in such a state of undress, Elizabeth first removed his bedclothes and then removed the bandage the surgeon had placed there. Recoiling momentarily at the uneven stitches and the infection that oozed from the wound, she determined to clean the area with the tincture before applying the goose grass. Blessing the memory of Grandmère, Elizabeth was grateful for having received these time honored secrets.

Mr. Bennet and Rabbi Meyerson announced their arrival with a quiet scratch at the door. Elizabeth acknowledged them with a smile, but turned back to her patient, whom she would not leave. She heard them stepping in and out of the room for the rest of the afternoon and throughout the night, concerned not only for the afflicted gentleman but for the stringent dictates of propriety. The servant snored quietly from her chair in the shadows. Elizabeth, with no thought to her audience, coaxed Mr. Darcy to sip the medicinal tea and, when he would not comply, she dipped her fingers in the liquid and wet his parched lips. Applying cool linens to his forehead, she prayed that his fever would break and whispered encouragements throughout the night.

"Please, my love, wake up. I have come to you, William. I have come!"

At length, the first few rays of morning light broke through heavy drapes that obscured the chalk white cliffs and the melodic kittiwakes that nested there. The flittering light danced across his sandy eyes and Darcy awoke to find Elizabeth lying by his side.

"Wha...what are you doing here?" he mumbled.

Elizabeth startled upon hearing his voice and was at once alert and coherent. "Mr. Darcy! *William*! Do you mean to frighten me by making me come all this way and finding you thus? Are you attempting to renege on your commitment, sir?"

"I—I do not—renege..."

In her relief, she had begun to tease him, but Elizabeth quickly recognized the error of her ways. He was not yet himself. It was not becoming to make a mockery of their predicament. Pressing her lips upon his brow, she whispered, "Rest, dearest. We will have plenty of time to do battle in future."

He slept peacefully now, yet she would not leave his side. When Mr. Bennet entered the room, he found his daughter asleep at the foot of the bed. He did not have the heart to wake her. "To the devil with propriety," he thought as he quit the room.

When, hours later, her patient stirred, Elizabeth dutifully awoke and felt his brow. She smiled at his disheveled appearance and wondered what William would think of his state *of déshabillé.*

"You are laughing at me again," he croaked.

"Not at all, dearest. I am—relieved. I am *grateful*. Pray, believe me, it was quite a shock to find you in this manner. When we arrived in Brighton, we had not a clue of what had befallen you. I had sent a message as soon as Mr. Meyerson informed us of your whereabouts..."

"You sent word to me? I did not have the pleasure of receiving it."

"No, of course not, William. You were otherwise engaged," she said, unable to check her impish reply. "Papa would not allow us to call, but I could not wait another moment without letting you know—"

"Why did you come all this way? What did you have to say that could not wait until I return to Longbourn?"

Seeing her beloved's eyes filled with torment, Elizabeth fetched the envelope she had inscribed with his name. It had been delivered on a silver tray and placed on the desk by the window, awaiting his attention. She carefully opened the document, unfolded the page and, without taking her eyes off of his, recited the message word for word.

"And there you have it, my love. I leave it in your hands to decide how we are to proceed," she whispered.

"Can you doubt my response? Even still? Tell me, what made you distrust my love?"

"I did not distrust you, I distrusted *myself*. I did not trust that we were well-matched, that I was the wife you deserved—that Pemberley deserved."

Mr. Darcy was much aggrieved that they once again had suffered due to his inability to communicate his emotions. How could he express something so profound, so *otherworldly*, that even the greatest psalmists could not do it justice? Gazing at her glistening eyes, he knew he must try.

"My heart aches to hear your doubt, for there does not exist, nor will there ever exist, two people better suited. When I was given life, the good Lord sent only a shell of a man to dwell on this earth. My love for my excellent parents, my cherished sister, or for Pemberley could not fill the void that existed in my heart. Our souls reunited that night at the Meryton assembly and, although I behaved abominably, the angels in heaven were celebrating our reencounter. We are connected, Elizabeth. Of that there can be no doubt. It is something akin to your love of nature, of soil and roots and water and sunlight. Your seedlings could not thrive without one of these components...as I could not thrive without you."

Unable to speak, Elizabeth permitted her tears to flow without shame, without fear. He had spoken from his heart before. That day on Oakham Mount, he bared his soul and lay it at her feet. She had been stunned by the emotion, astonished by his declaration, and overcome with relief. Today was an altogether different experience. He revealed his truth to her and, this time, her heart believed.

CHAPTER SEVENTEEN

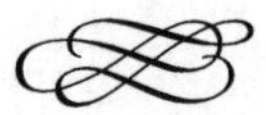

23rd of November

It was a cold and blistery afternoon when Mrs. Bennet decided to order the carriage and ride into Meryton. The house was quiet with only Jane and Mary at home, and she could no longer bear the silence. With whom could she bicker without Lizzy being present? By whom could she be entertained without Lydia about? She was for town and would pay a visit to her sister, Mrs. Phillips. They had not had the chance to catch up on all the gossip these long weeks, and Mrs. Bennet found she had much to tell.

Mrs. Phillips was always glad to receive visitors, and her sister, due to her recent absence, was particularly welcome. She was quite aware of the comings and goings at Longbourn but, to Mrs. Phillips chagrin, she did not have knowledge of the essentials. Why had Mr. Bennet disappeared? What relation did the family have with those Meyersons? Mrs. Phillips had been quite in awe of the Londoners at first, but her contemplation of the strangers was soon put to an end when she learned they were foreigners and, worse yet, dissidents.

While she had been long known for being hospitable and welcoming—even Mr. Collins had admired her manners and politeness and commented on her elegant civility—she could not be expected to open the doors to her home to *Hebrews*. It was with this air of intrigue and condescension that Mrs. Bennet was received, for Mrs. Phillips only wished to riddle her with questions and seemed quite determined to dislike her new friends.

"What I cannot comprehend, Sister—and you will forgive me for being so forthright—but how can you permit Kitty to spend so much time alone with those people?" Mrs. Phillips admonished. "Heaven only knows what they are about!"

Mrs. Bennet lowered her cup from lips in order to respond, but she no sooner set down the delicate saucer when her hostess continued with her disparaging line of questioning.

"I could hardly keep my countenance when we first saw the lot of them prancing about in the street! Whatever did they mean by such a hoydenish display?"

"Mrs. Meyerson explained their unusual behavior as being celebratory in nature. It is their custom to rejoice when bringing the Word of God to their new home—"

"But that is my point...*whose* God?"

"Such a question! I am ashamed of you, Sister. There is but *One*." Mrs. Bennet pursed her lips in the attempt to curtail further provocation. "You and I have had our share of rejection and ridicule, have we not? When our papa was not long for this world, he called us to his side and bade us to heed his will. Do you recall?"

"I was to marry Mr. Phillips so that he could continue with Papa's work," Mrs. Phillips muttered. "And you—you were allowed to marry Mr. Bennet, a landed gentleman, so that your children could rise above the taint of trade."

"Precisely—*the taint of trade.* I still recall receiving the cut direct from the Misses Sutton when we arrived at Limbrick Hall. Not a soul would speak to us! Our dance cards were left untouched. No gentlemen would dare approach the lowly Misses Gardiner."

"I cannot credit your lack of comprehension of the matter, for it is to *that* point which I speak! What has become of Mr. Bennet? Hmm? Am I the only one concerned with poor Jane and Lizzy? You have achieved that which was impossible for us. The girls have secured their future—or at least, they had done so, until those people arrived. Would you have me believe it is a coincidence their nuptials were postponed just as the Meyersons came to Meryton?"

Mrs. Bennet rolled her eyes and laughed. "For once in your life, I dare say, you do not have knowledge of all the particulars. The Meyersons are not at fault! Shall I remind you of the picnic in Harpenden Bury or the Michaelmas celebration at Bamville House? We were detested and set upon for being interlopers in their society. Such cruelty! Perhaps, seen in this prudential light, you can remember the Golden Rule, Sister, and treat the Meyersons with Christian kindness."

"I tell you, those people are cursed and bring a trail of bad luck wherever they go."

Mrs. Bennet arose and gathered her wrap about her, the bite from her sister's venomous speech more shocking to her person than the chill outdoors. "I must be on my way," said she. "I have forgotten a previous engagement with a dear friend."

Mrs. Phillips was all astonishment. Never had her sister spoken to her in this manner. "But Fanny, you have only just arrived. We have not had an opportunity to speak for days and days! How can you set me aside for *that* woman?"

"It pains me to hear you speak so, for Mrs. Meyerson and I have grown quite close in the short amount of time we have been acquainted. They are different, to be sure," Mrs. Bennet admitted, "but not in the ways that you think. It would behoove you to search your soul and find what is lacking there. What compels you to lash out to these newcomers who have shown nothing but friendship and allegiance?"

Overcome with grief and vexation, Mrs. Bennet left her sister's parlor and decided that calling on Mrs. Meyerson would help fill the void. There would be an added benefit for Kitty, as mother and daughter would be conveyed home together, snug and warm in Mr. Bennet's coach. Satisfied with her new plan, she provided the coachman his instructions and set off.

Mrs. Meyerson was found in her parlor unpacking a box of bric-à-brac just as the Mistress of Longbourn was announced. Kitty and Rachel looked up from the picture book they were perusing and welcomed her in from the cold with cries of delight and surprise.

"Mama, is everything well at home?" Kitty asked, quite startled at her mother's impromptu arrival.

Mrs. Bennet soon found herself settled by the fire with tea and cake by her side. "Yes, dear, all is well, but dreadfully dull. Jane and Mr. Bingley keep company at Netherfield surrounded by his relations, and Mary keeps to her books."

"Then I am glad you are come, Mama!" Kitty exclaimed. "For we are ever diverted here in this house, are we not, little Rachel?"

"We are glad you are come," the child echoed and returned her thumb to its favored place.

"Tell me, whatever are you about?" Mrs. Bennet asked, curious at the overflowing crates filled with homespun and tattered linens.

"I am still unpacking," Mrs. Meyerson sighed, "although my interest in the project is but a little."

"It is sometimes pleasurable to unfold a long forgotten item from its wrappings. Do you not find it so?"

With a shrug of her shoulders, Mrs. Meyerson discarded a half-opened package. "To tell the truth, your visit is a welcome diversion, my dear. I own my strength and courage are waning with each day that passes without word from my husband."

"We all of us have been worried," Mrs. Bennet soothed. "How could we not be?"

"It is unbecoming for a rabbi's wife to be so fearful," Mrs. Meyerson owned. "My lack of faith does not set a good example for my husband's congregation."

"Oh! But you are mistaken, Mrs. Meyerson," Kitty exclaimed. "Even I, who am not of your husband's flock, have been inspired by your example. Indeed, I have begun a course of reading on my own."

Mrs. Bennet was all astonishment at this statement. She had done her part as a dutiful mother and had attempted to see to her offspring's' spiritual education. How many times had she reprimanded the girls for their irreverent behavior whilst the vicar gave his homily? Other than dear Mary, she had not been sensible of her daughters sharing any great passion on that score.

Kitty blushed under her mother's gaze and felt the need to expand on her surprising comments. Her family had become accustomed to thinking her such a ninny but, this time away from Lydia and from the scrutiny of Longbourn had been put to good use. With her sisters being married off one by one, Kitty had begun considering her own prospects—not that she had many from which to choose—but she was not as silly as her father supposed.

"I had been appraising my chances of securing a good match, Mama—"

"Oh! Kitty, with one sister soon to be at Netherfield and another at Pemberley, I dare say you might find yourself with many young men from whom to choose."

"Yes, but what if I do not find a Mr. Bingley or a Mr. Darcy? I began to consider what would happen if I did not marry. As a gentleman's daughter, there would be very few options. Something that Mrs. Meyerson said, that first evening we were together started me thinking..."

"What was it, my dear?"

"You had mentioned the school for girls—for those who had to earn their living. You spoke of a curriculum for nursing, I believe. My thoughts were befuddled. I was at once envious of the opportunity being afforded them and ashamed for my ingratitude. Here I am, quiet and comfortable, while they have to toil for their daily bread. I wondered, could it be that God made them poor in order for His plans to unfold? How are we to determine what is just? These thoughts gave me pause."

"I am not certain I follow, my dear," Mrs. Meyerson confessed.

"Our families suffer from the same affliction," Kitty continued with some hesitation. She was uncomfortable sharing her thoughts, for she was afraid of being ridiculed or, worse yet, of being told to be silent. "A set of circumstances have unfolded which have caused our loved ones to be away from home. We neither can understand nor control the outcome. We simply must have faith as we learned last Sunday when we read Proverbs. Do you recall it, Mama?"

Although she never thought slightingly of her children, Mrs. Bennet was overcome with this sudden change in Kitty's character and could only nod her head in agreement.

"Trust in the Lord with all thine heart and lean not unto thine own understanding," Kitty recited. "I had heard this before, of course, but never had I thought about its meaning. Perhaps we are to partner with the Almighty by working faithfully with whatever is our portion and trust in Him to see us right."

"Kitty, my dear, what are you saying?" asked Mrs. Bennet.

"Simply this: if we have faith that the Lord watches over us, then we should trust that He knows best. Who am I to understand? I cannot even foresee when Lydia will devise a plan which will cause us to fall into disfavor with one and all!"

Mrs. Meyerson was shaken by this unexpected soliloquy. Finding a seat, she slowly lowered herself into the comfort of its support. "My dear, you have stirred my soul! While I have striven for *emunah*, I have lacked *bitachon*," she whispered. "Kitty, you have reminded me of an important lesson. Faith and trust are two different things."

The Bennet ladies watched as Mrs. Meyerson arose and began frantically pulling items from an abandoned container.

"Oh dear!" she cried. "Where is it?"

"What are you looking for, Mrs. Meyerson? May I be of assistance?" Kitty asked with great alacrity.

"The *chanukkiah*!" the lady responded. "It should be here. I must find it for, on Sunday eve, on the twenty-ninth, we will light the first candle of Chanukah. I have been so consumed with worry, I had forgotten."

"What is this *Chanukah*?" Mrs. Bennet asked. "It cannot be dissimilar to our winter holidays, which, I dare say, are still a month away."

"Oh, but it is, for we are commemorating something that occurred nearly two hundred years before the birth of your savior. In fact, he would have lit a *chanukkiah* to remember the great miracle."

"Mrs. Meyerson, you will need to explain!" Kitty giggled with delight, bringing little Rachel upon her lap. "It is too provocative to leave us guessing."

"I would be happy to relate the story, if you are certain..."

"Please," begged Kitty, "proceed *rebbetzin*."

"Very well. It was during the time of the second Temple. The Holy Land was ruled by a cruel people. They forbade the study of our holy texts, robbed the Jews of their property, and set up idols in our holy house of prayer. No one could stand up against them, until Mattathias ben Johanan—"

"My goodness, such a commanding name!" Mrs. Bennet could not help but interject her observation.

"It befits his role in the story, my dear, for he and his powerful sons rose up and rebelled. There were many battles. It took nearly three years but, in the end, this small band known as the Maccabees defeated the mighty armies."

"*Maccabees*, what does it mean?"

"It is the Hebrew word for hammer. They were named thusly because they fought fiercely against their enemies. The evil men, in a last attempt to humiliate and insult the Jews, desecrated the temple and destroyed the consecrated oil needed to light the *Ner Tamid*, the everlasting light."

"That was the episode to which Rachel referred?"

"Precisely! When the last battle had been won and the Jewish people were able to rededicate the holy sanctuary, a single vessel of oil was found—it was enough to last one day. So great was their trust, their *bitachon*, the Maccabees lit the lamp and prayed. Lo and behold, the oil burned for eight days! Our people commemorate these events by lighting a *chanukkiah*, or rather, a nine-branch candelabrum—and here it is!" she exclaimed holding up the venerated object at last.

Mrs. Bennet had no compunction in admitting she had never heard of such happenings. "I see now, Mrs. Meyerson, that it is unseemly to compare our holidays simply because they occur at the same time of the year."

"Not at all, Mrs. Bennet, for each has its merits and, closely scrutinized, each holiday speaks of bringing Light into a dark world. Kitty has reminded me: We must keep our faith in front of us and we shall reap the rewards."

Mrs. Bennet brought a delicate handkerchief to her lips and muffled a fit of giggles. "Mrs. Meyerson," she whispered, "I believe I shall be *reaping* my own reward in four or five months."

"Oh, my dear! Your morning ailments...?"

She nodded and stole a glance towards Kitty, not wishing her to overhear. "Who would have thought it? At my age?"

"You are a woman in her prime and, in any case, it *is* the season of miracles, is it not?"

When it was time to take their leave, the women hugged and cried upon saying their goodnights. Kitty could only assume they were anxious for their husbands. She commiserated with the sentiment and, in the spirit of the lessons learned in the Meyerson household, sent a prayer up to heaven.

That evening when the house was still and all were abed, a courier came to Longbourn. Jane, who had remained awake and overheard Hill at the door, quickly descended the stairs to receive whatever urgent news was heralded their way. Retreating quickly back to her chamber, she ripped open the note, for she could no longer bear to not know what was happening. She recognized her father's handwriting.

Dear ones,

We will be home by Friday morn, not being able to travel on the Sabbath— neither the rabbi's nor our own! Have everything at the ready, for the weddings will take place, God-willing, on Sunday the twenty-ninth.

CHAPTER EIGHTEEN

29th of November

"... Therefore marriage is not to be entered into unadvisedly or lightly, but reverently, deliberately, and in accordance with the purposes for which it was instituted by God."

Elizabeth fought to suppress an errant giggle. It seemed the Book of Common Prayer had been written with the Bennet family in mind. What would the vicar do if she laughed *now* in the middle of the wedding ceremony? What of William? Oh no. That would not do—but it was too provoking. Here she was being charged not to enter into marriage unadvisedly or lightly. Heavens, if she had deliberated over the matter for one more day, she might have lost him forever! Elizabeth put all levity aside upon hearing the vicar address her directly and focused on the solemnity of the cherished moment. After all, it was not every day one married one's Mr. Darcy.

"Elizabeth, will you have this man to be your husband; to live together in the covenant of marriage? Will you love him, comfort him, honor and keep him, in sickness and in health; and, forsaking all others, be faithful to him as long as you both shall live?"

She uttered the words that seemed so small yet represented all her heart, all her being. "I will." The vicar then posed the question to Fitzwilliam Darcy, and he responded with a hale and hearty, "I will."

Jane and Mr. Bingley, who stood to her right, were wed in the same manner, but Elizabeth noted none of her own humor in her sister's tranquil countenance. She could not deny her sister's felicity, for she knew her better than anyone else—Jane and her Mr. Bingley would do very well together. They were each of them so complying, so generous. *But*, she thought, *I am the happiest creature in the world. I am happier even than Jane; she only smiles, I laugh!* And then at once, Elizabeth's attention returned to the solemn matter at hand as the vicar put the final question to the congregation.

"Will all of you witnessing these promises do all in your power to uphold these persons in their marriages?"

The couples heard a resounding "We Will!" from dear family and friends, including the Meyersons, who had been accepted and included in all of Meryton's affairs.

Mrs. Phillips, unable to control her ignoble disposition, rolled her eyes at seeing the Hebrew clergyman seated amongst the congregation but, when the vicar himself acknowledged the man and his wife *and* had them escorted to an advantageous location, Mrs. Phillips had to admit defeat and resignation.

At least she would have sufficient gossip to share, for the party were all astounded when Lady Catherine de Bourgh and her daughter Anne arrived, escorted by the distinguished Colonel Fitzwilliam himself. It seemed that Kitty had sent word to Rosings—how could she not, her niece later exclaimed, when she was given leave by the lady to remain in communication?

It appeared the grand lady's presence brought some much needed relief to Miss Caroline Bingley and her sister, Mrs. Hurst, for their sour demeanor transformed quite considerably when Lady Catherine chose a seat by their side. The party had been rather small and insignificant, in Miss Bingley's estimation, but taken into account that the congregation consisted of an earl's son and a noblewoman, she no longer feared being rebuked by Society for attending such a rustic affair.

The wedding breakfast was to be held at the Bennet residence. The blissful couples were seen off with great fanfare in festooned carriages, trimmed with boughs of evergreen and colorful ribbons. As family and guests made their way to Longbourn, Kitty found herself walking beside Mr. David Meyerson. They had been much thrown together during her afternoon visits to his mother's home, and she had missed his company while he had been at Brighton. Truth be told, she had missed more than just his witty conversation and knowledge of the world. Kitty Bennet believed herself to be in love.

"I am glad you are come back, Mr. Meyerson," she murmured. "I did not have the opportunity to thank you for your kindness in helping my sisters. I fear things might have been different had you not been along."

"You need not thank me, Miss Catherine, for I did but a little. Your sister, Miss Elizabeth—or rather, *Mrs. Darcy*—was the true champion. It was her quick thinking that saved the day! You are truly blessed to have such a sister. Pay attention to her guidance. She will not lead you astray."

"While that is true, sir, I believe I have learned a great many things in *your* household. I believe I would enjoy learning more of your ways—"

David Meyerson was not a conceited young man, but he knew that Miss Catherine Bennet had formed an attachment to him in the last several weeks. He knew her to be a sweet, generous girl, but there was nothing for it. His eager acceptance to escort the sisters to Brighton had not been a selfless act. Naturally he wished to be of assistance to his father and Mr. Bennet, but there had been something else. He was no London rogue. He had no desire to injure the young lady's tender heart, and so, he gladly accepted the opportunity to put some distance between them. It was his hope that, during his absence, she would see things in a more sensible light.

"Now that my father has returned," he said, hoping to sound cavalier, "I am for London. I should not return to Hertfordshire for quite some time."

"Oh! I had not thought...that is to say, must you go so soon?"

He nodded and tried to swallow the knot that had suddenly developed in his throat. "I must finish what I have started and make my way in the world."

"I plan to study with your mama," Kitty declared. "I wish to learn more of Judaism. I wonder, do you approve?"

Mr. Meyerson noted that the rest of the party were busy chatting amongst themselves. No one paid them any mind, so accustomed were they to seeing Miss Catherine with his family.

"I find it commendable that you wish to study and appreciate new ideas and philosophies, but you should do so because *you* wish it and not—and not because you believe it would please anyone else," he said, wanting to take hold of her hand to show his fraternal regard. Knowing that propriety would disallow such an action, Mr. Meyerson remained stoic and walked on, keeping his eyes on the road ahead.

Uncomfortable with her silence—which said more than if she had given voice to her thoughts—he continued.

"You honor me, Miss Bennet, with your friendship and your confidences. I would humbly offer this advice: seek out Mr. Ainsely and learn from his wisdom. Put your questions to him. Allow the vicar to enlighten your path."

Kitty shook her head and grinned. "Mary has been the family member most inclined to seek his counsel. To be sure, Lydia and I have giggled our way through most of his sermons. It has only been since her withdrawal from Longbourn that I have come to recognize my folly."

"I would have you begin your studies with Mr. Ainsely then. After all, one must have a solid understanding of one's own philosophies before looking to take on another's. And, if I may, do not allow Mary's views to dictate your convictions. You must forge your own thoughts, your *own* relationship with the Lord. And then," he paused and smiled gently, "the journey within can truly begin. We *must* be true to ourselves, Miss Bennet. Do you understand my meaning?"

Kitty had listened, but her love only grew stronger at his kindness. His rejection was all the more bittersweet. She nodded and smiled as a teardrop fell upon her cheek. Kitty looked away so that he would not notice. She preferred his respect rather than his pity. Calling out for little Rachel, she clasped hands with the child, and the three walked along, following in her parents' path.

When the happy couples at length were seen off and the last of the party had departed Longbourn, Mr. and Mrs. Bennet were found in the dining room quite alone, sharing the last bit of port between them.

"What shall we do now, Mrs. Bennet, with three daughters married?"

Surprised at being asked her opinion, Mrs. Bennet gave the

question some thought before replying. "I suppose we have earned a respite, husband. Let us see what Life has in store for us."

"No rest for the weary, my dear, for soon Mary will leave us and then Kitty. We shall have to make arrangements for the inevitable. Perhaps you can live with one of the girls when I am gone and Mr. Collins inherits the place."

"Mr. Bennet," she giggled, "you should have more *bitachon.*"

"I beg your pardon?"

Perhaps it was the port, or perhaps it was pure exhaustion, but Mrs. Bennet found she had no scruple in sharing the entire tale of Chanukah with her most astonished husband. "Pray Mr. Bennet," she concluded, "what was the true miracle of this holiday?"

"The logical answer," he replied dryly, "would point to the miracle of such a small group of men overcoming a fierce and mighty army."

"No, that is not it." She giggled, as a hiccup escaped her lips.

"Well then," he sighed, "the esoteric answer would point to the miracle of the oil lasting eight nights."

"No, Mr. Bennet. Again, you are incorrect."

"Pray, tell me, wife, what then was the miracle, for I can see that you may burst with anticipation for the sharing of it!"

"The miracle, sir, was that they had *bitachon.* I do hope I am pronouncing correctly. At any rate, it means *trust.* They knew they only had one vial of sacred oil and had no means to create more. They lit the candle and left the rest up to the Almighty. And that is exactly what we should do."

"My dear, it is a lovely tale and I am certain that it has inspired many generations before us and will inspire many generations after we are long gone, but it does not change the fact that Mr. Collins is to inherit Longbourn..."

"Longbourn is entailed to Mr. Collins *if* we do not produce a son."

"Yes, and well you know that we have produced five daughters, although you are as handsome as any of them, Mrs. Bennet. A stranger might believe I am the father of six!" he said with sincere admiration.

"You flatter me, Mr. Bennet. I certainly have had my share of beauty, but I wish to say..."

"You were but a child when we wed," he waved her silent, "not much more than Lydia's age, if I recall. But, my dear, that is neither here or there, for in all this time a son has not been produced and there's nary a thing to do for it!"

"Mr. Bennet, there *is* something I have been meaning to tell you," she said, suddenly quite subdued. "If you could only spare a moment of your time, or does your library call you away?"

His wife's anxious smile made him feel quite the blackguard. Had he not made a promise in Brighton? Did he not vow he would change his ways? Mr. Bennet decided it was high time he put the good rabbi's advice into practice. Bowing low, he replied, "Madam, I am your humble servant."

Happier words had never been spoken.

EPILOGUE

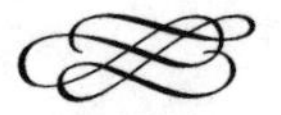

20th of August

"Where is she, Mrs. Reynolds? The stubborn woman is supposed to be in confinement!" Mr. Darcy bellowed as he fairly raced down the grand staircase of Pemberley. "How difficult can it be to keep an expectant mother *confined*?"

"William, dear, be at ease," Georgiana Darcy cried, nearly running into her brother as she exited the music room. "Elizabeth is in the lower gardens. She and Cook are inspecting the summer harvest."

"I left her resting comfortably on the chaise in the library," Mr. Darcy said, running a shaky hand through his hair. "I was gone for five minutes—*five minutes*!"

"You must calm yourself, Brother. Women have been bearing children since...well, since the beginning of time."

This comment did nothing to appease the gentleman, for now his attention was solely on his sister. "And what do you know of it?"

Georgiana blushed and then turned ghostly pale, so wholly unprepared was she for this line of questioning. Elizabeth had enlightened her on several intriguing subjects of late—subjects which, according to her sister-in-law, all young ladies were entitled to appreciate, considering it was their own physiology in question. How was she to explain to her brother? Just when Georgiana could not bear his stern regard for another moment, Fitzwilliam Darcy released a deep resounding laugh that echoed throughout the hall.

"What is all this?" asked Elizabeth, smiling at observing her husband so exceedingly diverted. "Whatever you have done, Georgiana, I give you leave to do it again and again! At least the master of the house is not traipsing after me with a footrest for my swollen ankles or a glass of cool milk."

"I desire to see you resting comfortably," Darcy confessed. "You should not be running around the estate picking wildflowers, or weeds, or whatever you wish to call them."

Elizabeth nestled herself in her husband's embrace, receiving all the comfort and security she required in his arms. "All is well, William, pray do not concern yourself overmuch. I was preparing a basket for Fletcher to take to Jane. She will be in need of my *wildflowers* long before my time comes..."

"Elizabeth, I would not speak of these things in the vestibule."

"Are you blushing, husband?"

"I do not blush!" he decreed and hid his smile while making his way into the drawing room.

Elizabeth and Georgiana shared a laugh as they threaded their arms together and followed in his path. While the three settled down, Mrs. Reynolds brought in a tea tray and the periodical for Mr. Darcy. Mr. Fletcher, who was now happily employed by her generous master, had just ridden in from Lambton with *The London Times* and a batch of afternoon mail. Because the mistress of the house was to be pampered in all things, Georgiana poured, while Mr. Darcy read a letter from Longbourn.

Dear Ones,

We send our love and best wishes and hope all is going well. With so much activity at home, you can well understand, Lizzie dearest, why we do not come to Pemberley and pay you a long overdue visit. Your baby brother, Jonathon is an angel of a child and your father—oh my goodness, Lizzy, you father is a sight to be seen! For all the years he condemned my girls for being silly and censured me for being ridiculous, you would not believe the change that has come over that man. He makes noises and faces all the day long! He dances and prances about, never once tiring of the babe's cries or complaints. It makes me wonder what alterations you will see in Mr. Darcy when your time comes!

Darcy rolled his eyes at this comment, cleared his throat and continued with his recitation.

The banns have been posted for our dear Mary and her Mr. Ainsely. It seems we shall soon have reason to celebrate once again! I have never seen Mary so content—it does my heart a world of good. My poor nerves could not bear it if my girls were not well and settled.

Kitty has surprised us all by continuing her correspondence with Lady Catherine. Together with your beloved aunt and uncle Gardiner, the lot of them have conspired and have enrolled your sister in a private seminary in London. While instruction will be focused on the conventional accomplishments to which genteel ladies are accustomed, I am told that the newish Rousseau approach allows for study in natural sciences and philosophy. Our Kitty—a scholar! Can you imagine?

As you know, Mr. and Mrs. Collins have had their parsonage taken over by their three little girls. I declare I was all astonishment when I heard Charlotte had been delivered of triplets, but no more than Mr. Collins when he heard the news of our Jonathan's arrival—I believe the poor man might have fainted!

And now I come to Lydia. As you know, Mr. Wickham was sent to the ends of the earth and our sweet girl followed him all the way to Buenos Aires. Her letters speak of handsome 'caballeros', who, I suppose, are the gentlemen who live there. They have been nothing but kind and solicitous while Mr. Wickham serves his sentence. Lydia has petitioned a major of the regiment—whom she met and won over at one of their local assemblies—and the gentleman has agreed to have Mr. Wickham's cruel and menial assignment changed. Although we are pleased to hear this good news, we must remember that, while Mr. Wickham may be eventually pardoned, he will never be able to return to England.

"Thank the good Lord!" Mr. Darcy decreed.

I best conclude now, for Jonathon is crawling around quite like a ferocious Maccabee—and your dear papa is following in his destructive path! It would seem the little master is inspecting his territory, getting to know his terrain, as it were, which I suppose is rightly done as this little Bennet will inherit Longbourn... a long, long time from now. God has been good to us, dear Lizzie. We are all truly blessed.

Mr. Darcy looked up from the missive, gazed at his wife's glistening eyes and humbly said, "Amen."

AUTHOR'S NOTES

I hope you enjoyed this Pride and Prejudice variation as it is truly a topic very near and dear to my heart. Due to my partiality for period novels such as the works of Jane Austen, Elizabeth Gaskell, and the Bronte sisters, I became obsessed with wanting to fuse my passion for all things Judaic with my penchant for historical fiction.

I found that too often renowned authors, such as Shakespeare, Dickens, Chaucer and Heyer offer Jewish characterizations which are superficial or insulting. On the other end of the spectrum, we can read George Eliot's heavy work that portrays Jews—for lack of a better definition—as practically perfect in every way. I couldn't help but wonder: what if there had been a rabbi in Hertfordshire or a *yeshiva* (a Jewish academy) in the Lakes district? How would the Bennets interact with Jewish families living in the neighboring town of Meryton?

If you'll indulge me to *wax poetic* on the subject—at the risk of sounding much like a text book—there have been well-recorded communities in Kent since the year 1066, when Jews from

Normandy followed William the Conqueror into England. As a history buff myself, I was astounded to find that while the edict of 1290 expelled the entire Jewish population; by September 1655, Rabbi Menasseh Ben Israel of Amsterdam came to England to discuss their resettlement. He and three other rabbis were lodged as personal guests of Oliver Cromwell, lord protector of England, Scotland, and Ireland during the republican Commonwealth.

Here are a few more interesting tidbits! The synagogue in Plymouth—where the Mayflower set sail for America—has been in continuous use since 1762. In Dover, Rabbi Ash began keeping a register of Marriages and Circumcisions taking place in that locality as early as 1768. Moses and Judith Montefiore were so enchanted with Ramsgate after honeymooning there in 1812, that they purchased an estate in the sea-side resort and commissioned a Regency-style synagogue to be built for the local community. Both Lady Judith and Sir Moses are interred next to the synagogue in a white-domed mausoleum, a reproduction of the historic tomb of Rachel. Brighton's synagogues pre-date the first Catholic or Methodist places of worship in the city. By 1875, the Middle Street Synagogue was opened to meet the needs of an ever increasing Jewish population. It was dubbed "an opulent jewel in the crown of the South Coast's most elegant Regency resort." Clearly, there is a plethora of Jewish history to be found in England!

While doing research for *The Meyersons of Meryton*, I found that there were many eminent Jewish families in my focus Regency period, such as the Montefiores, the Rothchilds, the Goldsmids, and the Mocattas. Their role in society cannot be denied and should not be forgotten. Nathan Rothschild is a prime example.

Beginning in 1811, Rothschild was contracted by Commissary-General John Charles Herries to set up a network of agents in order to transfer funds to Arthur Wellesley, the famed general of the

Peninsular Campaign. By 1815, once again with the help of Rothschild & Sons, the-now Duke of Wellington was able to pay his 200,000 soldiers assembled in Belgium and subsequently, was able to defeat Napoleon at Waterloo.

Nathan Rothschild played an extraordinary role in assisting the British Empire. Needless to say, there have been anti-Semitic and slanderous commentary attached to his name. Commissary-in-Chief Herries responded to Rothschild's accusers with the following statement: "I, who know him so well, and who in the discharge of my public duty received so much assistance from him, can safely pronounce him to have been most capable, skillful, upright and liberal in the whole of course of his employment as an agent of the state."

Sir Moses Montefiore and Lady Judith were arguably the most influential Jewish couple throughout the Georgian and Victorian era. Montefiore (a Sephardic Jew) collaborated with the Duke of Norfolk (a Catholic) by working on removing religious prejudice from areas of national life. By the time Montefiore served as a captain in the 3rd. Surrey Local Militia in 1810, he was not required to pledge an oath *on the true faith of a Christian*. In 1812, Montefiore married Judith Barent Cohen, which made him Nathan Mayer Rothschild's brother-in-law.

After retiring from the business world in 1824, Montefiore devoted his time to community and civic affairs. He was named Sheriff of London in 1837 and was knighted by Queen Victoria the following year. In 1846, he received a baronetcy in recognition of his services to humanitarian causes on behalf of the Jewish people. A giant among men, Sir Moses Montefiore was highly respected and admired throughout England and across the globe.

The "First Lady of Anglo Jewry," Judith Montefiore (an Ashkenazi Jew), was known for her philanthropic work and devotion to the Jewish community. She was highly educated, spoke several languages and assisted her husband in his communal affairs and public activities. Lady Judith wrote of their experiences when she and Sir Moses visited Damascus, Rome, St. Petersburg and the Holy Land, but more than travel logs; these works were later hailed as spiritually inspiring and educational. In addition, she has been credited for writing a cookbook, which in actuality is a "how-to" manual for ladies of her social position.

She adapted recipes to conform to Jewish dietary laws, replacing ingredients such as lard, so much used in English kitchens, and eliminating shellfish and forbidden meats. Lady Judith was decidedly a Victorian when she wrote this book. She recommended simplicity in dress, considered delicate hands a mark of elegance and refinement, and carefully assessed the effect of diet on the complexion. Her philosophy was that "the face and body are indexes of the mind."

Now, with regards to that dastardly Mr. Wickham and his transportation to a penal colony, I will plead guilty to one count of gross overuse of creative license! The British did attempt—unsuccessfully—to seize control of the Viceroyalty of the Río de la Plata (present-day Argentina and Uruguay) as part of the Napoleonic Wars. Unable to secure a holding, the British instead continued to foster a productive, commercial relationship with the fledging nation. I suppose I should have had Wickham transported to Australia but, I chose Argentina for selfish reasons. Why you ask? Because, Argentina was the land of my birth and like Mr. Meyerson, I am an Ashkenazi Jew. My ancestors emigrated from Russia to Argentina in the late 1890's.

ENDNOTES

CHAPTER FOUR

1. **The *Shehechiyanu* blessing is recited on special occasions and on holidays**:

   Blessed are You Lord our God, Ruler of the Universe who has given us life, sustained us, and allowed us to reach this season.

2. **The Blessings before the reading of the Torah**:

   The one honored with being called up to the Torah calls out: *Blessed the Lord, who is blessed.*

3. The congregation responds: *Blessed be the Lord who is blessed forever and ever.*

   The chanter continues: *Blessed are You, Lord our God, King of the universe who has chosen us from among all the nations by giving us His Torah. Blessed are You, Adonai, who gives the Torah."*

CHAPTER FOURTEEN

1. **The Blessings before partaking of food:**

   Blessed are You, Lord our God, King of the Universe: Depending on which food group, you conclude with:

   Who creates the fruit of the vine.

   Who creates the fruit of the earth.

   Who brings forth bread from the earth.

   by Whose word all things came to be.

ACKNOWLEDGEMENTS

Writing is a lonely process, but one cannot do it alone. I'm extremely fortunate to have an understanding husband, one that is self-sufficient and can manage on his own—when I simply cannot pull myself away from the keyboard. I'm grateful for the tremendous support from my family and friends. Their words of encouragement have meant the world to me.

I owe a debt of gratitude to Debbie Stone Brown who graciously provided editing services to this project. In addition, I would like to thank Sister Diana Doncaster and Jeanne Garrett for their proofreading and beta-reading talents. I couldn't have completed the novel without the knowledge and generosity of these amazing women.

I would also like to acknowledge the following books and websites:

Pride and Prejudice

~ Miss Jane Austen

The Jewish Manual; *Practical Information in Jewish & Modern Cookery with a Collection of Valuable Recipes & Hints Relating to the Toilette*

~ Lady Judith Cohen Montefiore

The Kosher Gourmet in the Nineteenth Century Kitchen: *Three Jewish Cookbooks in Historical Perspective*

~ Barbara Kirshenblatt-Gimblett

The Jews of Georgian England*, *1714-1830: *Tradition and Change in a Liberal Society*

~ Todd M. Endelman

janeaustensworld.wordpress.com/

jewishgen.org/JCR-UK/

jtrails.org.uk/

Thank you for your interest and support of this work. If you are so inclined, please leave a rating and/or a review on Amazon and Goodreads. As an "indie" author, I rely on word of mouth and visibility on these websites and social media outlets. Your feedback is most appreciated!

For more information, please visit me at:

http://www.facebook.com/mirtainestrupp

Or send me an email: indieauthor4life@gmail.com

ALSO BY MIRTA INES TRUPP

Destiny by Design~ Leah's Journey

Becoming Malka

With Love, The Argentina Family~

Memories of Tango and Kugel; Mate' with Knishes